THE
TRUTH-
SEEKER'S
WIFE

ANN GRANGER

HEADLINE

First published in 2021 by
HEADLINE PUBLISHING GROUP

First published in paperback in 2021 by
HEADLINE PUBLISHING GROUP

1

Cataloguing in Publication Data is available from the British Library

ISBN 978 1 4722 7065 8

Typeset in Plantin by
Palimpsest Book Production Limited, Falkirk, Stirlingshire

Printed and bound in Great Britain by Clays Ltd, Elcograf S.p.A.

HEADLINE PUBLISHING GROUP
An Hachette UK Company
Carmelite House
50 Victoria Embankment
London EC4Y 0DZ

www.headline.co.uk
www.hachette.co.uk

This book is dedicated to my dear granddaughter, Josie, with love and very best wishes for your future, in whatever you do.

Chapter One

*I have very little time left and I do not need Dr Wilson
to tell me. But I will settle all outstanding matters
before I die. It is an obligation, is it not, to leave
one's affairs in order? I shall take care of everything.*

Elizabeth Martin Ross

THE SCATTERING of grey-and-white feathers on the
road marked the murder scene.

When I opened the curtains at the bedroom window
this morning I'd looked down to see a young pigeon,
waddling along the pavement. It started to plod across the
road. Then, in the middle of London's brick and stone
forest, against the noise of the great engines in nearby
Waterloo Station, from out of the smoke-veiled sky dropped
a peregrine falcon. It seized the pigeon and carried it off.
It happened so quickly that I couldn't quite believe it, yet
the morning breeze from the river was already blowing
away the evidence.

Sometimes murder comes like that, quick and ruthless, seizing the moment. Or the killer can be a careful predator, watching and waiting. In either case the prey, man or beast, is doomed. I am still trying to put out of my mind the events of a few weeks ago, when Aunt Parry and I paid our ill-fated visit to the south coast. But I shall never forget it: neither the shock of the first crime, nor the ghastliness of the last.

Spring is always welcome and that year, 1871, it was particularly so. The past winter had seen a fog-shrouded world. Londoners had been trapped, suffocated by foul air. But now the snow had gone, the fogs were fewer and less dense, the coughs and sneezes were a fading memory, and green shoots had appeared on trees and bushes in the parks. At Scotland Yard, so my husband Ben told me, the atmosphere was positively cheerful. Well, at least compared with what it had been for the previous few months.

'It won't last,' he added. 'You'll see.' He was addressing his reflection in the shaving mirror; I wasn't entirely sure whether he was telling me or reminding himself.

In either case, he was almost certainly right. Not only were honest citizens making plans for the better weather; every kind of criminal in the city was doing the same. The social season would soon begin for the wealthy. They were shutting up their country houses and the servants had been sent ahead to open up their town residences. Hostesses were setting the dates for balls and parties; appointments were being made with fashionable dressmakers and smart tailors. I am glad I never had to go through the Season. My father was only a doctor in a small mining community.

Together with the rest of their luggage, the wealthy brought their jewel boxes to London. Thieves are like magpies, attracted by bright, shiny things. For them the London Season meant easy pickings. Housebreakers and receivers of stolen goods were probably rubbing their hands in gleeful anticipation. Like the professional gamblers, and all kind of confidence tricksters, they saw the coming influx of the well-to-do with the cheerful anticipation of trawlermen spotting the silvery gleam of shoals of fish.

'In a couple of weeks' time,' prophesied Ben, wiping the remains of shaving soap from his chin, 'we shall be run off our feet. Not only at the Yard, mark you! But every police officer in town.'

My former employer, before I married, Mrs Julia Parry was also making travel plans, but these involved leaving London. She was the widow of my late godfather, who had left her comfortably off. Her own business acumen had increased her wealth. After spending the winter sequestered in her London house, she now had an urge for travel. There was however a problem. The war between Prussia and France had only just played out its last desperate scenes, but the end of hostilities had not brought peace. France was still in turmoil. Blood ran on the cobbles of Paris, which was seeing an uprising of revolutionary elements and ruthless actions by the authorities to suppress them.

Needless to say, Aunt Parry viewed the events across the Channel, with their tragedies and violence, strictly from her own viewpoint. It was as if she held a Stanhope device to her eye and viewed the Continental scene in detail but in miniature, events reduced to the strict boundaries of her own interests.

'There is no question of my travelling abroad,' she lamented. 'I shall remain in England, but make a journey to the coast somewhere, to take the sea air.'

The conversation was taking place in her comfortable home in Dorset Square, to which she had invited me to take tea with her.

'Take care!' warned Ben that morning at breakfast, after I passed him the note the lady had sent me asking that I come. 'She wants something.'

'Aunt Parry is a rich woman and there's nothing she can possibly want from me that she can't acquire easily for herself,' I pointed out.

But I was uneasy. Ben was right, as I was soon to find out.

The room in Dorset Square was overheated. The windows were tightly sealed, and the lack of air made me sleepy. I'd eaten too many toasted teacakes. It was difficult to make any intelligent conversation; much less stay alert for whatever Mrs Parry was planning. So her next question took me by surprise.

'That police inspector you married, he is occupied with his duties, I dare say?'

I was a little annoyed, because she always refers to Ben by occupation and not by name. But I agreed that Ben was, as always, very busy.

'And you still employ that maid you took from me when you left my home to set up your own household?'

I replied that yes, we did. She spoke as if I had lured away a valued servant, but the truth was that Bessie had been a humble kitchenmaid in Dorset Square. Aunt Parry had barely been aware of her existence.

She tilted forward (her corset did not allow her to bend), and asked in a confidential whisper, 'Could he spare you for a month?'

'Spare me!' I exclaimed.

'For a month,' repeated Aunt Parry, raising her voice a little, as if I were deaf. 'You still employ the maid and she could look after any household needs for that length of time?'

'No! I mean, not for a month . . .'

'Three weeks?' bargained my hostess. She tilted her head to one side as she waited for my answer. Her hair was elaborately dressed and not all of it was her own. Her gown was brightly coloured cobalt-blue with ivory lace trimmings and yellow satin ribbons. It was like being observed by a large exotic bird.

'It would hardly be fair on Ben . . .'

She sighed and said crossly, 'Oh, very well, Elizabeth, two weeks! Although that is hardly any time at all if I am to benefit from the sea air.'

'Oh, you want me to go to the coast with you!' I exclaimed as I saw the reasoning behind her request.

'Well, yes, Elizabeth. I have been planning a little time by the sea, as I was saying only minutes ago. Were you not paying attention? Unfortunately, I am again without a companion.'

I had lost count of the number of companions she had engaged and dismissed since my time in that role.

'Oh? I'm sorry to hear that,' I said. And I was sorry, extremely sorry, because it sounded as if she intended to engage me as a substitute. 'It would be difficult,' I protested. 'Bessie is good at housework; but to run a household is a different matter. She's an indifferent cook. Besides, when Ben comes home of an evening, he looks forward to a little companionship, someone to discuss his day with—'

'So do I,' she interrupted. 'I shall take Nugent with me, of course.' (Nugent was her long-suffering personal maid.) 'But she has no conversation. I need a companion, if only for *such a short time,* and Nugent wouldn't fill the role at all. The girl, Bessie, can run a little house like yours, surely? And there must be pie shops in the area.'

I drew a deep breath. 'Where are you thinking of taking the sea air, Aunt Parry? Brighton?'

'Good heavens, no!' she exclaimed, raising her pudgy hands in horror. 'Far too crowded and all manner of people go there nowadays. I blame the railway. They offer cheap tickets for a day's excursion. Whole families descend on the resort, with babies, small and unruly children, elderly relatives, picnic hampers and all manner of paraphernalia. I have therefore decided to rent a house in a quiet, out-of-the-way spot on the south coast, somewhere that combines the sea air and the rural landscape. I need peace and quiet. I hope you will approve.'

She fell silent, possibly hoping I'd ask her where this gem of a summer resort might be. But I was determined not to show any enthusiasm for a trip I had no wish to make.

Suddenly, Mrs Parry looked up at me and beamed. It

was such a radiant smile and so unexpected – her usual expression was one of discontent – that I was completely thrown off my guard. That, of course, was her intention.

'Dear Elizabeth,' she said. 'You do already know the New Forest area, in Hampshire . . .'

I exclaimed in dismay, 'You cannot possibly suggest I return there? Have you forgotten what happened last time? There was a murder!'

Aunt Parry shuddered. The various ribbon and bow trimmings on the blue gown all quivered in harmony so that her whole form appeared to shift about like the onset of an earth tremor. She raised her hands, palms outward, and gestured as if she would wipe away some stain.

'There is no need to *name* the awful event, Elizabeth. Now, I have been offered the use of a delightful property on the shoreline, about a mile away from – from where you were before. The house is the summer retreat of acquaintances of mine, by the name of Hammet. They do not require use of the property for some months. I believe they are to undertake a tour of Italy, even though it means risking the perils of Continental travel. They are delighted to make the house available to us. Disuse does no property any good, so it would suit the Hammets very well to allow me the use of it for as long as I need it.'

Ah, I was beginning to understand. Though Mrs Parry was now a very rich woman there had been a time when she had been the daughter of an impecunious country curate. The thinking that springs from a thrifty upbringing is hard to shake off. Our accommodation would cost us nothing, other than the food we ate.

'The house,' she went on, 'is called The Old Excise House. Years ago, oh, when I was a child and we were at war with Old Boney, smuggling was rife in the area. Well, the house was built by the government of the time, as an office and accommodation for an excise officer, together with somewhere to store confiscated goods. But there is no longer that kind of lawless activity in the area, thank goodness, and so the building was sold off. The Hammets have spent, I'm told, quite a sum of money to turn it into a very comfortable summer home. Moreover, there is a gentleman's residence nearby, belonging to a Sir Henry Meager, which means you will not be without a neighbour. Mrs Hammet has written to tell him that I shall be coming and he has expressed the hope that we will dine with him during our stay. We shall have some company, Elizabeth. You need not let a lack of it worry you.'

I said, imprudently, 'I have heard the name of Sir Henry Meager. I never met the gentleman, but I did meet a family connection of his, when I was there last.'

'You see?' cried Mrs Parry in delight. 'You will feel quite at home there!'

I was now more than annoyed: I was truly angry. It seemed that everything had been thought out and settled before the idea had even been suggested to me. What was more, in confessing I had heard of Sir Henry Meager, I had now sealed the matter by my own unguarded tongue. *Oh, why could you not have kept quiet, Lizzie?* I told myself.

Mrs Parry swept on, disregarding my agitation. 'As for The Old Excise House itself, there is a cook-housekeeper and I am informed there is a quaint but attractive garden. The cook and gardener form a married couple, I understand, living in a small cottage nearby, so everything is provided.'

She now deigned to recognise my lack of enthusiasm but managed, as ever, to turn it to her advantage. 'It would do you the world of good, Elizabeth, to come with me. You are looking a little peaky and lacklustre, quite unlike your usual bright spirits. It would be very selfish of Inspector Ross to deny you the opportunity to benefit from the sea air with me. It will be so peaceful, and relaxing, and two weeks,' concluded Aunt Parry, in minatory tone, 'is a *very* little time. I am sure he could spare you for *three*.'

Later, I recounted all this to Ben over supper. 'Of course, I told her it was out of the question. I couldn't leave you for three weeks alone here with only Bessie to take care of you! You would find Constable Biddle in the kitchen every evening, as the two of them are still walking out. She would be fussing around him and not around you.'

'I don't think,' objected Ben mildly, 'that I want to be fussed around.'

'You know what I mean. I told Aunt Parry it couldn't be done.'

Ben leaned back in his chair and surveyed me. 'Now, don't mistake my meaning, Lizzie, but perhaps it's not such a bad idea.' He raised both hands, palms outward, to ward off my reaction to this unexpected lack of support. 'I do appreciate most sincerely that you're concerned for my welfare. But I'm equally concerned for yours.'

9

'I don't think being packed off to Hampshire with Aunt Parry and poor Nugent will do any good for my welfare,' I muttered resentfully. 'Much less with the only entertainment being the occasional dinner with the local squire followed, no doubt, by cards.'

'Well, I'm not so sure, Lizzie, dear. It has been a very bad winter and you do look a little pale. As pretty as ever, of course,' he added hastily.

'I am not *pretty*. I don't even like the word! It makes me sound vacuous.'

'Handsome, then,' he amended.

'Thank you. But I still don't want to leave you here alone. Three weeks, Ben! You with only Bessie's company of an evening and me with only Aunt Parry to talk to. I shall be incarcerated in an isolated, windswept house, the tide surging in and out inundating the pebble beaches before me, and the heather and gorse of the heathland behind. Add in the dismal cries of gulls overhead . . . Don't *laugh*! No entertainment of any kind, except for the promise of dinner with this old fellow Meager, who is probably soaked in port and suffers from gout.'

'You'll come back completely reinvigorated,' Ben insisted. 'And I do believe we are going to be very busy at the Yard and I shall arrive home late most evenings.'

'But, Ben, you can't have forgotten what happened the last time I went to that area?'

'Of course not. But you are going to another house. The owners are about to depart or have already left for Italy. There will be only you, Mrs Parry, Nugent and the husband and wife who form the permanent staff. I don't think any one of those is likely to be murdered while you are there.'

'I am not so sure,' I muttered. 'I might murder Aunt Parry.'

'Oh, you can manage Mrs Parry, my dear,' said my husband comfortably. 'You always did so. Only don't go seeking out mysteries, will you? This will be a pleasant seaside break for you. Keep your detecting instincts under lock and key.'

'Going off to the coast then,' observed Bessie in the kitchen as we cleared up the supper things. She had obviously been listening in to the conversation with Ben. 'My, that will be exciting.'

'Will it?' I muttered. 'It was exciting the last time I was in the area, but it wasn't any sort of excitement I relished.'

'Oh, that murder!' returned Bessie cheerfully. 'Don't you worry, missis, lightning don't ever strike in the same place twice. That's what they say, isn't it?'

'They may say it. I am not sure it's the truth,' I snapped.

'I can take care of the inspector,' countered Bessie, undeterred. 'If that's what's worrying you!' She gave me a sly look. 'Not like you, missis, to give up the chance of having an adventure.'

So that is how I came to travel again to the south coast, this time with Mrs Parry and Nugent. Of course, it didn't work out as relaxing and peaceful as promised. But then, nothing undertaken in the company of Mrs Julia Parry ever did.

Chapter Two

Some plan holidays and others plan murder. It is the attention to detail that matters. Then seize the moment! The opportunity is coming. They are making their arrangements; and I shall make mine.

Elizabeth Martin Ross

I HAD made one last desperate attempt to persuade Mrs Parry to abandon the idea, or to choose another destination. The train service to Southampton was frequent and reliable. But, as I knew from my earlier visit to the area, to reach the New Forest it was necessary to cross Southampton Water. The choice was either by means of the regular ferryboat service or a long detour by road. I hazarded a last throw of the dice.

'I understand, Aunt Parry, that the proposed landing stage for the ferry on the Hythe side has still not been built. To land from the ferry involves a hazardous descent on to the stony spit called the Hard. It runs out from the shore to the spot where the water is deep enough, even at low tide, for the ferryboat. Climbing down the little gangplank from the boat to the Hard is bad enough. The movement of the sea makes it bounce about distressingly. Making one's way on foot to the shore, along the Hard, is nothing short of perilous. You cannot think of risking it.'

'I shall not,' retorted Mrs Parry serenely. 'I have made inquiries and we shall go round by road. There is a bridge across the river at a higher, very much narrower, point. That is the route all the road traffic takes. Mr Hammet, the owner of the house to which we go, has been in communication with Sir Henry Meager. Sir Henry has kindly offered to send his coachman to meet us at Southampton railway station. He will drive us to The Old Excise House.'

She beamed at me. 'So, you see, Elizabeth, there is absolutely nothing for you to worry about. It has all been arranged.'

It was always a mistake to underestimate Aunt Parry. I was foiled. In my mind's eye, the dice I had thrown rolled across the table and dropped on to the floor.

She had left me little time to make ready. I made sure the larder of my home was well provisioned and a menu of simple meals drawn up for Bessie to prepare for Ben. Both of them assured me they would manage very well without me.

'Although,' my husband added earnestly, 'I will miss you very much.'

So off we set. First of all, we had to board the train at

Waterloo Station in London. I dressed as suitably as I could for the journey, in walking dress. But Aunt Parry considered herself a woman of fashion. Fortunately, the crinoline was no longer de rigueur; but skirts were still very full and gathered in a bunch at the back, just below the waist. The most rigorous lacing of a corset could not reduce Aunt Parry's generous figure to slender lines. She had sailed down the platform at Waterloo like a galleon, followed by a veritable baggage train of our personal belongings and other necessities. A compartment had been reserved for our use and we more than filled it.

'Why do they not construct the entry to the carriages more conveniently?' Mrs Parry wailed as Nugent and I struggled to push her through the door. 'I shall write to the railway company and complain!'

The journey itself passed without any mishap. But if getting Mrs Parry into the train had not been easy, decanting her and our bags and boxes from the train at Southampton called for considerable manoeuvring, and the help of a porter and a boy. Eventually she burst from the compartment on to the platform like a jack-in-the-box.

Following that, our boxes must be unloaded. Several seagulls had arrived and patrolled around us, rightly realising that we had brought food. They were taking a particular interest in a Fortnum & Mason's hamper, deemed essential by Mrs Parry. One gull was so bold as to peck at it with its wickedly sharp beak.

'I don't like this, Mrs Ross, not one bit,' observed Nugent gloomily. She took a tight grip on her umbrella and pointed it defiantly at the gull.

I did not care for the gulls, either. 'We should seek out our onward transport, Aunt Parry,' I urged. 'And not keep Sir Henry's coachman waiting.'

Fortunately at that moment an elderly man appeared. He wore a voluminous caped coat such as might have been seen on a coachman thirty years earlier, and held his hat in his hand. He hailed us, bowing deeply.

'You'll be the party for The Old Excise House, then?' he asked, as he straightened with a grunt of pain. ''Tis the joints,' he added in explanation for the expression of discomfort. 'I'm all right going down and not so good standing up straight again.'

'Yes!' I told him in some relief. 'You must be Sir Henry Meager's coachman.'

'That's it, ma'am. Tizard is the name. It's a good thing we brought the dogcart along, as well as the carriage,' he added, gazing past me at our pile of luggage. 'The master said we would need it. "Tizard!" he said to me. "When ladies go travelling, mark my words, they take a baggage train of boxes and trunks with them. You'll need the dogcart. Go and find Davy Evans. He can drive it and help with moving the boxes." So I did.'

'We are very grateful to Sir Henry,' I told him.

'If you will follow me, ladies, the coach is outside, as is Davy with the dogcart. Just leave the luggage. Davy will come down for it here and manage it all.'

I gave a suitable gratuity to our porter and the boy who between them had managed to decant our luggage and ourselves. The porter thanked me, adding: ''Twas worth it! The lady there is a fine sight.' He nodded towards Mrs

Parry who, fortunately, didn't overhear. 'The lad and I will stand guard over your baggage,' he went on.

I saw that the lad in question had taken a seat on the Fortnum & Mason's hamper. He gave us a cheery grin. I returned a severe look to him. The wicker hamper was buckled with leather straps but not locked and I suspected the imp's intentions were the same as those of the gulls.

Tizard had already set off. We trooped after him out of the station to the main road. There, sure enough, was a venerable berlin carriage drawn by a pair of horses that looked very much as if they had been brought from the farm for the purpose. But I supposed there was little call for an expensive matched carriage pair in the rural surrounds to which we travelled. There also was the dogcart, drawn by a sturdy dark bay pony. A man stood at the pony's head and was stroking its neck.

'Davy!' called Tizard. 'Here's the ladies. Boxes is back there on the platform.'

The man moved away from the pony. He looked us over quite openly and a grin spread across his face. He was a strongly built, dark-haired fellow, good-looking in a weather-tanned, slightly piratical way. He might have sprung from one of the penny dreadful novels Constable Biddle gave Bessie to read. I supposed him a year or so short of thirty. To my mind he had not the demeanour of a servant; certainly not in the way his grin broadened as he studied Mrs Parry.

I heard myself ask Tizard, in a low voice, 'Is that Sir Henry's groom?'

The coachman chuckled. 'Bless you, ma'am, no. Davy

Evans don't work for no man. But he's available, as you might say. Available as needed. Here, Davy! I'll go on ahead with the ladies.'

We now reversed the procedure followed to get down from the train to manoeuvre Mrs Parry into the carriage. It wasn't roomy and once we were all three women packed into it, we could hardly move at all. I thought with sinking heart of the quite long journey ahead of us.

Tizard slammed the door on us and stood outside; with just his grizzled head showing at the window as if it floated free of his body.

'Oh, mustn't forget!' He drew a deep breath and recited an obviously rehearsed speech. 'Sir Henry presents his compliments and hopes you had a good journey. He'll let you settle in tonight and hopes that tomorrow you will dine with him, at six thirty. He trusts you will forgive him for not calling on you beforehand, and inviting you in person, but his gout is troubling him.' He clapped his hat on his head to signify the speech was over.

I knew it! I thought unworthily. *I knew he'd be gouty! I must tell Ben when I write.*

Tizard's head disappeared with disconcerting suddenness and the berlin shuddered as he climbed on to his perch. He whistled at the horses and with a jerk we bounced forward and began a lumbering progress.

'I have not dined at six thirty,' observed Mrs Parry in a nostalgic tone, 'for more years than I care to recall.'

She was facing forward. Nugent and I were crammed in, side by side, with our backs to the horses. Over Mrs Parry's shoulder, through a small rear window, I had a glimpse of Davy Evans standing in the road and watching us depart. As yet he had made no move to load our luggage into the dogcart. But I understood why Sir Henry had sent it. If all our boxes had been stacked on the roof of this old carriage, the springs would not have withstood the weight.

We creaked and rattled along, and I did begin to worry that we might break down mid-journey, especially as the sun was setting, touching the scenery with an ochre glow. Soon after quitting the town, and rattling across the stone bridge over the estuary of the River Test, we turned southwards again in a hairpin movement and found ourselves following the shoreline on the Hythe side, with Southampton now across the water to our left.

The journey brought back memories of my previous visit. The area known as the New Forest is a lonely place, and not all of it forested. There are wide areas of heathland roamed by ponies and other livestock turned out on it to graze by foresters who hold the rights to pasture their animals on such poor land. But the light was failing and we had little to view. We passed an occasional flint-built cottage and, once, an inn. Its mullioned windows glowed with the warm tones of lamplight, a beacon on the darkening highroad. Any sight of the sea was now lost to us, with trees between and everything veiled in a mauve dusk.

Mrs Parry had noticed the darkening sky: and also the lamplit inn. 'It is to be hoped that the house to which we travel has the benefit of gaslighting,' she observed. 'But I begin to think it will not. Lamps or candles, as well as dinner at six thirty, oh my, it quite takes me back to my youth.' She didn't sound displeased.

Nugent, a Londoner through and through, was not so sanguine. 'If there are no gas lamps,' she grumbled, 'I'm not setting foot out of doors after dark.'

Where we travelled though patches of woodland it was as if we trespassed on the domain of some lurking monster that had stretched out its branched arms to seize unwary travellers and had swallowed us up.

'There could be anything out there!' muttered Nugent.

She need not have worried. For most of our journey we appeared to be utterly alone. This might have encouraged us to talk to one another but the reverse was the case and we fell into an apprehensive silence.

After a journey of great discomfort, we reached the coast again and drew up on a deserted stretch of road. The extensive heathland was lost in the shadows. I could see no lights from other dwellings.

'Why have we stopped?' demanded Mrs Parry querulously.

The berlin shuddered again. Tizard was climbing down from his perch. He now appeared at the door, holding up a lantern.

'Here we are, ladies,' he said. 'The last few steps of the way you will have to do on foot.' He turned away and pointed out into the shadows. 'The Old Excise House is a little below us there. It's not a long way, but to take the carriage down would be a good sight trickier than I would like. There is little space to turn and anyway it's too dark. But if you would just step down, I'll guide you to the door.'

'What?' exclaimed Mrs Parry in dismay.

I heard Nugent grumble that this was a strange old place to choose to come, and that was for sure.

But at that moment we were hailed from the direction of the house, and a light came bobbing towards us.

'Ah!' said Tizard. 'Here's Jacob come to lend a hand.'

A figure emerged from the shadows, holding aloft the lantern, bowing and uttering words presumably in welcome. I couldn't quite make out what exactly he'd said.

'Give us some light, Jacob!' urged Tizard. He turned back to the berlin and addressed Mrs Parry. 'Just give me your hand, ma'am, and I'll have you out of there in two shakes.'

Mrs Parry did not receive this suggestion with anything like gratitude. She had no intention of giving her hand to the coachman, or of going anywhere 'in two shakes'.

'Elizabeth, my dear,' she said to me. 'Be so kind as to descend first. Nugent can follow. Then, between you, help me down.'

I scrambled out inelegantly, feeling that I was stepping out into the unknown and quite happy to grab Tizard's arm. I was followed by Nugent, still gripping the umbrella ready to fend off any danger lurking in the darkness. Aunt Parry was then prised through the door and we all three arrived on terra firma. Behind us, the carriage horses snorted and stamped. Theirs had been a long day and they sensed they were not far from their home stables. I could feel the heat rising from their steaming flanks.

'Lead on, Jacob!' urged Tizard.

We set off, Nugent and I one to either side of Mrs Parry and supporting her by the elbows. Beneath our feet the soil, a mix of sand, peat and stones, muffled our footsteps. I thought I could smell pine trees. Jacob went ahead with his lantern and Tizard brought up the rear. The moon was out now and lent its pale sheen to help us, but I understood the coachman's reluctance to bring the carriage down from the road. Mrs Parry complained non-stop that we should all break our ankles and that she should certainly have stayed overnight in Southampton if she'd had any idea of the remoteness of the locality.

With relief I saw we were approaching a house, quite a substantial one. Perhaps the present owners, the Hammets, had caused the original building to be extended. The flint exterior had been whitewashed and seemed to glimmer in the moonlight. The lower windows glowed a brighter yellow and an oil lantern swung before the entrance door, though that appeared to be at the side of the building, not in the front. But the side of the building was what faced the path. This had not been built as a gentleman's summer retreat, after all, but as a working office for the Excise. A warm glow enveloped us as the door opened. A female form appeared and dropped a deep curtsey. Behind her was a second female figure, also curtseying.

'Welcome, ladies. I'm the housekeeper, Mrs Dennis. And this is my daughter, Jessie, who helps out. I hope you had a good journey.'

'No!' gasped Mrs Parry. 'We've had a dreadful journey!'

Perhaps this reply was no more than the housekeeper expected, because she said in comfortable tones, 'But you're here, safe and sound, and that's what matters.' She indicated our guide with the lantern. 'That's Jacob, my husband. He looks after the outside of the place, and I look after the inside, as you might say.' Mrs Dennis turned to our coachman. 'Well, Tom Tizard, what have you done with the ladies' luggage?'

'Davy is behind us, with the dogcart,' explained Tizard. He turned back and addressed me. 'I'll be back tomorrow, at half-past five, to take you and the other lady to dine with Sir Henry.'

'Thank you,' I told him. 'But the dogcart has not yet arrived with our luggage. I hope there's been no upset on the road.'

'Oh, Davy will be along shortly,' Tizard assured me. 'He's very likely stopped to take a mug of ale along the way. Davy does things in his own fashion. But he'll be here, never fear.'

'Extraordinary!' observed Mrs Parry to me. 'I wonder Sir Henry employs the services of such a fellow.'

'Oh, he's a very useful sort of chap, is Davy,' said Tizard. 'I'll bid you all goodnight, then.'

Mrs Dennis urged us indoors. Her husband had disappeared back into the surrounding bushes. I knew him to be the gardener, but he couldn't surely lurk about the garden all night. Then I remembered that the couple was housed in a cottage nearby.

It was difficult to settle in without our luggage. But the housekeeper assured us it would arrive safely before long. Perhaps we would like to dine? We must, she said, be hungry.

This reminded Mrs Parry that she was, indeed, very hungry.

As feared, there was no gas lighting. We were provided with a candle apiece and climbed a narrow stair to inspect our rooms and take off our outer garments. The stairs led up to a square landing from which two long corridors ran the length of the house, from side to side. I was reminded again that this had not originally been built as a family home, but as a base for government revenue activities. This made the living arrangements a little inconvenient, as both corridors were narrow. Mrs Parry had been allotted what was obviously the master bedroom. It lay off the corridor to the left of the landing, and had a dressing room attached. In this little annex a bed had been made up for Nugent. My room lay along the corridor to the right. Thus we were at opposite sides of the house, some distance apart. My room, though smaller, was well appointed, and although darkness now deprived me of a view I calculated that in the morning I should have a fine sea vista, possibly affording a glimpse of the Isle of Wight.

I took off my hat and outer garments and placed them on the bed. A knock at the door heralded the arrival of Jessie carrying a jug of hot water, which she poured into the basin on the washstand. She was a sturdily built girl I judged to be about sixteen. Her mane of thick red hair was tied back at the nape of her neck with a ribbon.

'Ma says you'd want to freshen up,' she said brightly.

I duly freshened up, although in the absence of our luggage I couldn't change my gown. I went back downstairs to the dining room, where I found Mrs Parry, also perforce still in her travelling clothes, already seated at the table. It was prettily set, with crisp linen, and a large oil lamp with a cranberry glass shade casting a pink-tinged glow. We were served with a substantial and delicious meal, beginning with soup, followed by fresh fish, roast chicken and potatoes and finishing with syllabub. I hoped that Nugent, in the kitchen, was being served with as good fare. During the chicken course, a general racket outside signified our luggage had arrived. We heard it being carried indoors and up the stairs, with many a crash and thump.

'They appear to be very careless!' observed Mrs Parry, as a particularly loud collision, followed by a brief argument in male voices, sounded above our heads. 'Do you suppose that fellow who drove the dogcart has arrived drunk?'

This was quite possible, but I spoke up in Davy's defence, pointing out that the staircase was very narrow, as were the upstairs corridors. 'And the ceilings low.' I couldn't help but add, 'Poor Nugent will be very unhappy at being without gas lighting.'

'It is a very odd house,' ruled Aunt Parry. 'Mr Hammet should have warned us of its peculiarities.'

By the time we rose from the dinner table, weariness, hastened by such a good meal, was overcoming both of us.

'I shall retire!' declared Aunt Parry.

I agreed it was a good idea and I would do the same. Mrs Dennis came in at that point and asked us if the meal had been acceptable. We told her, yes, excellent.

'I hope you sleep well, ladies,' she said. 'My husband and I, we don't stay overnight in the house. We're just a stone's throw away in our cottage. But you won't be without anyone to call on. Jessie will sleep here and be on hand if needed. There is a bell rope by the bed in both your rooms.'

It had been a long and exhausting day. I was glad to climb into my bed. I had intended to write to Ben before I retired but decided to do this in the morning. I would have plenty of time, as Mrs Parry never appeared before noon.

Yet, despite my weariness, I did not fall asleep at once. In my own home near Waterloo Station in London the night was punctuated by noises from the great railway. The sounds I heard now were altogether different and perhaps it was their strangeness that kept me awake and listening. The tide was in and the waves below murmured their distinctive refrain, a soft growl, punctuated with the occasional slap of water against some obstacle. It had not been possible to tell in the darkness of our arrival, but the house must have been situated to give the Revenue officers a good view out to sea and along the coast in both directions. I had drawn back the curtains before blowing out the candle, and only silvery moonlight bathed the room. A wind had sprung up, blowing unimpeded across the water. It found its way into the roof space and the rafters creaked so much above my head it was as if I were aboard ship, not on land.

As I listened I began to imagine that the creaks and rattles were not all due to the wind, but to someone moving surreptitiously in the roof space. There must be attic rooms overhead, I thought. Perhaps someone slept there. It could not be either of the Dennises, because I knew they had both returned to their cottage for the night. *Imagination!* I told myself. But a louder creak than the others, more of a sharp crack, made me sit up in bed in alarm. There was definitely someone up there. Then I remembered.

'Why, Lizzie!' I muttered to myself. 'It must be Jessie Dennis who sleeps up there. You are letting your imagination run away with you.'

Nevertheless I reached out for the shawl I had left draped across the foot of the bed, threw it round my shoulders and swung my legs out of bed. I felt for my slippers with my toes and, when I had located them, crept across the floor to the door of the room. I decided there was no need to light the candle that stood in a pottery holder by my bed, together with a packet of lucifers. The moonlight provided its clear cold light. I opened the door as quietly as I could and stepped out into the passageway. Here I had no benefit of the moonlight, and I was sorry I had not bothered with the candle after all. I felt my way along until I came to a small door at the very end, blocking any further progress. It seemed to be fastened by a primitive latch. I raised it but could not see what lay ahead. I put one foot carefully ahead of me – and promptly stubbed my toe. Stooping, I felt for the obstacle. A narrow wooden step rose directly before me, and above that another – and another. A narrow stairway. This must be the access to the attic room above. Now I had satisfied myself, I was about to close the little door again when the murmur of voices drifted down towards me. There were whispers and a female giggle. Following that, I just made out another voice, definitely not female. Jessie Dennis slept up there, but not alone. No wonder she had been happy to remain 'should she be needed'.

Well, I thought, *Jessie had been needed, but not by either Mrs Parry or myself.*

I closed the stairway door quietly and made my way back to my room. This time when I climbed back into my bed I fell asleep at once.

I awoke again at first light. I rolled over towards the window and was startled to see a gull perched on the ledge outside, peering in at me with a hostile yellow eye. The little travelling clock on the table told me it was still too early to rise, but I slipped out of bed anyway and went to the window. The gull flapped away at my approach. Outside, a cold early light bathed the approach to the house and gave me my first sight of what lay on the other side of the garden wall. A stony path ran by, and beyond that a stretch of rough grass and low bushes. Then the land fell away with alarming suddenness down to the beach perhaps twelve to fifteen feet below.

I was about to turn back to bed when unexpectedly a man appeared. He walked round the side of the house, which he must have left through the kitchen door. He did not turn the corner to walk up the track to the main road along which we'd travelled the previous evening, but crossed the scrap of garden and left through a wooden gate on to a narrow path above the beach. He turned left and set off downhill. I had recognised him instantly. There was no mistaking Davy Evans.

Chapter Three

Well, it is all settled now, details worked out, no room
for error. I should not have left matters so late.
But perhaps Fate intended this moment.
At any rate, I shall not miss it.

Elizabeth Martin Ross

IT HAD never been Mrs Parry's habit to appear before
midday. In London she always breakfasted in her room
and read any letters that had arrived that morning. Assisted
by Nugent, she would then make an elaborate toilette and
appeared in full splendour at twelve, ready for a 'light
luncheon', as she cared to call the meal. Having moved
temporarily to the coast did not mean she had changed
her ways. So it was that I breakfasted alone that morning.
I didn't know whether Mrs Dennis had expected Mrs Parry
to be at the breakfast table with me, or whether she thought
I had a very good appetite. There was certainly enough
food for two, at least. I did my best, in order not to distress

the housekeeper, but I could make no more than a dent in the amount.

'Not hungry, then, ma'am?' inquired the Mrs Dennis with a worried frown. 'Did you not sleep very well?'

'I am quite well,' I assured her. 'And I've made a very good breakfast, thank you. I don't eat much so early in the day.'

'Oh, well, you'll be ready for your luncheon,' was the reply.

If I was to be ready for any kind of meal at midday I needed to take some exercise before that. Accordingly I postponed my letter-writing until the afternoon, and dressed for an expedition to explore the coastal footpath. I chose my sturdy balmorals as footwear, and tied on my hat with a scarf lest it blow away out to sea. Jessie appeared just as I was about to leave.

'Mam says to be sure you take a walking stick. Otherwise, you'll most likely turn an ankle.'

She looked bright and cheerful, with her abundant red hair tied back as before at the nape of her neck and wearing a blue cotton gown and white apron. She held out a stout stick of the sort old gentlemen usually carried.

'Thank you, Jessie,' I said, taking it.

She bobbed a curtsey and walked briskly back towards the kitchen. If she had had limited sleep the night before, it didn't show. I felt myself to be in a difficult situation. I had no idea whether her mother had any suspicion about Jessie's behaviour when the girl wasn't sleeping under the family roof, though I supposed she didn't. Should I mention to Mrs Dennis that I had seen Davy Evans leaving the house at first light? But, if I did, Davy and Jessie would probably both deny the incident and Davy would be ready with some glib reason for his presence on the shore path. Besides, I was newly arrived, and I didn't know these people. There was something else too. My instinct was not to make an enemy of Davy Evans. To do so might upset others besides the Dennis family. I remembered Tizard's description of Davy as a 'useful chap' and 'available as needed'. I would only be in the area for three weeks. Any attempts on my part to 'upset the applecart' would not be welcome.

My first action on leaving the house was to step back and take a good look at the building in daylight. That it had not originally been designed as a dwelling was already clear from the interior. Now I could find my own bedroom window from outside and, at the other end of the house, what must be Mrs Parry's room. My real interest was to see what kind of an attic floor there was and sure enough, above the first-floor bedroom another row of very small windows confirmed the presence of rooms up there, including the one in which Jessie and her visitor had slept the previous night. Perhaps, once upon a time, confiscated smuggled goods had been stored in the attics. I walked to the corner of the building where I'd seen Davy earlier. From here I could see up the slope rising to the road. A little way off, perched like a gull's nest, was a small cottage. A pathway ran from it down to The Excise House. This, I decided, was where the caretaker's family lived.

After only a few steps I reached another wooden gate, on the seaward side of the coastal path. This gave access to a narrow and steep footpath that turned at an angle to lead down on to the beach below. The tide was ebbing fast, already well below the high tidemark of seaweed and debris. The smell of ammonia and rotting fish rose from the mix, and gulls patrolled up and down, scavenging. They were not the only seekers after bounty. Jacob Dennis was down there, digging energetically in the patches of soft mud between the pebbles. He had a bucket beside him, but I couldn't see what it contained.

The path along which I now walked was narrow and bordered with heather and bracken, divided by clumps of brambles that must be chopped down and beaten back soon or they would encroach on the path itself. Behind these edgings grew a wall of trees and bushes, the taller branches stretching out over my head so that I walked through a tunnel of entangled vegetation. Only regular use could keep the path open. If it fell out of use, the wild growth would soon reclaim it and make it impassable. Even now, I was forced to use the stout walking stick to knock back intrusive growth that snatched at my skirts.

Suddenly the direction turned inland. I emerged from the tunnel into sunlight, and here the secluded path joined a wider, more permanent road. There were buildings here, cottages, and in the distance the square tower of a Norman church. It seemed familiar and I realised I had reached the village near which I'd stayed on my previous visit. But this time I was approaching it from the opposite direction. Suddenly I came upon a dilapidated dwelling, set back from the road by a long and untidy vegetable garden. Before it, on the roadside, was a wooden bench and, seated on this, two women.

I was so startled at the sight of them that I stopped. It was not that it was so strange to see someone enjoying the sunshine. It was the aspect of the two watchers, for that is what they clearly were. They were elderly, so alike in their stumpy build and facial features that they had to be sisters, and dressed head to toe in black. I did not know if this betokened mourning, or whether it was just their choice. I suspected the latter, because they were festooned (it was the only word for it) with an astonishing variety of jewellery. They wore jet necklaces and silver chains; brooches and pins. From their ears dangled silver earrings and the fingers of their hands, resting clasped in their laps, were be-ringed with heavy gold and silver bands. Whether it was by design that they wore all their valuables, and so kept them on their persons, or whether there was some other significance in the profusion of decoration, I had no way of knowing. But there was deliberateness about the fashion that was unsettling. The skin of their faces was pale and almost silken in texture. These were not women who had spent their lives as labourers in the fields. Beneath hooded eyelids, their dark eyes shone as brightly as a hawk's and were as predatory. They sat perfectly still and silent, watching my progress towards them.

They are guarding the approach to the village, I thought wryly, *like the sentry at the gates of Pompeii who perished at his post.*

I felt an atavistic need for some token of protection and without realising it raised my hand to touch the gold cross and chain I wore round my neck. They saw what I did; and one of them smiled slightly. Then she spoke.

'Well, truth-seeker's wife, you have come back to us.'

'You know me?' I asked, shocked.

'You were here before, were you not?' she returned calmly.

'Yes,' I admitted, 'five years ago. But I was not married then.'

She nodded acknowledgment of the fact, but returned: 'You came first, but the truth-seeker followed after.'

I wasn't nervous now and I was becoming a little angry. She was playing me like an angler plays a hooked fish. 'When I was here on my previous visit,' I said loudly and firmly, 'I came to be a companion to a young married lady. Unfortunately a crime was committed during that time and, as a result, a police detective was sent down here from Scotland Yard. That, I assume, is the gentleman you describe as the "truth-seeker".'

Neither replied, only sat there like a pair of black-clad sphinxes. It was time to seize the initiative.

'May I presume to ask your names?' I asked a little sharply.

The one who seemed to be spokeswoman for the pair of them nodded. 'Our name is Dawlish. I am Aunt Tibby and she— ' She pointed at her companion. 'Is Aunt Cora Dawlish.'

Aunts to whom? To the whole village? Even given that families in small communities were often linked by an intricate web of connections, it seemed unlikely. But the title of 'aunt' can be bestowed on almost any older lady.

After all, I called Mrs Parry 'aunt', at her request, and we were not in any way related by blood or marriage. I would find out more in good time.

Now I asked, 'How do you know I am married now, and to that detective?'

'We know many things,' she replied. Indicating her silent sister with a jerk of her head, she added calmly, 'My sister is a witch. She sees things.'

I managed not to snap out in reply, *In the tea leaves, I suppose?* Instead, I said as calmly as I could, 'Does she, indeed? Well, I am not a village woman and where I was born, in the north of England, we are a practical people. If you have learned somehow that I married Inspector Ross, it was not from— from anything Miss Cora knew through any occult practices.'

Cora Dawlish spoke for the first time to say sharply, 'I help people!' She accompanied the words with a glare.

Aunt Tibby looked sullen and said, 'Jessie Dennis told us. She had it from her mother.'

'And Mrs Dennis had it from where?'

Tibby rallied and retorted, 'Why, Mrs Ross, from the gentleman who owns The Old Excise House, Mr Hammet, of course! He told Jacob Dennis and his wife that the house was let out for a month to a pair of ladies, and one of them was married to a police inspector.'

There was a touch of triumph in her gaze when she told me this. I was discomfited, because I should have been able to work it out for myself. But it did not completely answer my question. How did the sisters know it was Ben Ross I had married, and not another police inspector? They were right, but it was probably no more than an inspired guess on their part.

This is how it works, I thought to myself. If you are told someone has supernatural powers, you begin to believe that what they, or anyone connected with them, says, originates in those powers. But usually it is no more than simple observation and deduction; or some scrap of privately acquired information. They had a good memory for faces, and Aunt Tibby had recognised me, though it was five years since I'd shown my face hereabouts. That is how Aunt Cora and others, who make claims of being witches, work their 'magic'. They are like conjurors. You see something you know is impossible; but cannot help, for a moment, believing it.

But did it also explain their being known to all as 'aunt'? I realised it was a term of respect and authority. These were what would once have been known as 'wise women'. When the villagers, particularly the women, were in need of help or advice, they still came, not to their parish priest, but to one of the sisters.

If I had seen either of them on my previous visit, I should certainly have remembered them. But I had been fully occupied with other matters at the time and had no memory of them. The inattention of others also plays into their trickery. Well, I had no more time to waste being made a fool of by them.

'Good day, ladies!' I said firmly, with a nod of my head.

I was about to walk on when I looked past the two women, down the length of the overgrown garden behind them to the cottage. The front door had opened at some point, I was not sure when, and a man now stood in the doorway, watching the exchange by the gate. He was grinning broadly. It was Davy Evans.

Now I was seriously angry, because I realised all the information the sisters possessed had come via him, and he had it from his lady love, Jessie Dennis. I ignored him and stepped out briskly on my way. But even then, Aunt Cora had the last word.

As I walked away I heard her call after me. 'When you came before, you brought death with you. And on this visit, truth-seeker's wife, you will bring death again.'

As a last word it was an unanswerable one, so I made as if I hadn't heard her gloomy prophecy. But she knew I had and, if I were to look back, both sisters would be smiling. Davy would be laughing openly.

Then I realised the sisters had inadvertently let slip a detail of real information. Mr Hammet, the house owner, had told Mrs Dennis that the house was let for a month. So much for my believing I had negotiated my stay down to three weeks. Something else to tell Ben when I wrote! Mrs Parry had wanted to stay a month, and stay a month she would; and I, perforce, with her.

I had only a faint memory of the village from my previous visit and nothing had struck me then as particularly interesting. It did have, as such places so often do, a very old church. But I'd visited that the last time. I might not be very interested in the village, but the villagers I encountered seemed fascinated by me. They probably seldom saw a strange lady walking down the street. They smiled and nodded. Their welcome helped me to overcome the ruffled feelings my meeting with the Dawlish sisters had left me with. I was pleased, too, to observe a wooden sign on the fascia of what appeared to be a general store, declared that this was also the post office. Writing to Ben was what I should be doing.

Outside the post office was a saddled horse, the bridle held by a scruffy, tousle-headed boy in hand-me-down garments a little too large for him. I guessed the rider must be inside the building. On cue the door opened, the bell positioned above it jangled and a man walked out. He was certainly handsome, perhaps in his mid-forties, with well-tailored clothes, but without the casual manner of a man of independent means. Rather, he had a capable air about him, as if he carried practical responsibilities. To this was added a degree of wariness when he saw a strange lady standing in the street by his horse.

I realised I was studying him, and felt myself blush because no wonder he was puzzled. He took off his hat, bowed and said, 'Good morning, ma'am.' His voice was educated.

I returned the greeting and we stood a little awkwardly. The boy who held the horse's head stared at us both with a complete absence of any interest that was more disconcerting than if he'd shown curiosity.

'You are a visitor, I think, ma'am,' the rider prompted.

'Yes, indeed, I am staying at The Old Excise House, together with another lady,' I told him.

He relaxed and smiled broadly, 'Then you must be, I fancy, Mrs Ross? And the other lady must be Mrs Parry. We shall meet again, ma'am! My name is Harcourt. I believe we shall be dining together this evening.'

'Oh,' I said, taken aback. 'At Sir Henry Meager's home?'

'Yes, yes,' he said. 'Until then, Mrs Ross.' He set his hat firmly on his head, gave the boy who'd held the horse a small coin, remounted and, with a touch of his hand to the brim of his hat, clattered away.

I turned and set off back to The Old Excise House. I was curious about the horseman and puzzled. Something about him had seemed familiar, but I couldn't think what it was. Well, my curiosity would be answered later that evening.

Passing by the cottage, I saw that the wooden seat by the road was now vacant. The sisters had either gone indoors to prepare their luncheon or they were about other business. Davy was nowhere to be seen, either. I was heartily relieved.

On my return, I took my writing materials into the garden where I found a pretty sheltered arbour. Climbing roses twined about a wrought-iron framework, though they were only just beginning to come into flower. There was a paved floor and, standing on it, a small round table with a gaily coloured tesserae surface. I guessed the Hammets had brought that with them from Italy on one of their previous tours.

I had promised to write Ben a full account of our adventures as our holiday progressed. But this first letter would set the tone, and I did not want to worry him. So, although I described Davy Evans and the dogcart, I made no mention of the Dawlish sisters: and certainly none of Aunt Cora's grim prophecy.

I had just about finished when Mrs Parry appeared,

ready for the day. She wore a gown patterned with broad lilac stripes. It had trumpet-shaped sleeves reaching down to a little past the elbow, teamed with separate crisp white lawn ballooning sleeves to cover her forearms from elbows to wrist. This fashion she clearly considered holiday wear.

She exclaimed, 'Ah, there you are, Elizabeth! Quite hidden away. Will you not come indoors? Mrs Dennis has set out a quite delightful luncheon.'

We went in and, sure enough, Mrs Dennis had set the table. Jessie was bringing in the soup.

'And how have you been occupying yourself this morning?' asked Mrs Parry, shaking out her napkin and studying the table with approval.

I told her I had walked down to the village and located the post office, and that I had encountered a gentleman by the name of Harcourt, who had told me he would also be at Sir Henry's dinner table that evening.

'Who is he?' asked Mrs Parry. 'Another landowner?'

'I have no idea,' I confessed. 'He didn't say. I don't think so. He would have said. He has some other—'

But I didn't complete my sentence because I didn't quite know what I did think about Harcourt.

'Schoolmaster? Clergyman?' she asked.

'Oh, no, neither of those.' Of that I felt quite sure.

Fortunately Mrs Parry lost interest in the subject.

I did not tell her of my meeting with the black-clad sisters, or my fleeting sighting of Davy Evans. It struck me that, what with having to be careful what I told Ben, and careful what I told Mrs Parry, I would need my wits about me for the whole time we were here.

'And already you are so much brighter in manner, more *yourself*, Elizabeth,' she observed. 'I knew our sojourn here would do you good.'

I couldn't let that pass without a mild challenge. 'Mrs Dennis,' I said, 'seems to think we are to stay the full month.'

'Of course,' said Mrs Parry comfortably. 'That was what we agreed, was it not?'

I wanted to shout that no, it wasn't. But it would have done no good. She had convinced herself that I had agreed to stay the full month, because that is what she wanted to believe. I was so annoyed that, just for a fleeting moment, I contemplated telling her of Aunt Cora's declaration that I had brought death with me. However Mrs Parry was not, to my knowledge, superstitious; nor was I. I said nothing. Nobody likes the bringer of bad news, and in particular they don't want to hear that news over luncheon.

Chapter Four

Be careful now.
Don't make a mistake at this late stage.

Elizabeth Martin Ross

THERE IS a marked difference between meeting a complete stranger unawares and meeting, for the first time, someone you are expecting to see, of whom you have been told a little.

In the first instance, a chance meeting with strangers, such as with Aunts Tibby and Cora, one's opinion is informed by what one sees and hears for oneself.

In the second instance one may already have constructed a mental image. This in turn leads to certain expectations. Such was the case with Sir Henry Meager.

I knew his name and who he was. I had met a member of his family, Andrew Beresford, five years before, and liked him. Accordingly when we set out to dine with the gentleman that evening I expected an elderly, white-haired gentleman of old-fashioned style and kindly manner. He might be corpulent from good dining and lack of exercise and, because of the gout that afflicted him, it would not have surprised me to see his bandaged foot propped on a stool.

Married to a police detective I should have known better. 'Expect everything and expect nothing!' Ben had once said to me. 'Always base your conclusions on the evidence of your own eyes and ears, and proven facts.'

I would have done well to remember that. My first sight of Sir Henry would then have come as less of a surprise.

But before this happened I had my first view of 'the Hall', as Tizard named the house, and was fascinated by it. The carriage turned into a long drive, a little neglected perhaps because the berlin, once again sent to carry us, lurched over an uneven surface. We drove between a ceremonial guard of tall elms to either side. Beyond them, someone had introduced a much more modern fashion in gardening in the shape of rhododendron bushes. Now, in late spring, they were still resplendent in their white, pink and red blooms, and seemed to float like islands on the green lawns. But if someone had tried at some point to bring the gardens up to date, no one had seen any need to touch the house itself. The drive brought us to the door of a once-splendid Elizabethan mansion, extended in Jacobean style but left in peace by later Georgian fashions in architecture. That this, like the driveway, could have done with a little better maintenance did not matter. It seemed to grow so naturally from the landscape that its weatherworn exterior made it of a piece with the venerable elms. Seeing it, I now thought the rhododendrons out of place and understood that whoever had ordered their planting had realised this and abandoned any further attempt to impose the taste of the present day.

It would be a mistake to assume from Mrs Parry's self-indulgent appearance that she was an unobservant woman. She was not. Little escaped her sharp gaze and she, too, had taken note of the elm avenue.

'When I was a girl,' she said unexpectedly, 'country people still held to various superstitions connected with that species of tree. Their roots lead down into the underworld, many believed, and supernatural beings were drawn to them. Fairies and so on, you know. Such nonsense, of course, but one cannot help but wonder whether here, so far from London, there are not some who still believe it.'

I thought it quite likely hereabouts. It was the sort of tale Tibby and Cora would tell. But we had little time to observe any more. We were ushered into the house, led across a square entrance hall and shown into a long, narrow drawing room. The lower sections of the walls were oak-panelled and very dark, clearly of a date with the house. The ceiling was of stucco and painted. But two centuries of smoke from the splendid open hearth with its carved stone surround, from the gentlemen's tobacco and from the candles that had preceded the gas lighting now installed, had discoloured the images above our heads and it was not possible to make them all out. I hoped I might get the opportunity to view this room in daylight. Family portraits adorned the walls above the wainscot, together with paintings of sailing ships of a type much less seen now in the age of steam. The air held the lingering scent of an old English country house: tobacco, fine port and dogs. The dogs had been banished for this evening, however, and there was one unexpected note of sophistication. The room contained a piano. It was not draped, as so often, in some sort of oriental shawl, and crowned with an array of photographs. These things are signs that the instrument is there as a fashionable piece of furniture only. This fine grand piano was bare and well polished. I wondered if, later, someone would be invited to play. I hope the request wouldn't be made of me.

A reception party of four other people awaited us. Two of them I recognised at once. One was Andrew Beresford, whom I'd met on my last visit to the area. He greeted me with a smile of genuine pleasure as he rose to his feet. I was not surprised to see him, because I already knew that his family and the Meagers were connected. There was a young woman who had been seated by him, perhaps in her late twenties, with plain but not unpleasing features. Would she be the pianist?

The other man, who had risen to greet us, was Harcourt, whom I'd encountered that morning. He bowed and fixed me briefly with a conspiratorial look. I fancied it carried a message. It might be advisable not to admit I'd met him already. Well, if he did not wish it, I would not mention the encounter. Aunt Parry wouldn't refer to it because she would already have forgotten what I'd told her before lunch that day. I decided that Harcourt seemed an odd person but I liked him.

That left our host, who rose to his feet as we entered,

with the aid of a cane but without other assistance. The gout was not so bad as to incapacitate him. He was of commanding aspect, a little thick in the body but not corpulent, only strongly built. I judged him in his mid-sixties. He still rejoiced in a full head of thick, iron-grey hair and splendid side whiskers, with the result that he might look a little younger than he really was. Still, he was a fine-looking man, I thought, who must once have been very handsome. If he were born around 1810, then what we saw here was a Georgian buck, still with all the dash and swagger of his youth, even leaning on a cane. I glanced at Mrs Parry and saw she was impressed.

'My dear ladies!' said Sir Henry. 'I have the honour of receiving Mrs Parry beneath my roof, I believe? You are very welcome in my house. I am delighted you are able to dine this evening.' He bowed in the direction of Aunt Parry.

He stretched out his hand in a gallant gesture. Mrs Parry placed her plump little white hand on his, and he raised it gracefully to his lips. Mrs Parry, already quite pink from pleasure, now dimpled, glancing up at him beneath fluttering eyelids, and I wondered if I ought to stand by to catch her if she fainted.

Fortunately he released her hand. He turned, leaning a little more heavily on the cane, and fixed me with a gaze that made me feel I could have no secrets from such a man. 'And this must be Mrs Ross? You are most welcome, ma'am.' He bowed again, a little more stiffly; there would be no kiss of the hand for me. Instead, he indicated Beresford and the young woman.

'You have met my nephew, Andrew Beresford, I believe?'

'Indeed, I have,' I said. 'On a previous visit to the area some five years ago.'

'It's a pleasure to see you again, ma'am,' said Beresford. He put his hand on the arm of the plain young woman in what struck me as a reassuring gesture. 'May I present my wife, Agnes?'

Well, he had not been married when I was here before. Agnes Beresford blushed and looked down. She is shy, I thought. Is it because she knows herself to be plain? Pretty girls soon get used to being the centre of attention. She is embarrassed by it. Yet she has made a good marriage and ought to have more confidence. Or is she worried about being asked to play for us after dinner?

It only remained for the other gentleman to be introduced and Sir Henry did this now, with a somewhat casual gesture towards him. 'My estate manager, Robert Harcourt.'

Robert Harcourt bowed again and said, 'I hope you will enjoy your stay in our county, ladies.'

He didn't smile this time, and still made no reference to our earlier meeting in the village, so neither did I. If anything, I thought he seemed a little put out. This, I thought, is why he didn't explain himself more fully this morning. He has been invited to make up an even number and ensure that there are three ladies and three gentlemen, and he knows it. Still, estate manager was an important position and carried much responsibility.

And so the evening began. I have often thought back to it and tried to remember everything that was said and the impressions I received. We learned early that Sir Henry was a widower. Our way into dinner led us past a number of family portraits, gathered in a display. We were invited to turn our attention to one of them. 'My dear late wife, Madeleine.' He added: 'We were married only five years before her untimely death.'

The portrait showed a young woman I judged to be in her early twenties. Her features were regular and her expression somewhat wooden. But perhaps that was the fault of the artist and not a true reflection of the sitter. Her most distinguishing feature was her hair. That had been drawn up into an elaborate wired topknot, balanced by thick bunches of glossy curls either side of her face. Either the profusion of curls or the topknot must be false, or the late Madeleine Meager had been blessed with more than the usual amount of natural hair. This way of dressing the hair, and the style of her gown, confirmed the portrait to have been done in the 1830s. Had it been for the new young wife, I wondered, that the rhododendrons had been introduced to the gardens? With her early death, had the interest in novelty been extinguished? Now they were her monument.

'And have you children?' asked Mrs Parry, after she had expressed her condolences on his early bereavement.

'Sadly, ma'am, my dear Madeleine and I were not blessed with children.'

I don't know why at that moment I glanced towards Robert Harcourt, but I did, and caught a fleeting, angry expression on his face. Then he saw that I looked at him and he smiled at me in a friendly enough way.

Sir Henry was drawing our attention to another portrait; that of a dashing young fellow in naval uniform, posed against a background of rocks, crashing waves and distant ships of the line. 'My father, as a young man', he said. Then, indicating a companion portrait, 'And later on in life.'

This second version of the late naval hero showed him with fine white whiskers, a red face and a slightly mad look in his eye.

'And who are the two young boys in that painting?' asked Mrs Parry, pointing to a smaller oil.

'That, ma'am, shows my late father and his brother, Henry, in childhood. Both were sent into the navy. My Uncle Henry, after whom I was named, died of fever in the West Indies.' Sir Henry walked on and we had perforce to follow.

When we had settled at table, Mrs Parry took our host's words concerning his childless marriage as a cue. She began to tell the gentlemen about her nephew, Frank Carterton, who was a Member of Parliament and at the beginning of what would surely be a distinguished career. What was more, he and his delightful wife, Patience, had just been blessed with an infant son.

At that, Sir Henry raised his glass of wine and proposed a toast to the new arrival.

'And you, Mrs Ross, have you and Mr Ross a young family perhaps?' Harcourt asked me unexpectedly.

'No, unfortunately, we do not,' I told him.

Sir Henry had overheard and said, rather abruptly, 'My nephew, Beresford here, will be my heir.'

It was difficult to tell, in such a warm room and by artificial light, but I thought Harcourt flushed and did not look best pleased for a second or two. Nor did Andrew Beresford. Suddenly, the lingering unease I had sensed in the gathering when we arrived crystallised into a something I could pinpoint. There had been some kind of dispute before Mrs Parry and I arrived. Probably Agnes Beresford had not been involved in it, but the three men certainly had.

After dinner, we returned to the drawing room.

'And will you not play something for us, Agnes, my dear?' asked Sir Henry with a smile and a bow of the head towards Mrs Beresford.

Agnes flushed rather pinker than the warmth of the room and the good dinner we had eaten might have accounted for. Again I saw her husband touch her arm lightly. He also turned his head to smile encouragingly at her.

Agnes rose to her feet, went to the piano and seated herself. Beresford followed her and positioned himself to turn the sheets of music for her. I was expecting her to be accomplished. Young ladies are taught these things. What I had not expected, but knew from the first notes, was that she was a true musician, a gifted performer. When she was at the piano she was no longer shy and awkward, with little to say for herself. As the notes rippled beneath her fingers the piano spoke for her, communicating her thoughts and emotions through the music. I glanced at Mrs Parry and caught a look of surprise on her face, though she quickly concealed it. Then I looked at Sir Henry. He was leaning back in his chair, his fingertips together in front of his cravat, his abandoned cane propped against a small bureau behind him. He watched Agnes as she played, a slight smile on his lips and something in his eyes I did not quite like.

But where was Harcourt? I realised he was not with our seated group. I turned my head and saw that he had removed himself to stand by the fireplace, with his arm resting on the mantelshelf. He may have been listening; but he was not watching Agnes. He was looking towards the portrait of our host's late wife, and I could not read his expression.

'Well, that was a most pleasant evening,' declared Mrs Parry, as we rattled homeward in the creaking old berlin. 'Sir Henry is such a charming gentleman.'

'Yes,' I agreed, as it was expected I should. But I had not found Sir Henry charming. If urged to express what I felt about him, I might even have confessed that something about him had frightened me.

A good dinner, wine, a little later to bed than usual, and a great deal of new information to sort through in my brain, together with the sea air, all combined to send me into deep slumber. I was awoken by a dreadful shriek.

I sat up in bed with a start. My first instinct was to think I must have been dreaming, and had cried out. But, no, what I'd heard was real enough. There were raised voices on the floor below and wails of disbelief and dismay. I scrambled from the bed and after donning my shawl and slippers hurried out into the corridor. As I made my way towards the head of the stairs I met Nugent, hurrying towards it from the other direction. She was at least dressed, but her hair was still tied up in rag curls.

'You heard it, too, then, did you, Mrs Ross?' she

demanded. 'Whatever could be the meaning of that?'

'Something's wrong,' I said. 'But it may be nothing more than a dropped dish.'

'Not a scream like that,' said Nugent firmly. 'No one ever yelled out like that on account of a dropped dish of kidneys!'

Remembering Mrs Parry, who had not joined us, I began to ask, 'Where is—?' But I did not complete the sentence. Nugent was ahead of me.

'Still fast asleep,' she told me. 'It takes a fair bit to waken her in the morning.' Recalling that she spoke of her employer, she added, more respectfully, 'Madam was very tired last night when she returned. She was falling asleep as I got her ready for bed. I dare say she won't have heard it.'

Below us, a pattering of feet caused us both to lean over the balustrade. A flash of red hair indicated Jessie Dennis, evidently the source of the shriek. She stopped at the foot of the staircase, becoming aware that there were spectators on the landing above, and looked up at us, her mouth agape, eyes wild.

'Oh, madam!' she exclaimed. 'Oh, Mrs Ross, a terrible thing has happened up at the Hall.' She clasped her hands at her breast. 'Like nothing before, never!' She drew in a deep breath. 'You'll never believe it, ma'am, but it's true. Oh, ma'am, Sir Henry is dead!'

My heart sank like a stone and I hope my dismay did not show in my face. In my mind's eye I saw Cora Dawlish, in her black gown and jet necklaces, seated on the bench and loudly prophesying that I would bring death. Death, it seemed, had not tarried.

Chapter Five

*Well, well, now we'll see what they all do. They do so
love their secrets, that family. They have them all
penned up like water behind a dam. But now there is
a crack in the dam wall. They will be seeking to stop it
up before it widens and a spate of truth rushes out.*

Elizabeth Martin Ross

JESSIE WAS clearly in deep shock at the unexpected news,
but it struck me she was also excited. Her eyes sparkled and
her mouth hung open. Her breath was ragged and fast. It
was the undercurrent of thrill that worried me most. From
high excitement the emotional barometer could plunge to a
panicked low; and it could happen in a trice. She might
faint or begin to sob uncontrollably. At the very worst, she
might have a fit. Did I attempt to soothe her? Or slap her?

'Let me, Mrs Ross.' It was Nugent who spoke. An
experienced upper servant, she knew how to deal with
hysterical underlings. She stepped forward and took charge.

'Pull yourself together, my girl!' she ordered Jessie crisply. 'And stop making an exhibition of yourself. No more squawking! Do you hear me?'

Jessie closed her mouth and blinked, as if someone had shaken her awake.

Nugent then turned to me and said, 'I'll go down, Mrs Ross, and get some details. If you don't mind my suggesting it, perhaps you could slip into something you'd prefer to be seen wearing.'

She gripped Jessie's arm. 'Come along, my girl. Back to your mother!' She marched the girl away in a fashion an arresting constable would have been pleased to copy.

I returned to my room and wriggled hurriedly into a day gown. I brushed my hair and twisted it into a coil, well secured with pins at the back of my head. Then I made my own way downstairs at a dignified pace. I hoped my demeanour would pass muster, as inwardly I was now anxious to learn whether such shocking news could be true. But something had happened and, in the continued absence of Mrs Parry, I must give the appearance of authority. I went into the small parlour, seated myself, folded my hands in my lap and waited. I had not to wait long.

Nugent returned with Mrs Dennis. Somehow, in the time during which I'd dressed, skilled lady's maid that she was, Nugent had found time not only to fetch the house-keeper, but to untie the rag knots dotted about her own head. The result was a haphazard tangle of greying curls. As for the housekeeper, she was pale but not, I was pleased to see, hysterical.

She bobbed an awkward curtsey, and said, 'I am sorry,

ma'am, for the disturbance. It's my girl, she was that scared when she heard the awful news. I was took aback myself.'

I thought the housekeeper's outward control was maintained with difficulty and she might give way at any moment.

Nugent, after a minatory glare at the housekeeper, took over. 'I am afraid, Mrs Ross, there has been an accident, a fatal one.'

'What kind of fatal accident?' My own voice echoed in my ear as though the words were spoken far away by someone else.

Mrs Dennis, now visibly trembling, replied: ''Tis the squire, ma'am. He's been found dead in his bed!'

This did not tally with the first report. People died in their beds in the course of nature. It was not usually termed an accident. I began to suspect the news might yet turn out to be unfounded rumour. 'Are you sure of this?' I asked sharply. 'This would be a very serious story to spread.'

'It's the truth, ma'am. There's Davy Evans in the kitchen, brought us the news not twenty minutes ago. I'm afraid my girl let out a great screech. She was frightened. It's given me a terrible shock, as well.'

I tussled with the housekeeper's undoubted certainty, and was forced to accept it. She was a sensible woman. She would not repeat something she did not believe to be the truth. I sought to clarify the facts, such as were known. 'When you say Sir Henry has been found in his bed, then has he died in his sleep?'

'He didn't die natural, ma'am. He was shot. There was blood everywhere, so they say.'

'*Shot?*' Into my mind leaped the memory of that tension between the three men I had noticed the previous evening. 'How so, shot?'

'I don't know, ma'am,' the housekeeper confessed. 'I don't think Davy knows exactly. Only that Sir Henry's manservant found him this morning, lying there dead, with blood all over the pillow and a pistol on the coverlet.'

Had Sir Henry shot himself? He had not struck me as the sort of man to take his own life. Nor had he seemed to be in any kind of despair the previous evening. But the alternative sent a cold shiver running along my spine. If it were not suicide, and it could hardly be an accident, we were left with murder.

The housekeeper was standing before me, awaiting my reaction to the news. Her red country face gazed at me as if awaiting orders about the menu for the day. It brought me to my senses. In the absence of Mrs Parry, I was in charge here and expected to show it. I stifled my alarm and made a quick decision. Nothing could be accepted without all the facts, or as many as could be learned. 'Is Davy still here?' I asked.

'Yes'm. In the kitchen,' confessed Mrs Dennis.

Consoling the distraught Jessie, no doubt, I thought. 'Bring him in here,' I ordered, 'I want to hear his account myself.' Then, realising that it would help the housekeeper if she had something to do, I added, 'Perhaps you could make some tea? It will help us all.'

Mrs Dennis, as I'd guessed, brightened at having a task given to her. She bobbed a curtsey and hurried out.

'Just wait here with me, would you, Nugent?' I asked.

'Of course, Mrs Ross. I wouldn't leave you here alone with that scallywag!' declared Nugent, drawing herself up and ready for battle, if necessary.

It was not the thought of being left alone with Davy that worried me. It was the prospect of Mrs Parry being awoken and told the news by her lady's maid, with gory details of blood on the pillow and a pistol lying nearby. But rumour quickly adds detail to a bare skeleton of fact. Perhaps there had been no blood, no pistol, only the lifeless body of an elderly man who had eaten and drunk well the previous evening. A heart attack? That was much more likely. In any case, surely, someone would have sent for the doctor, if only to certify the death. We should soon hear what had really happened.

'We must not leap to conclusions, Nugent,' I said firmly. 'First we must hear how Davy Evans learned the news. It will help assess how accurate it may be. I would not wish Mrs Parry to be frightened by kitchen gossip.'

We heard the clump of heavy male boots outside and Davy Evans appeared. He held his hat in his hand, and ducked his head beneath the low lintel of the doorway. Ignoring Nugent, he made an awkward bow in my direction.

'Morning, ma'am. You sent for me.'

He looked and sounded sombre and the mocking gleam I remembered in his dark eyes was gone. But his gaze was still sharp and wary as he glanced around the room before returning his attention to me. I wondered if he was checking no one else had joined us. Had he expected Mrs Parry? I drew a deep breath.

Ann Granger

'Good morning, Evans. I understand that you have brought some very shocking news regarding Sir Henry Meager?'

Davy nodded his head. 'Aye, he's dead.'

'From whom do you have this information? Is it reliable and not some foolish rumour?'

'No,' said Davy simply, 'he's a goner, all right.'

'That is no way to speak of the gentleman!' snapped Nugent, shocked.

Davy was not in awe of a middle-aged lady's maid. ''Tis true, even so.'

'So, from whom do you have this tragic news?' I demanded sternly, repeating my original question. At the back of my mind lingered the fear that he had it from Cora Dawlish or her sister. Where Cora might have learned it, goodness only knew. She would claim it was by second sight, if asked.

He nodded his mop of dark curls again. 'From Tom Tizard.'

This was serious. A member of Sir Henry's staff should know the facts. At the same time, I felt a sense of relief that the news had not originated with the sisters. I said, 'Go on.'

'Well, then,' resumed Davy. 'I was walking up on the main road, meaning to cut across the heath to Hythe. I sometimes help out on the ferryboats. The dogcart came rattling along, Tom driving. He pulled up the pony and shouted down to me that the squire was dead, and by his own hand. He was driving over to Mr Beresford's house, to break the news, and ask him to go at once to his uncle's,

60

to the big house. Tom was intending to drive on afterwards and fetch the doctor, to come and certify the death. Mr Harcourt had told him it would be necessary.'

'Mr Harcourt is presumably at the house and has taken charge?' I asked.

'So Tom Tizard said.' Davy nodded. 'Until Mr Beresford gets there, Mr Harcourt is giving out the orders. Someone has to, I reckon. Warton, the butler, is an old fellow and he's got religion. He reckons the end of the world is nigh and this is proof. You'll get no sense out of him. The cook has her hands full with the maids. They're all wailing; and that valet of Sir Henry's had a funny turn when he saw the blood and hasn't got over it.' Davy allowed himself a grin and looked, briefly, as he had when I'd spotted him in the doorway of the Dawlish sisters' cottage. 'They're running round like chickens when the fox is in the henhouse.'

'You mind your tongue!' snapped Nugent, incensed. 'Speak respectful when talking of a death!'

Davy gave Nugent a careless glance. 'All right, m'dear, keep your wig on!'

At that Nugent looked so furious I feared she might set about the fellow, and box his ears, if she could have reached them. It was fortunate she did not have her trusty umbrella to hand, or she might have attempted to belabour him with that. Still, I had to admit that Davy had painted a lively picture of the scene. Harcourt had plenty to deal with. Nevertheless he'd struck me as a capable man, and must be, if he ran Sir Henry's estate and business matters.

'Thank you, Evans,' I said loudly and firmly. 'You can go now.'

He bobbed his head at me and left.

'That rogue,' spluttered the still enraged Nugent, 'is nothing but trouble! Mark my words.'

'You are probably right,' I agreed with her. 'But I am afraid the moment has come to wake Mrs Parry and tell her the bad news.'

We gazed at one another, united in apprehension. 'I'll wake madam,' said Nugent. '*You* tell her.'

I elected to wait outside the bedroom door until Nugent called me in. But it didn't work out as we had planned. The hustle and bustle had reached her ahead of us. As soon as Nugent entered the room, Aunt Parry broke into voluble speech. She began by demanding to know why she was being awoken at such an early hour (it was now a little after ten), and what was going on downstairs?

'I am very sorry, madam, but someone has brought some very bad news,' the maid began.

'What sort of bad news?' snapped Mrs Parry, unimpressed by Nugent's soothing tone. 'It must be desperate indeed to cause such a racket.'

Nugent told her the bare facts. There was a moment's delay and then Aunt Parry exploded in rage.

'Gossip, Nugent! After all these years, you come and worry me with malicious servants' gossip? And about Sir Henry! It's wicked to say such a thing.'

'It's a fact, madam, and there's no mistake, I'm afraid. That fellow Evans has been here to bring the news.'

'Well, I certainly wouldn't believe anything *he* says!' Mrs

Parry vehemently repulsed the suggestion. 'He is making mischief, and probably already drunk. How would he know, anyway?'

'He had it from the coachman, Tizard, madam. He met him on the road, driving to break the bad news to Mr Beresford.'

At the mention of Andrew Beresford being brought into it Mrs Parry fell silent for a moment or two, before demanding, 'Where is Mrs Ross?'

It was time for me to put in an appearance. Nugent greeted me with a wry expression and muttered, 'I had to tell her, ma'am. She was already awake and aware something was going on.'

'Tell me?' Mrs Parry had excellent hearing. 'I should think so! Who should be told, if not me? Why, I sat at the gentleman's dinner table only a few hours ago! How can he be dead?'

'I am so very sorry, Aunt Parry. This is dreadful news and you are naturally very shocked, as are we all . . .' I began.

'Shocked?' burst out Mrs Parry. She was propped up on the pillows, swathed in a salmon-pink satin wrap, her hair invisible beneath a lace cap. Her face was much the same colour as the wrap.

'Nugent,' I suggested, 'perhaps you'd be so good as to go down to the kitchen and see if Mrs Dennis has made that tea.'

When we were alone, Mrs Parry announced, 'It is the beginning of a revolution, mark my words. The lower orders are about to slaughter the landowners! There is no other explanation.'

'I don't think anyone else has died, only Sir Henry and we don't know—'

'Who found him?' she interrupted.

'Apparently his valet did. Dead in his bed with a pistol beside him.'

Mrs Parry leaned forward and said firmly, 'Sir Henry was not a man to blow out his own brains! Whyever should he? He was a most gracious host this last evening, charming. He would hardly hold a dinner party and then go to bed and shoot himself!' In a last rebuttal, she added, 'If he wanted to make away with himself, why go to bed first? It would be much more seemly to be found fully dressed, not in a nightshirt.'

It was a good point to make. I was reminded that Mrs Parry was a very competent woman in her business affairs. Another elderly lady might have swooned away, as a suitable reaction, or burst into tears. Not so Mrs Parry. If anything, she seemed to be taking the idea that Sir Henry, who had kissed her hand so charmingly the previous evening, should have blown out his brains a few hours later as preposterous, as well as downright insulting. Actually, I was inclined to agree with her about the inexplicable nature of the event.

'You are an astute woman, Elizabeth,' continued Aunt Parry, in a rare compliment. 'Does it make any sense to you that a gentleman of breeding and property would host a dinner party, behave naturally in every way, bid his guests goodnight, go upstairs and make ready for bed, get into bed and then finish the evening by putting a bullet in his own head?'

'No, Aunt Parry, it doesn't.'

'Quite so.' Mrs Parry pulled the satin wrap tighter around her plump form, and leaned back on the pillows. 'A younger man, perhaps, who'd got himself entangled in some unseemly affair; or gambled away his inheritance, well, he might overdramatise the situation and do something desperate. But not Sir Henry!' She paused for breath. 'To think,' she continued resentfully, 'that I came down here to the seaside for rest and recuperation.'

Nugent returned, with a subdued Jessie behind her, bearing the tray. There was a pause for a restoring drink. The British widely believe tea to be a support in all emergencies. It certainly seemed to have a beneficial effect on Mrs Parry. After a few minutes of silent reflection as she sipped, she set down the teacup. She dabbed at her lips with a handkerchief and suddenly appeared much brisker and more matter-of-fact.

'Elizabeth!' she said. 'This is a very bad business. There is a murderer about the area somewhere. You must write to Inspector Ross and tell him he is to come *immediately*!'

'He can't start an investigation, Aunt Parry, until it is requested of him officially,' I protested, startled. 'After all, we don't know exactly what happened. In the meantime, if any investigation is to be made, the police will begin it under the direction, probably, of a senior officer at Southampton.'

'*I* am requesting it!' said Mrs Parry. 'Send a telegraphed message at once to your husband. The police at Southampton will not do at all. I know nothing of them.'

I sought for an acceptable delay to this request. 'Perhaps,

Aunt Parry, we should wait and see what Mr Beresford has to say. He is a member of Sir Henry's family and also, we learned last night at dinner, heir to Sir Henry's considerable estate. He will want a thorough examination of the facts. We should not, perhaps, act in any way that might suggest we are, um, interfering in a family matter.'

To my great relief this was received with a nod of agreement. 'Although it is still very early in the day,' Mrs Parry decreed, 'I shall get up and, against my usual habit, I shall come down to breakfast. Have you breakfasted yet, Elizabeth?'

'No, the household routine has rather—'

'The servants losing their heads, I dare say. It is always the case in any emergency,' interrupted Mrs Parry. 'First hint of an upset and they go to pieces. Go down and make sure they are putting out the breakfast. I shall join you shortly.' She turned to Nugent. 'Lay out my grey gown. What are you wearing, Elizabeth? Well, I dare say that dull shade of blue will do. People will expect us to show respect.'

By the time she had come down, dressed and ready for to face whatever might happen next, it was nearly midday. I ventured to suggest we treat the table of cold and hot meats, set out by Mrs Dennis, as our luncheon. 'After this, we shall not be ready to eat again until this evening. Well,' I added hastily, 'we can have tea and some little cakes later in the afternoon.'

'I suppose so,' said Mrs Parry discontentedly. 'I am so much put out by this awful business. I doubt I shall be able to do more than pick at something. A slice of that roast ham, perhaps? What do you think those sausages contain? Are there eggs under that lid? What happened to the pork pie we brought down in the Fortnum's hamper?'

We finished a substantial meal and retired to sit in the garden in the arbour, where I had sat the day before to write my letter to Ben. By now, Mrs Parry was in a better mood but still fretting at the lack of any more news.

'I don't understand why we have not received any message from Mr Beresford. He is aware we dined with his uncle yesterday. He must know we are anxious to have proper information, not just something told by the coachman to that disreputable-looking fellow who drove the dogcart with our luggage on the day we arrived.'

But I had become aware of a distant regular thud of hooves, coming ever nearer. A horseman suddenly appeared, the animal slithering down the downward slope from the road above, dislodging dirt and stones. Jacob Dennis came hobbling out to take the reins and Andrew Beresford swung down from the saddle and came towards us, hat in hand.

'At last!' exclaimed Mrs Parry. 'My dear sir, we are dismayed to hear the tragic news. Sir Henry will be greatly missed in the county.'

I hastened to add my own condolences on the family tragedy.

'Yes, yes,' agreed Beresford rather brusquely. 'The news has certainly got around.'

'Davy Evans came to tell us this morning,' I informed him. 'I believe he had met Tizard on his way to your house.'

'That's so. The doctor had to be brought, also, to certify the death.' He paused and added briefly, 'A single gunshot wound to the head.'

'Awful,' exclaimed Mrs Parry. 'We were all so merry yesterday evening. I cannot believe—'

He interrupted her. 'If you are going to say, ma'am, that you find it hard to believe my uncle shot himself, then I have to tell you I agree with you. There is no reason at all why he should. Apart from anything else, he was a tough old fellow and it would not be in his nature.' He paused.

I realised he was torn between satisfying our curiosity and not saying more than might be wise.

'Mr Beresford,' I said. 'You may be absolutely assured that neither Mrs Parry nor I will repeat anything you may tell us to anyone else hereabouts. I am a police detective's wife and I understand the value of evidence. If you don't want to answer, I shall understand perfectly.' It was my turn to hesitate. 'One thing does . . . I confess, there is one thing I would like to know.'

Beresford gave a faint smile. 'You are curious about the weapon, whether it was known to belong to my uncle.'

I felt my cheeks redden. 'Well, yes,' I admitted.

'A duelling pistol,' he said bluntly.

'A duelling pistol?' cried Mrs Parry. 'Do gentlemen fight duels any longer? In this country, I mean. When I was a girl, one heard occasionally . . . but it was already an unusual event. On the Continent, of course . . .'

'As soon as I saw the pistol, I recognised it as one of a pair, as such weapons usually are.' Beresford's voice was grim but also a little resentful. 'These were made in Spain; and brought from there by my uncle when he was a younger man. He was rather proud of them. They are highly decorated with damascene work. They were kept, in their case, in a locked desk in the library, together with a supply of ammunition. It occasionally amused my uncle to take one of the pistols outside and discharge it at a target, for the entertainment of visitors. Both weapons are reasonably accurate. I have, in the past, fired one myself at a target. I went at once to check that the weapon on the pillow was indeed one of the library pair. The opened case is still in the desk, and the companion pistol still in it. But the drawer appears to have been forced. If my uncle had opened it, he would certainly have used his key.'

He might have mislaid the key, I thought, and not wanted to spend time hunting for it. But why the urgency? 'Is it not a curious weapon to use? If, indeed, Sir Henry took his own life?' I asked.

'Very odd!' agreed Beresford. 'But if the weapon was loaded by my uncle, one supposes he did it in the library and took the pistol to the bedroom. He must have done this surreptitiously, because of the risk of it being seen by his valet. The man denies seeing it that evening. It is another thing that makes no sense. Did my uncle have some strange compulsion to die in his bed? If he loaded the weapon in the library, he might just as easily have shot himself there to be discovered fully dressed, rather than in a nightshirt. He had a strong sense of dignity.'

Beresford hesitated and gave Mrs Parry an apologetic grimace. 'Begging your pardon, ma'am, for distressing you.'

But Mrs Parry was not distressed by gory detail. She gave a little wave of her hand to indicate his apology was not necessary. 'Did no one hear the shot?' she demanded with a puzzled frown.

'Apparently not. It isn't perhaps as surprising as might seem. My uncle's staff, from the butler to the cook, the housemaids, and his personal valet, Lynn, have nearly all been in his service for some years. None of them is particularly young, except for the skivvy who washes the dishes, and she is a little simple. If she had heard anything, she would not have done anything. She'd have waited for orders. The dinner party had made extra work for them all. All the household staff sleep on the attic floor, and last night they slept soundly, it seems. None of them heard a thing. Or, if wakened by such a noise, they might have put it down to poachers outside. Dear ladies, I cannot stay long. I am on my way to Hythe, where there is a telegraph office. I must inform my uncle's lawyer in London, Pelham. He will want to come down.'

I managed to quell an exclamation of surprise. Could this Pelham be the same man of law whom Ben had had reason to encounter in a couple of cases?

Beresford was talking. 'And after I have sent the telegram, I must take the ferry across to Southampton and inform the police there. There is a constable at Hythe but this will be beyond his remit.'

'Then the coroner will be involved!' said Mrs Parry sharply. 'There will be an inquest. Well, it is to be expected. Sir Henry was a gentleman of some consequence locally.'

Beresford turned to me, suddenly looking embarrassed. 'Mrs Ross, I am also considering requesting that Scotland Yard send down a detective. I am hoping that your husband might be able to come and assist the Southampton police, as he did so competently in a previous case of murder in the district.'

Before I could reply, Mrs Parry leaned forward and said triumphantly: 'That is exactly what I was saying to Elizabeth before you came. Did I not, Elizabeth? We must have Mr Ross.'

Beresford rose to take his leave. I accompanied him until we had nearly reached Jacob Dennis, who stood waiting at the horse's head. 'Mr Beresford,' I said quietly, 'when I expressed my condolences on your uncle's death, it wasn't just because it's expected on occasions of loss, but because I am, truly, very sorry. Also, I know, as a police detective's wife, how intrusive the investigations into these matters can be. I am afraid that you and your wife are going to be inconvenienced in so many ways. It is inevitable. You are very shocked now, of course, and your wife must be too. But, for a time, things may get worse.'

He sighed. 'It's difficult for Agnes. She didn't care at all for the old fellow. She didn't tell me so, but I could see it. Now, well, our family affairs will be dragged into the limelight. We all have skeletons in the closet, don't we? Not that I am saying we have any that should lead to murder, in the normal way of things! But it is the knowledge that privacy will be stripped away . . . I sincerely hope that Mr Ross will be able to come and take charge. He is acquainted with us a little, and it would be far better . . .'

I had meant my words well, but they had touched on something too personal. Beresford fell silent, his manner changed abruptly. He placed his hat on his head, swung himself easily into the saddle and raised his right hand to touch his hat brim in a farewell salute. 'We shall meet again soon, ma'am, I am sure!' he said crisply.

With a clatter of hooves, he was gone.

'Well, now,' said Jacob, who obviously had sharp hearing despite his general gnarled state. 'This is a pretty puzzle, I must say.'

'You must not repeat anything you may have overheard,' I told him sharply.

'Right you are, ma'am,' he assured me.

I was not convinced. I returned upstairs and wrote a hurried note to Ben, briefly explaining what had happened and to forewarn him. I gave it to Jacob and asked him to take it immediately to the post office in the village. I couldn't trust Jessie not to open it and read its contents, and Mrs Dennis was busy in the kitchen. I certainly would not have given the task to Davy Evans, even if he had still been on the premises. But I hadn't heard his voice for the past hour and it seemed he'd left, no doubt to spread the news around.

Skeletons in the closet . . . I mused. Just what did Beresford fear might come to light?

Chapter Six

Inspector Ben Ross

'THIS IS a confounded ticklish business!' declared Superintendent Dunn.

'Yes, sir,' I agreed, standing before his desk with my hands clasped behind my back. The desk was positioned before the window. Thus I could see past him to where one of London's numerous pigeons was sunning itself on the windowsill outside. As I watched, a second one joined it. The new arrival was showing signs of amorous interest. Spring was indeed in the air. I quelled a sigh and wondered what on earth had possessed me to urge my wife to go away with Mrs Parry, particularly as she had apparently arrived only the day before a suspicious death. The news of Sir Henry Meager's sudden demise had reached us at the Yard later the previous afternoon, via a telegram from Inspector Hughes at Southampton. It lay on Dunn's desk together with further correspondence on the subject. The early post that morning had confirmed it for me in a letter from Lizzie.

'Pigeon fancier, Ross?' asked Dunn sharply.

'No, sir, I was just thinking. It is, as you say, a very strange and awkward business.' It was best to calm down Dunn by agreeing with him.

It was not the first time I'd been required to explain myself to Dunn; but this time I felt more than usually like a schoolboy, called to justify himself before an irate headmaster. I had no idea what had been going on down there in Hampshire. Lizzie wrote that she would have let me know by faster means than the penny post, had she had any way of reaching the telegraph office at Hythe. She did not know about the efficient Hughes. She went on to tell me there had been a death, a suspected suicide, but with enough unexplained detail to raise the possibility of a murder. The two ladies had dined with the victim only that evening, together with three others, including Beresford, his heir. 'You must remember Beresford!' wrote Lizzie. Mrs Parry was demanding my presence. Lizzie had explained to her that I had not a free hand in the matter. However, she, Lizzie, also wished dearly that I could be there. So did I. I do not like unexplained violent deaths in the vicinity of my wife. What's more, she normally has a neat hand when it comes to writing letters; but this missive could fairly be described as scribbled, with a couple of ink blots as well.

Dunn leaned forward, his fists clasped and resting on his desk. 'As you will know, I have the greatest respect for Mrs Ross and her judgment.'

'Yes, sir.'

'But this would not be the first time she has involved herself in police business.'

I attempted to defend my wife. 'I must protest, sir. She hasn't actually involved herself, as I understand it. It is not her fault that she was invited to dine, with a party of others, with a gentleman greatly respected in the county, and whom no one expected to, um, blow out his brains.'

'If he did so!' said Dunn tersely. 'General opinion down there, including the Hampshire coroner's, is that someone performed that task for him.'

'Yes, sir, quite.' I hesitated. 'The coroner has now ruled it murder, then?'

'I understand the matter was treated as urgent by the coroner; and he has, or so this telegram tells me, ruled it murder by person or persons unknown. Thus it is a criminal matter and has been placed in the hands of the police, that's to say, this Inspector Hughes at Southampton.'

Dunn tapped the telegraphed message lying on the desk. 'Hughes finds himself in a fix and has requested our help. I believe you have some acquaintance with the inspector?'

'I have met Inspector Hughes,' I admitted.

'And also this gentleman by the name of Beresford, who, I understand, is the deceased landowner's nephew. He wants Scotland Yard to send an experienced man and suggests you. You were there once before. So, you know him, too, don't you?'

'Not well, sir, but I have met him.'

'Sensible fellow?'

'I would say very sensible and very capable, sir.'

'Not the sort to panic?'

'Absolutely not, sir.' I thought it best to qualify my words. 'That's to say, in normal circumstances he'd be level-headed. But if it's murder and as Lizzie writes, if he's the heir, it's a ticklish situation for him.'

'To top it all, there is also a lawyer by the name of Pelham, here in London. He's been on to us, too. He's making representations on behalf of the estate; and the heir whom you say is Beresford.' Dunn gave me a quizzical look. 'All this in addition to the information you have received from your good lady. It begins to look to me as though you're taking an interest in the case already.'

At this I began to protest but then thought better of it.

'Hm!' Dunn glared at me as if I was in some way responsible for everything. 'You know this fellow Pelham too, don't you?'

'Had dealings with him, sir. He handles the business of some wealthy people. I have found him a cold fish and devious.'

Dunn leaned back in his chair and placed his stubby fingertips together. 'Then, if you know that much about Pelham, you won't be surprised to learn we are dealing here with what is generally called the county set.' He pursed his lips. 'You know what they are like in the country!' He peered at me. 'You appear to be smirking, Ross.'

'No, sir! Absolutely not!' I hastened to deny.

But I had been briefly amused. Dunn, who was a Londoner by birth and had, as far as I knew, no family members in the country, always dressed like a countryman up for the day. He favoured tweed. His complexion was ruddy as if he spent most of his time outdoors, not at his desk, and his wiry hair stood up on end as if he'd just come in from tramping round his fields. 'Sit down, Ross!' he ordered.

I knew immediately what that meant. I was to be sent down to Hampshire. If not, this was the point at which I would have been dismissed. But the decision had been made 'higher up'. I was now to be given the facts of the matter. My initial reaction was one of relief. I would see Lizzie for myself; and be sure she was in no danger and remained so.

'The deceased, Sir Henry Meager,' began Dunn, speaking rapidly, 'was aged sixty-two, born locally and residing there all his life, with absences necessitated for business reasons, and for tours to the Continent when younger. He was of an old, established family. He was wealthy and he was generally respected, if not actually liked. He was a magistrate. On the evening preceding his death, he hosted a small, private dinner party with only five guests. But you will already know all about that, Ross. You say your good lady has written to you.'

'She wrote to tell me he'd been found shot dead in his bed. She had no other information.'

Dunn sniffed. 'No doubt Mrs Ross will be deploying her investigating skills even now. Well, you will know, then, that his valet found him dead the morning following the dinner party. A weapon, a duelling pistol, was found lying on the coverlet, fairly recently discharged. The weapon is one of a pair of such pistols, property of the deceased. They were kept in the library and occasionally displayed to visitors. Therefore their existence and whereabouts were common knowledge. Meager could not have imagined anyone would use one of them to kill him, or he'd have taken more care to keep them properly locked away in a gun cabinet or safe.

'That is the trouble with country houses,' Dunn added in a kind of controlled fury, 'too many weapons of death available. Age-old blunderbusses displayed above the fire-places, military men's favourite service revolvers lying around, to say nothing of articles for use in hunting, shooting, fishing and, on this occasion, murder.'

'Now the coroner has ruled that someone did shoot Meager, there must be some reason for it,' I pointed out.

Dunn grunted and scratched his head of bristly hair to signify agreement. 'I can understand the coroner's ruling. Apart from the suspicious absence of a farewell letter such as people usually leave if they kill themselves, the forcing of the lock of the drawer in which the pistols were kept indicates another hand fired the pistol. Apparently, the deceased occasionally kept correspondence in the same drawer, anything he didn't want lying about for curious eyes to read. Thus it was kept locked, and Sir Henry kept the key on his watch chain. This means he would have had no need to break in. Inspector Hughes took possession of the watch chain and has established that the key is still on it. The coroner made much of that. Nor does there seem to be any motive for suicide. The coroner was pretty insistent about that, too.'

I ventured to say, 'Families don't like verdicts of suicide, sir. The coroner may have been under some pressure to bring in the murder verdict. The local parson would have been entitled to refuse burial in consecrated ground for a suicide, and no local family would want that. There is probably a family plot in the local churchyard. Although the coroner could have decided that the balance of Sir Henry's mind was disturbed at the time. Then he could be buried without any fuss.'

Dunn nodded. 'You are right, of course, but there is no known reason why he should commit suicide. All who knew him, and that includes the coroner, consider it quite out of character. Oh, and families – county families – don't like doubts raised about the balance of the mind. Any suggestion of madness in the bloodline, you know, would set the cat well and truly among the pigeons. No, they want this cleared up quickly, and they want a murderer found, someone to blame. That, Ross, is why they are so keen to have the assistance of Scotland Yard.

'Now then, in normal circumstances, your former acquaintance with Beresford, and your wife's presence at the house before the death occurred, would mean *you* would *not* be sent to investigate. Personal involvement can sway any man's judgment. But, I repeat, we are dealing with a set of people who close ranks against outsiders. They have a marked objection to answering questions about their private affairs, since they consider such inquiries to be impertinence. But Beresford and others might, just, be prepared to talk to you. Only keep in mind, if you can, that you will be there as an investigating officer and *not* as a family friend, something you almost seem to be already!'

Dunn cleared his throat and added awkwardly, 'There is a Mrs Beresford, Hughes informs us. She is young and might be moved to impart confidences to your wife. In any case, Mrs Ross is a witness to Sir Henry's state of mind and she may have noticed other things of interest. She generally does.' Dunn frowned. 'Don't take that as licence to let Mrs Ross have her head. The expression "a loose cannon" is one that comes to mind.'

At this I was moved to object more strongly that I usually dared. 'That is unfair, sir! You place Lizzie, my wife, in an awkward situation. On the one hand, you want her to befriend Mrs Beresford, under pretences of sympathy, and then report what the lady may tell her to me. Yet you repeatedly insist she is not to investigate. And I am not a family friend!'

Outside on the windowsill, the second pigeon's advances were being rebuffed.

'Besides,' I added, 'it would be shabby thing to do and Lizzie, Mrs Ross, is a woman of high principles.'

'Don't make a fuss, Ross,' Dunn said wearily. 'Of course I don't want her to *investigate*. That is what you will be going there to do. I just want Mrs Ross to keep her eyes and ears open. I would not presume to ask your wife to behave in any way that is underhand. Frankly, I wouldn't dare to. But you and I know well that Mrs Ross has an active curiosity about criminal matters. Now then, I have spoken to the commissioner and he is in agreement. So, off you go to Hampshire. Oh, you cannot accept the hospitality of any of the persons concerned, of course, or any witnesses. That means you cannot stay under the same roof as Mrs Ross. Sorry about that.'

He did sound as though he meant the last words. I decided to be gracious.

'Yes, sir,' I agreed. I did regret I couldn't lodge in Lizzie's company; but felt glad I hadn't to share a roof with Mrs Parry.

Both pigeons took wing and flapped away to another roof; where the male pigeon might have better luck, or not.

'There is an inn where I lodged the last time, sir. I could probably stay there again. I could hire a pony from them to enable me to move about the area,' I continued.

Dunn's bushy eyebrows twitched alarmingly. 'Didn't know you were a horseman, Ross.'

'Nor am I. Sergeant Morris was with me last time, and he rode the pony. But I did ride a horse one day while I was there, and managed, just, not to fall off. So, with a bit of luck, the pony won't set me on the ground.'

Dunn pursed his lips. 'Mrs Dunn and I have been married for twenty happy years, Ross.'

'Congratulations, sir.'

'Mrs Dunn is an intelligent and capable woman. She has never, *never*, Ross, become involved in a police investigation. Mrs Ross, on the other hand, seems to make a habit of it. You will need to keep not only the pony but your wife under control this time, Ross.'

'I will do my best, sir.' Of the two, the pony might prove the easier, I thought.

Elizabeth Martin Ross

'In the circumstances,' said Aunt Parry at breakfast, 'we can hardly call and leave cards at the home of Mrs Beresford, though I should very much like to do so, of course, and socially it is expected of one. But we have no means of transport. I wonder, Elizabeth, do you think that if I sent a note to Mr Harcourt, Sir Henry's estate manager, he would make the carriage available to us?'

'It might be needed,' I pointed out. 'There will be a good deal of coming and going at Sir Henry's home.' I spoke firmly because I had no intention of being a nuisance at this distressful time for the Beresfords. Mrs Parry, naturally, had no such qualms. The idea that she might ever be considered a nuisance would never enter her head. But she reluctantly accepted my argument.

'Yes, I dare say you are right. Well, then, we shall have to make do with letters of condolence.' She sighed. 'This distressing event quite takes away the appetite; but I think I might manage some scrambled eggs.'

Accordingly, after breakfast, we set about writing our individual letters to express sympathy to the Beresfords on their loss. Mrs Parry chose to settle herself in the small parlour. I took myself outside again to the little rose arbour. The day was very mild. There was only a gentle breeze and the sea murmured softly below making a friendly background sound. There is a formula to writing sad letters of this sort, but, even so, I found it difficult to begin because I could not rid my mind of the memory of the evening spent dining with Sir Henry. I am ashamed to confess that I wasn't thinking so much of the shock and distress of his sudden and gruesome death as of that underlying tension between the three men at table; and how Harcourt, when Agnes was playing the piano so beautifully for us, retired to a separate area of the room to listen. Would it not have been more natural for him to take his seat with the rest of the small audience? Why hadn't he? Because, I decided, he had been upset about something; and it was not just that he knew himself to be there to make an even number. Harcourt was the estate manager, so it had probably been a business matter.

As for Sir Henry, it is bad form to speak ill of the dead and perhaps even to think it. But I had not liked him. Now, shocked as I was at the manner of his death, I still could not help wondering if Sir Henry had not in some way 'brought it on himself', in the popular phrase. To think this way, even as I sat here with the intent of writing to the Beresfords, made me feel ashamed, but also resentful. It was as though Sir Henry, in death, had placed on the table a winning card. Whatever his faults, we were all now obliged to speak well of him. *I come to bury Caesar, not to praise him* . . . Shakespeare had understood how to phrase it. I however was no Shakespeare.

Lizzie! I told myself. *Keep your mind on the task before you!* I picked up my pen, only to be interrupted. Heavy footsteps were crunching along the coastal path towards me. The garden gate creaked and a postman appeared, in his blue-and-red livery, with a satchel of mail slung across him. He must have tramped up the hill from the village. Seeing me, he hesitated. At the same time, the front door opened and Mrs Dennis appeared.

'Good morning, Charlie,' she greeted him. 'You've got letters there, I see. For the ladies, I dare say?'

'Two ladies,' confirmed the postman. 'A Mrs Ross and a Mrs Parry. Oh, and there is a postcard for you, Mrs D.

It's from Italy.' As he spoke, he took a pack of letters from his satchel. 'Here we are.'

'Well, there!' exclaimed the housekeeper in delight, taking possession of the postcard. 'That will be from Mrs Hammet. She always sends me a postcard from wherever she is. She's a great one for travelling and I've got an album nearly full of all the cards she's sent.'

'Gone to Italy again, eh?' asked the postman. 'What have they got in Italy, then, that we don't have here?'

'Monuments!' said Mrs Dennis firmly. 'Left by the Romans, and all in ruins. I've got two pages of postcards of those in the album already.'

The postman did not look convinced that the attraction of monuments would be reason enough to set off across Europe; especially if these were in ruins. He stared across the scrap of garden towards the arbour where I sat. 'That will be one of the ladies, will it?'

Mrs Dennis was recalled to her duties. She pushed the postcard into the capacious pocket of her apron. 'That's Mrs Ross,' she said. 'The other lady is in the house. Do you give those letters to me, Charlie, and I'll see they're safe delivered.'

It seemed a moment for me to join the conversation. I called out, 'You can bring my letters over here, postman!'

Charlie accordingly handed Mrs Parry's post to Mrs Dennis, then crunched his way over to the arbour and handed me the remaining two envelopes with a bow. 'There you are, ma'am.' He had a round, sunburned face with small dark eyes. He grinned and the boot-button eyes twinkled at me so brightly that I was put in mind of a photographer with his camera, and the flash of the bulb as the image was taken. Charlie would carry his mental post-card image of me, together with the latest information on the Hammet travels, to the next house at which he called.

I thanked him and, as he plodded away, I scanned the two missives in my hand. One was from Ben. The other envelope was addressed in a round, careful, childish script. It was very thin and must contain a single sheet of paper. Normally, I would have read Ben's letter first. But I was curious and opened the other one. It proved to be from Bessie.

Dear Missis, it began. *I hope you has both of you got there safe. We do very well here, the inspector and me. I made him a beefsteak pie for his supper last night. He ate most of it. I hope you and Mrs P. are both in good health and having a good time by the sea, even though the inspector says someone has been horribly murdered. We don't have no excitement here, only that the coal-shed door has fallen off. A man is coming to mend it. Respectfully yours, Bessie Newman.*

I was very touched by this missive, over which Bessie must have laboured. I did wonder about the beefsteak pie, though. I set the sheet of paper aside and opened Ben's letter. He would not have had time to reply by post to my letter. But he'd obviously heard about it all in another way. Mr Beresford's telegrams sent from the Hythe telegraph office must have sparked a spate of others.

The letter began: *My dearest wife* . . . After expressing satisfaction, as had Bessie's letter, that we had arrived in safety, it continued: *I am truly sorry I encouraged you to go with Mrs Parry to the coast, as Hughes at Southampton telegraphed the Yard about a case of murder in the locality, even before the arrival of your letter. Lizzie, I beg you, do not do anything! At least, not until I get there. I have reason to believe I shall be sent to help out with the investigations. I am more anxious to see for myself that you are safe than you can imagine. But I shall see you and I cannot wait until that moment. Alas, as my visit will be on police business, I shall not be able to lodge with you and Mrs Parry. It is planned that I stay at the Acorn Inn, as before.*

I, too, was impatient to see him and more relieved to know that he would be coming to investigate this matter than I could express in writing. I did realise, however, that his letter must have been posted after Bessie had sent hers, as she had made no mention of Ben's setting out to join me. Hum! I thought. So my little house will be left to the care of Bessie, Constable Biddle and the man who had come to mend the coalhouse door. Between the three of them, they would finish off the store of food I'd left in the larder and when I got back, like Mother Hubbard's, my cupboard would be bare.

At this point, I recalled I was supposed to be writing a letter of condolence to the Beresfords. Again I set about this task, this time with better success. When I had finished, I took it indoors to find Mrs Parry had also finished composing her letter, and was now dozing in the sunlight coming in through the small window and falling on the rocking chair in which she'd established herself.

'I hope you had satisfactory news in the post, Aunt Parry,' I said loudly.

She opened her eyes and sat up with a start, so that the

chair creaked in protest and rocked her forward. She gripped the arms. 'Very little at all of any interest!' she said discontentedly. 'I have put it all aside to read again later. I have finished my letter to the Beresfords.'

'You will be pleased to hear,' I told her, 'that there is a real possibility of Ben coming to join us. Unfortunately, he will not be staying here at The Old Excise House, because his visit will be official, to help with the investigation into Sir Henry's death. He will stay nearby at an inn.'

'How very odd and unsatisfactory,' returned Aunt Parry crossly. 'I am of course delighted to hear that the inspector will arrive soon to take charge of this matter, as I requested that he should. But I do not see why he cannot stay here. We are in need of protection. There is a murderer on the loose out there!' She waved a hand to encompass the surrounding countryside. 'We may be his next victims!'

'Since Davy came with the terrible news, the Dennises have been sleeping in the attics, as well as Jessie,' I reminded her. 'We are not alone in the house at any time. There is safety in numbers, they say.'

Mrs Parry's expression told me at once that she thought this poor consolation. It was true that Jacob and his wife had quitted their cottage and joined their daughter on the attic floor at night. This had led to a distinct loss of spirits on the part of Jessie, attributed by her mother to shock. I thought it more likely it was due to the absence of Davy Evans's company. I well understood the Dennises were afraid to be alone in their cottage after nightfall. Mrs Parry was right. Murder had been committed. Until the crime was solved, fear stalked the heath and woodlands, and crept into each lonely cottage. But panic is a voracious beast, and needs to be stopped in its tracks.

'I really don't see why *we* should be in danger,' I told her robustly. 'Why would anyone want to murder one of us?' I quashed the unkind thought that Mrs Parry might inspire thoughts of murder from time to time in the most saintly of people.

'Robbery!' declared Mrs Parry without hesitation. 'I have concealed my jewellery box beneath the mattress each night since this awful business began. I trust you do the same, Elizabeth.'

I thought it best not to confess I had no jewellery box; not a valuable one in Mrs Parry's league, anyway. I had a trinket box; but any murderer who came for that would be sorely disappointed, and wish he hadn't taken the trouble. In contrast robbery certainly could be a motive for an intruder to break into Sir Henry's home. Yet we had not yet heard that anything of value had been taken and even the pistol used to carry out the murder had been left behind. If anything had been taken, we should hear about it in due course. 'This is a very vexatious affair,' I said. I had not meant to speak aloud; I was only mulling it over to myself.

'I am glad you agree!' snapped Mrs Parry. 'If you will allow me to say so, Elizabeth my dear, you have seemed to treat our predicament with quite unnatural calm. It is being married to a policeman, I suppose, and hearing all the time about sordid criminal matters.'

I could have retorted that Ben did not 'bring his work home'. But she would not have believed it. Perhaps it was a good thing, after all, that Ben was to lodge at an inn and not at The Old Excise House, since Mrs Parry found anything connected with police work so distasteful. I decided to avoid further discussion of the matter.

'I intend to walk down to the post office in the village and post my letter of condolence,' I said. 'I can take yours with me, if you wish.'

Aunt Parry brightened at the thought of an excursion of any sort. 'Then I shall come with you, my dear.'

This had certainly not been my intention. 'It is a fair distance and, although it is downhill going there, returning will be uphill,' I warned. 'Also, the path is narrow and treacherous underfoot in places.'

She dismissed this with a wave of her pudgy paw. 'Oh, I was quite a walker when I was a girl.'

Possibly so, but that was a long time ago. I had never known her walk anywhere. 'I'll ask Mrs Dennis if she can find another walking stick,' I said, resigning myself to the non-stop litany of complaint that must surely accompany our visit to the post office.

Mrs Dennis produced a second walking stick, a much smarter item than the stout country stick Jessie had offered me. It had a silver knob as a handle and I guessed it belonged to Mr Hammett. I must make sure we didn't lose it.

It wasn't long before Aunt Parry began to complain about the path. I had made another attempt, before we set off, to persuade her to stay behind. But it had been in vain. Now, however, she was very discontented and, somehow, it seemed all to be my fault.

'I cannot think why you should choose to walk to the village along this dreadful track, Elizabeth. It is quite over-grown and the brambles catch at my skirts. Oh! There! I am caught up again and you will have to release me.'

I managed to free her from the entanglement and off we set again. Of course, before we'd managed another couple of yards, she was caught up again, or an overhanging branch had knocked her hat askew. It took us at least three times longer to reach the junction with the main road than it had taken me alone. When we reached it at last and came to the Dawlish sisters' cottage, I hoped they would be indoors. But no, there they were, side by side on the wooden bench by the road, watching us approach with their sharp eyes. They made no movement at all, but sat there in their black apparel, looking like nothing so much as a pair of basalt urns in a graveyard.

'Is it much further to this post office, Elizabeth?' demanded Aunt Parry, wheezing to a halt. She was perspiring freely.

'It will take perhaps another twenty minutes, but there are no more brambles or undergrowth to hinder us,' I assured her. Alone, it would have taken me ten minutes at the most, but I had no hope my companion would quicken her pace.

'Twenty minutes!' she exclaimed in horror. 'I cannot walk another twenty minutes without a rest. You shall take both letters to the post office, Elizabeth, and I shall wait for you here.' She pointed her walking stick at the bench where the sisters sat. Not waiting for my reply, she marched imperiously towards it and, to my amazement, the sisters shuffled along, one to either end of the bench, leaving a space between them. Aunt Parry lowered herself on to the bench, stood the walking stick before her on the earth and folded her hands over the silver knob. The effect now was of a mantelshelf garniture, a clock, perhaps, and a pair of vases either side of it. None of the three spoke.

'I shall be back as soon as possible, Aunt Parry,' I promised. I looked towards Cora Dawlish, but she stared straight ahead and did not even seem to see me. Tibby Dawlish had a ghost of a smile about her lips, but otherwise she made no move. I nodded to them in greeting. They did not return it. Well, I thought to myself, I fancy Mrs Parry is fully their equal when it comes to holding her ground.

I set off at the best pace I could for the village. When I reached it, I couldn't fail to notice the change in people's attitude towards me. Whereas, on my first visit, they had been curious and smiling; now they turned their heads away from me as I approached and hurried to the further side of the village's main road. The postmaster was polite but stony-faced. He said a brusque, 'Good day, ma'am!' on my entry, and took my letters from me with no more than a nod. A mother with a little daughter, who had been buying something in the shop, caught her child's hand and dragged her away from my unlucky presence.

I thanked the postmaster, to which he returned only another nod. I left the premises with, I hoped, a confident step. But I was very angry. The Dawlish sisters have done this! I thought. They have spread the word that wherever I go, I bring death with me. They would not say I was a murderer. They dared not accuse me of that. Besides, I had no reason to break into a house I had only visited for the first time that day, and shoot dead the householder. No one would have believed them. No, it was something much more difficult to refute: superstition. I made bad things happen. There are countries in the world where that is called 'the evil eye'.

I walked back as fast as I could to where I had left Mrs Parry, to find her still enthroned on the bench as I had left her. But the Dawlish sisters had gone. It was as well. I was annoyed enough to have accused them outright of spreading their nonsense with malicious tales about me.

'I hope you haven't been bored sitting here, Aunt Parry,' I said. I did my best to sound cheerful.

'Oh, no,' she replied serenely. 'It has been very pleasant.'

'Did you have any conversation with the two women in black?'

Aunt Parry looked vague. 'Oh, no, not a word. You mean the two old countrywomen who were here? They just got up, after you left, and went into their cottage.' She paused. 'I think I perhaps they were overawed by my presence.'

'I dare say they were,' I agreed, though I didn't for a moment believe it. 'Are you ready to set off home?'

She rose to her feet with the aid of the walking stick and off we went again. We reached the point where the track leading up to The Old Excise House branched off the main road, and had barely turned on to it when disaster struck. Aunt Parry exclaimed, 'Oh!' She lurched forwards and collapsed into a heap on the ground.

'Aunt Parry!' I cried out in alarm. I thought perhaps she had suffered some form of heart attack. The day was warm and she had been taking more exercise than was normal for her. But no, she had turned her ankle on the uneven turf. Now she sat there in a welter of skirts and glared up at me.

'I knew we should not have come this way! I don't know why you insisted on taking this path, Elizabeth. Help me up!'

But this I couldn't do. Even with the help of the walking stick and my arm she could not get to her feet; and her weight was such that I couldn't lift her.

She sank back on to the ground and ordered: 'You must go and find some help, Elizabeth. Go back to that cottage and ask if there is not some strong fellow who can be sent to aid me to my feet.'

I really did not want to do this. Silently I cursed my bad luck. If I had been a village woman, I might even have thought the mishap had been wished on us by Cora Dawlish, the self-declared witch, as a revenge on Mrs Parry for commandeering the bench. I quickly reminded myself that is also how 'witchcraft' works. Someone offends the witch. Someone else falls sick, or breaks a cherished possession. I would not fall into that trap, but I would need to fetch help. If I continued all the way to The Old Excise House there was only Jacob Dennis to call on, and I doubted he could haul Mrs Parry upright. The Dawlish sisters' cottage was the nearest habitation and so back there I must go. It was very mortifying.

Accordingly, I set off back to the cottage and walked

up the path through the untidy front garden and raised my hand to knock at their door. Before I could do so, Tibby Dawlish opened it. She must have seen my approach through her window. She stood before me, short, solid, glittering with her jet beads and her eyes fixed on me mockingly. I quickly lowered my hand, and opened my mouth to explain my reason for calling. But she forestalled me a second time.

'Well, now, truth-seeker's wife,' she said. 'You are in need of help, are you? And you have come to us, as indeed you must.' She gave a curious little smile, her lips turning upward, but her dark eyes malicious. 'All come to us eventually.'

It was at that moment, and it did only last a second or so, that I felt a tremor of fear. There was something of triumph in her attitude, as if the sisters had indeed played some deliberate practical joke on me, and were enjoying its success. I reminded myself again that if Aunt Parry had tumbled, it was because she was unused to walking, was overweight, and the turf uneven beneath her feet. Tibby and Cora Dawlish had not 'magicked up' the accident. I would not allow them to play with my brain. They had seen me leave with Mrs Parry and almost immediately I had come back alone and to their door. Only one thing could have brought me: some accident.

'I am sorry to disturb you,' I said firmly, 'but the lady with me has fallen and I need someone strong to help her to her feet. Is there some man nearby who could help?'

Even as I spoke, I knew the answer and who it would be. I had spotted a movement in the background. My eyes had become more accustomed to the dim interior of the cottage and seen that there was a door ajar into some further room. Someone stood there and was listening. As I ceased speaking, the door opened widely and Davy Evans stepped into the room, ducking his head beneath the low lintel.

'Mrs Parry taken a tumble, has she?' he asked in his familiar manner. 'I'll come along with you.'

Tibby Dawlish said nothing, only stepped aside to allow him to pass. The door was closed immediately behind him.

It took only a few minutes to get back to Mrs Parry. She still sat as I had left her, brushing away bothersome flies and muttering in an ill-tempered way.

'Well, now, m'dear,' said Davy, stooping over her. 'This is not a path for a fine lady like yourself to go walking along.'

He could not have said anything better. Mrs Parry threw me a look of triumph. 'Indeed, it is not!' she said. 'Be so good as to lend me your arm, young man.'

She raised her hand as if he should take it, but instead he bent down, slipped one muscular arm about her waist, ordered her to 'Just take a good grip on my shoulder, m'dear!' and hauled her to her feet with ease. Her hat fell off during this process. I picked it up; and remained, with it in my hand, transfixed by the incongruous sight of Davy Evans and Mrs Parry, locked together like a courting couple.

'How's the ankle, then?' asked Davy. 'Let me take your weight now, go careful!'

Aunt Parry tried the ankle and grimaced. 'I have twisted it somehow.'

'We'll get you home, never fear,' he promised her. He

looked towards me. 'Could I ask you, Mrs Ross, to just hand me the walking stick the lady dropped?'

Gritting my teeth, I retrieved the silver-headed cane and handed it to him.

'Off we go,' he said cheerfully, and added in a wicked whisper in Mrs Parry's ear, 'locally they do call this path Lovers' Lane!'

Now, at last, I thought Aunt Parry might snap some retort to put him in his place. But no. She gave a girlish laugh, practically a giggle, and off they went down the path, Davy knocking aside the encroaching vegetation with the stick held in his free hand, the other still firmly clasped round the lady's waist.

As The Old Excise House came into sight, Mrs Parry at last decided it would be fitting to detach herself from Davy's embrace. 'Thank you very much, young man!' she said briskly. 'I think I can manage to go the rest of the way, using that cane, and with Mrs Ross's help. Elizabeth! Give him something for his trouble.'

'Oh, no trouble for me,' said Davy with a broad grin. ''Twas a pleasure to be of service to you, ma'am.' He turned his dark eyes on me. 'And to you, Mrs Ross.'

At least he hadn't addressed me as the 'truth-seeker's wife'. He turned and set off briskly the way we'd come, not seeing – or ignoring – the coin I had taken from my purse.

'An obliging young fellow,' observed Aunt Parry, 'though what is usually called "a rough diamond", I believe.'

Rough he certainly was, I thought. But if any kind of diamond, it was one with a deep flaw running through it.

Our unorthodox arrival had been spotted from the house. Nugent, Mrs Dennis and Jessie all came running out. Nugent and Mrs Dennis helped Mrs Parry indoors, but Jessie remained at the gate, her hands twisted in her apron, and gazing wistfully in the direction Davy had taken. However he did not look back and was almost immediately lost in the tunnel of trees shielding the path to the village.

I went up to my room and took off my balmorals. I felt hot, tired and troubled. I was also, I realised, very angry. It was hard to decide at which target to aim my anger. I had a choice: Mrs Parry, the churlish postmaster, the Dawlish sisters, in particular Tibby, and Davy Evans.

'Oh, Ben,' I whispered, 'do come quickly. I need you here desperately.'

It was at that moment I realised how afraid I was. I had been out of temper because I had not wanted to make this trip in the first place. I was cross with Aunt Parry on that account; and because she would walk to the village although I had warned her about the path. I was angry with Tibby Dawlish, because she had again mocked me, and I had been forced to seek help from her. I was angry with Davy Evans, because there was something deeply untrustworthy about him, no matter what Mrs Parry might choose to think. But I hadn't, until this moment, been afraid. I sat down on the little chair by the window to gaze out at the sea in the distance. The tide was nearly out. Jacob Dennis was down there, digging in the mud again. Fishing bait, I decided, something that lived in the mud, worms, eels, or such. I didn't like the turmoil of my feelings and I wanted very much to explain them to myself before Ben arrived and I must explain them to him.

The news of Sir Henry's gruesome murder had shocked me. The notion of a murderer on the loose would make anyone uneasy. The Dawlish sisters had 'rattled me', as Ben would say. And what was Davy to them? Did he lodge with them? Was he related in some way? I had known, in my heart, that when I knocked at their door for help, it was Davy Evans I was about to call on. Nevertheless, until this moment I had not felt personally threatened. But now I was aware of something monstrous out there. For the second time that day, words of Shakespeare came into my mind, although from a different play.

> *By the pricking of my thumbs,*
> *Something evil this way comes.*

Chapter Seven

*You see what a fuss is made when
a person of importance dies? They have
brought a detective from London!*

Inspector Ben Ross

IT IS not often that anyone asks a police officer if he is happy in his work. Perhaps it is because they might find it disturbing, should he reply that he was.

'By Jove, sir or madam, I love it! There is nothing as satisfying as chasing a burly cut-throat down a dark alley; or supervising the removal of a bloated corpse from the Thames!'

No one has ever put the question to me, at any rate. If I were asked, I might have answered that I was satisfied I was doing a necessary job; and I tried to do it to the best of my ability. I could have added that I was proud to work out of Scotland Yard and that I shared my work there with some men of courage and intelligence, for whom I had a high regard.

Ann Granger

Not that the Yard is without its share of constables of modest ability who are unlikely to attain high rank. I regret to say that Constable Biddle, Bessie's swain, is one of those. It is a pity because, if he does eventually marry Bessie (or when his redoubtable mother allows him to marry her), he will need an income on which they can live, and promotion would help him in that. On the other hand, Biddle is hard working, conscientious, and loyal. He and Bessie should do very well.

Which brought me, as the train rocked southwards out of London, to thoughts of my own marriage. At that moment, I could honestly say I was very happy indeed being the officer sent to inquire into the death of Sir Henry Meager. Dunn disapproved of the interest my wife took in my work. I confess that from time to time it worried me because of the risks involved. On the other hand I had no reason at the moment, I told myself, to think my wife might be in any direct danger. But she was, like it or not, involved. She had been present at the dinner party in Sir Henry's home on the fateful evening. Anything she might be able to tell me about that dinner party, and those who attended it, would be useful. She is observant and shrewd. I trust her judgment. In any case, I should have to interview her as a witness. That wouldn't be difficult since she would tell me all about it anyway and probably throw in a few suggestions of her own. Although she and Mrs Parry had not been long in Hampshire, Lizzie would certainly have taken a good look round her environment and made some decisions. I would hear about those, no doubt. All in all, when I climbed down from the train and felt the sea breeze on my face, I was feeling optimistic.

I was also pleased to reacquaint myself with Inspector Hughes at Southampton. I apologised, when we met, for appearing to be trespassing on his turf. He had, of course, requested help from the Yard, but it was important in these circumstances not to appear to imply I was there because he couldn't cope.

'Not at all!' he told me earnestly, in his soft Welsh tones. 'I'm delighted to see you.'

I don't know when Hughes left his Welsh valleys for the south coast of England, but he had never lost his accent. People say the same of me. I am a Derbyshire man, and still sound it after years in London. I wondered whether, like me, Hughes was a collier's son.

'You will be thinking we have not made much progress in our inquiries,' he was saying. 'But we are run off our feet here, see? Travellers bound for all parts of the globe begin their journeys here; and every kind of thief and confidence trickster comes here hopeful of rich pickings. Then there are the warehouses storing goods imported from everywhere you can think of, and they are a target for gangs of thieves.'

'In London, what they call the society Season is about to begin and we see much the same sort of thing,' I told him.

Hughes nodded sympathetically. Then he became businesslike. 'Now then, this case of murder, well, it's going to take some sorting out. The victim is a gentleman of some consequence and results are expected! I can lend you a man, if you need one, but I can't be overseeing it myself.' He smiled and added, 'I have taken a room for you at the Acorn Inn, where you stayed before. I trust that's all right?'

'Excellent,' I said. 'Is the landlady still Mrs Garvey?'

Hughes confirmed that it was. He added, 'Now then, you'd like me to bring you up to date on the case, I dare say.'

'There is no doubt at all that it is murder?' I asked. 'Not a chance it might be suicide? I know the coroner has ruled it murder, and that must guide us. However, generally, when the weapon belongs to the dead man and is found lying beside the body . . .'

Hughes was shaking his head. 'No suicide note has been found; and there is no known reason why the man should choose to blow out his brains. No reason why he should say goodnight to his dinner guests, go upstairs, make ready for bed, get into the bed in his nightshirt and then shoot himself in the head. He was wealthy. He was respected.'

'And a close friend of the coroner, I understand,' I commented.

'That, too. But I think the coroner's verdict was the right one; and wasn't influenced by friendship with the victim. Someone broke into the house, smashed the lock of a drawer in the library where a pair of duelling pistols was known to be kept, crept upstairs and . . .' Hughes spread out his hands expressively.

'But nobody heard a thing?' I knew I sounded a doubting Thomas.

'The servants were all asleep. It's a large old house, very solidly built, and the servants' rooms are in the attics. If one of them had awoken, and thought it had been a shot that had disturbed his slumbers, he would probably have put it down to a poacher. There are deer in the wooded areas. Sometimes, at night, they leave the shelter of the trees and venture out into the open. I was told they have occasionally forced a way into Sir Henry's garden and caused considerable damage. Venison fetches a good price, no questions asked. Likewise, the ponies that roam the area have been known to find their way into gardens seeking to graze in the vegetable patch or on the lawns. A householder with a gun might fire a shot to scare them away. A single shot at night doesn't arouse the kind of alarm it might do in London.' Hughes sat back and waited for me to ask my next question.

I repressed the impulse to point out, 'But this shot wasn't outside the house, was it? It was indoors!' Instead I asked: 'How was entry to the house effected? Has anything been taken? There must be valuables in such a fine property.'

Hughes's features set obstinately. 'Nothing taken and we found no sign of forced entry. The coroner asked twice about that. The butler (you will meet him) is an old chap, and to my way of thinking not quite in his right mind. But he's worked there for many years and I don't think a silver teaspoon could go missing without his being aware of it. Also, my men took a good look round. Windows, doors, all undamaged. You may take my word for it. Believe me, the only intruder we found was a dead mouse in a trap in the still room.'

'Which would suggest he was shot by somebody already

in the house?' I was beginning to wonder whether Hughes, good fellow though he was, simply did not want the burden of investigating this case. He had enough on his hands. That was why I'd been brought in, and why he was happy to see me.

'Who?' Hughes spread his hands to signify he was at a loss. 'The servants are all of good character and there were no house guests at the time,' he returned promptly. 'Yes, Mrs Ross and the other lady were there as visitors, earlier in the evening, but for dinner only. They were driven home by the deceased's own coachman. You will not suggest one of them came back later to murder their host, a man they had only met that evening? Otherwise, Mr and Mrs Beresford attended the dinner party and they are family members, with no quarrel known between them and Sir Henry. They also drove home after the dinner party. The only other person present that evening was Harcourt, the estate manager. He has worked for Sir Henry for some time. It is a good position to have and he would not risk it. I dare say he hopes he will keep it when a new owner takes over. He is a single man, accommodated in a modest house on the estate, and returned there after the dinner party. No guests stayed overnight.'

Discontentedly, Hughes added, 'These country houses always have plenty of people wandering around them, family, servants, visitors.' He paused to pick up a sheet of paper and hand it to me. 'This is a list of names of all the servants; together with the approximate date they began to work in the house. Some dates are very approximate because the servants concerned have been there so long, no one knows quite when they joined the staff. All have worked there for some time, even the housemaids who have been there for two or three years apiece. The most recent addition to the staff is the kitchen skivvy, Susan Bate. She's just turned thirteen, but even she has been there nearly a year. Sadly, she's simple.' Hughes touched his forehead. 'She came to the house from an orphanage.'

'Indeed? I wonder how that came about,' I said. 'You said the butler was also a little muddled.'

'Not muddled, but he's got some strange ideas of a religious nature. Perhaps that's because he is of an age to be long retired. He has been on the staff since Sir Henry's father's day. All of them see their lives turned upside down by Sir Henry's death. They certainly have no reason to kill him, quite the reverse.'

Yes, I could see why he was so happy to hand the investigation over to me.

'Just an idea,' I said. 'I haven't seen the house and you have. Since it seems we must discount any idea of an actual break-in, causing damage, how easy would it be, do you think, for someone to slip in earlier in the evening? Just walk in and hide until Sir Henry had retired for the night?'

Hughes looked mournful. 'Not difficult at all,' he admitted. 'Large, rambling house, Tudor in origin I'm told. It's full of nooks and crannies. Might even have a priest's hole, or something like that. I don't know that it has, but these very old places have survived some very difficult times historically speaking, you might say. The servants were busy all day preparing for the dinner party that evening. If someone sneaked in, hid away, waited until all was quiet and everyone asleep . . . Yes, it's possible. Indeed, it must have happened like that.'

'Let us assume then that our murderer has got into the house. But he would have to leave by some exit or other, window or door, and you say they were all found locked in the morning.' I thought it over and Hughes waited patiently. 'Unless,' I said, 'our murderer has a particularly strong nerve, and it does look as though he is a very cool-headed fellow indeed. He hid away during the day, as you suggest. After the deed, he returned to his hidey-hole and waited until morning. The kitchen staff would be up early and the back doors would be unlocked. Maids would open the downstairs windows to air out the place. Our man slips out and no one is the wiser.'

'And provided he's a local chap,' Hughes picked up my theory, 'it doesn't matter if someone does see him around the grounds. He might be there for any reason.' Hughes shook his head mournfully. 'There you have it, then,' he concluded. 'It's a desperate business!'

So much for theory, for the moment at least. Time to turn to what physical evidence there might be.

Hughes had sent a photographer to make a record of the murder scene before it was all cleared up. The resulting pictures were stark, but also unsatisfactory, because they could tell me nothing I didn't already know.

'What about the weapon?' I asked next.

Hughes produced a prosaic cardboard box. When he took the lid off, I couldn't prevent uttering a low whistle. It was a beautiful object; a triumph of the Spanish gunsmith's craft; the damascene work came from the hand of an artist. And there were two of these beauties! I understood Sir Henry wanting to own them. Yet this prized possession had been the means of his death. The weapon told me something else. I needed to hear if Hughes thought the same.

'Tell me,' I asked him. 'In your opinion, what sort of a man might own something like this – and its pair?'

Hughes didn't hesitate. 'One who thought himself a very fine fellow indeed,' he said. After a pause he added, 'Rich, too, of course.'

'Meager had made his will, I suppose?' I asked. When a rich man dies, one always thinks of the will.

Hughes had the answer to that as well. 'Oh, yes, and had recently requested his solicitor to update it. He had signed the new version just a few weeks before he died. His man of law came down from London, bringing the new will with him. Pelham is his name, and he will know the details. So all is in order there. Sir Henry had no children of his own and his heir is his nephew, Mr Andrew Beresford, who was at the dinner. He lives not very far away at Oakwood House and, as I've told you, was driven home afterwards, with his wife, by his own coachman. He is acknowledged to be a most respectable gentleman, of ample means, and not long married.'

This final detail was news to me. Beresford had been single when I last met him. He was a rich man but I doubted he was as wealthy as his uncle had been. And, with a new wife, and new household, his expenses would suddenly have increased. 'I shall be calling on Mr Beresford,' I said. 'We have met before.'

With that, I shook hands with Hughes, and set out for the ferry across to Hythe.

The day was pleasant and I chose to sit on the deck of the little ferry with a gentle wind caressing my face as it chugged its way across the Southampton Water towards Hythe. The crossing was short but it gave me time to review the information supplied by Hughes. The first thing I discounted was the existence of a priest's hole or other secret nook in the dead man's home. Any house that is nearly three hundred years old is popularly believed to be full of secret corridors, hiding places of all kinds, sliding panels operated by pulling this or that piece of carved masonry, and any amount of such romantic nonsense. Not that these things do not exist, but if they do they are generally known about. Servants are well acquainted with every inch of a house in their care. Since no one had pointed out the location of a secret hidey-hole to Hughes, then Sir Henry's home probably did not include one. On the other hand, I reminded myself, this murderer does know the house very well. He knew about the duelling pistols in the drawer in the library. He knew to find his way to Sir Henry's bedroom. I would, of course, keep an open mind.

Having decided this, I turned to more pleasurable thoughts of seeing my wife before long. On my arrival at Hythe, my intention had been to hire a fly and driver from the livery service there. This was how Sergeant Morris and I had travelled to the Acorn Inn on my previous visit. To my surprise, this was not necessary. I scrambled 'ashore from the hard with all the other passengers and found an aged berlin carriage waiting. Its driver appeared equally aged and wore a strange old-fashioned caped coat. He studied me head to foot.

'Tom Tizard!' he announced himself. 'You'll be the police inspector from London we've been awaiting.'

I confirmed that I was the expected detective.

'Mr Harcourt sent me to meet you and take you to the Acorn,' he told me. 'Mr Harcourt is Sir Henry's estate manager, or he *was* Sir Henry's manager. Now, I suppose, you would say he is Mr Beresford's manager, since Mr Beresford has inherited the lot. Mr Harcourt says I'm to tell you the carriage is at your disposal during your stay.'

'It is thoughtful of Mr Harcourt,' I said. It also created a problem. If I went everywhere in the berlin, driven by Tizard, then Harcourt and Beresford would both of them know every move I made. So would every local inhabitant to whom this venerable conveyance would be a familiar sight.

Tizard gave me a knowing look. 'I fancy Mr Beresford told him to do it,' he said. 'Mr Harcourt will be taking his orders from Mr Beresford now, as we'll all be doing.'

'Once the will is proved,' I said mildly.

Tizard blinked. 'No reason why it shouldn't be!' he retorted.

If one or more of the beneficiaries turned out to be the murderer, that person would inherit nothing, I thought but didn't say aloud. Everyone believed Beresford was his uncle's heir; and Sir Henry had declared it at the dinner party. Even my wife and Mrs Parry, who had only met the deceased that evening, knew it.

'You just got the one bag, then?' asked Tizard. 'Well,

you get up into the conveyance and I'll hand the bag in after you.'

Any man of Tizard's age, who had spent his working life in the service of a gentleman of means, had his social priorities nicely judged. He had been sent to help me, as I was a visitor of some importance. But I was not a gentleman. At no point in our conversation had he once addressed me as 'sir'. I had been called in to do a job, as might any other tradesman. I climbed into the carriage unaided. He held up my bag at the open door. I took it from him and set it myself on the opposite seat.

'Let's be off, then!' said Tizard, slamming the door on me.

No wonder no one asks a police officer if he is happy in his work, I thought, as we jolted forward and rattled over the cobbles. High or low, everyone considers him a dogsbody.

At least Mrs Garvey, the landlady of the Acorn, was delighted to see me.

'Welcome back, sir! Jem, take the inspector's bag up to his room. Your sergeant not with you this time, sir?'

'He could not be spared,' I told her. 'But I am sure I'll manage alone.'

'Bless you, of course you will.' Mrs Garvey bestowed this accolade with a beaming smile. 'You'd like to take some refreshment after your journey, I dare say. Just go into the snug there, and I'll bring whatever you fancy.'

I thought I had earned a mug of ale and, since I had not yet started my inquiries hereabouts, no one should object. I retreated to the cramped room so named. It appeared to be unchanged from how I remembered it during my previous stay here; the only difference being the addition of another layer of dust. I had forgotten Tizard and the carriage. As Mrs Garvey left to fetch my ale I caught a glimpse of the coachman raising a tankard in the taproom. If asked, he would reply he was awaiting my further orders, since Harcourt had so shrewdly put the vehicle at my disposal.

Mrs Garvey was back, bearing a tray on which stood my ale and an envelope.

'Mr Beresford, from Oakwood House, rode by this morning and left this for you, sir. He was most particular that I should give it to you straight away.'

I opened the envelope and took out a brief letter. Beresford trusted I had arrived without any difficulties along the way. He would call on me at the inn in the morning, directly after breakfast, if I would be so kind as to wait for him. I might send my reply with Tizard. So that was why the coachman waited. I went out into the taproom.

'Mr Beresford is waiting for a reply to this letter.' I raised the sheet of paper in my hand.

'Yes,' agreed Tizard obligingly, wiping froth from his mouth with the back of his hand.

'Tell him, if you would, that I will wait for him here in the morning, as he requests. I would like to make an early start.'

'Don't need me no more today, then?' asked Tizard, a sharp gleam in his eyes.

'No, thank you, Tizard. I am obliged to you for bringing me here so quickly.'

'What about tomorrow, then?'

'I won't need you tomorrow.'

He still hesitated so I settled the matter by walking straight back into the snug and closing the door. Well now, I was in for a game of chess, was I? Beresford and Harcourt were determined to keep track of my inquiries and me. They had made their move. I had countered with mine.

It left me, however, with an immediate problem. I hoped to visit The Old Excise House that evening and see Lizzie for myself. But I had dismissed my means of transport. I waited until I was sure the berlin had rumbled its way out of the inn yard, then went to find the landlady again.

'Mrs Garvey, you don't, by any chance, still keep the pony you hire out? My sergeant rode it last time I was here.'

If she was surprised, or curious that I had dismissed the higher status of a private carriage in favour of her pony, she didn't show it. I fancied she understood.

'Bless you, sir, we can do better for you than that old animal. We have a new pony, a much smarter beast. Firefly is his name.'

I did not want a smarter animal, and the name given to the new pony raised alarm bells. I imagined myself clinging to the mane of an uncontrollable bolter. But if I requested the old pony in preference, I would, as I believe the Chinese describe it, 'lose face'. The honour of Scotland Yard was at stake.

'Thank you,' I said. 'My wife is staying at The Old Excise House. Do you know it? Is it very far?'

'Oh, I know it, sir. Riding straight across the heath, you

could be there in three-quarters of an hour.' She pursed her lips and studied me thoughtfully. 'But that's if you know the way; and you don't, I suppose, sir?'

I confessed I did not.

'Besides, there's coming back this evening,' she said, 'with the light fading. You would get lost easy; never find your way.'

Perhaps my chess move, dismissing Tizard, had not been such a clever one after all.

Mrs Garvey brightened. 'I have the solution, sir! There's Wilfred, the handyman. He looks after the ponies among other odd jobs. You take Firefly, and Wilfred will go along with you on the old pony, take you straight there. Wilfred knows the heath like the back of his hand. He'll wait at The Old Excise House while you visit your good lady, and then the two of you can return here.'

I would have an escort after all, but at least it wouldn't be one directly in Beresford's employ. I thanked her and said I would like to start out at once, as it was late in the afternoon.

Wilfred proved to be quite a bit older than me, although how old I couldn't judge. He was short, bandy-legged, had a skin tanned to the colour of a ripe acorn and very few teeth. He wore a bowler hat of the kind gamekeepers like, corduroy breeches and gaiters. His shirt was grimy and the elbows patched. Firefly, in contrast, was indeed a very smart pony, black, with white socks and blaze down his nose. Despite my fears, he did not seem ill disposed towards me.

'You don't want to worry about him, sir,' Wilfred assured

me, accompanying his words with a wink and what would have been a broad smile, if he'd had more teeth. As it was, it was a disconcerting display of gums, dotted with yellowing stumps. 'He won't set you on the ground.'

I wondered, as we rode out of the yard, whether my longing to see Lizzie that night might have led me into an unwise decision. It was late to be setting off. It had been a long day. We rode along the main road and then turned off up a rutted track, and passed by a couple of dilapidated cottages where a pair of scruffy dogs ran out, barking at us. Wilfred yelled a volley of abuse, and the curs withdrew; but no one came out to see what the noise was about. At last we emerged on to the heath. The track here was wide and seemed well used. Wilfred turned in the saddle to look back at me and asked, 'All right, there, sir?'

I called out that I was. Wilfred gave his toothless grin again and set off, his mount breaking into a canter. Firefly followed the lead of the pony ahead and soon we were making good going. Wilfred glanced back a few times to make sure I was still securely in the saddle. I found I was quite enjoying myself. Eventually he slowed, for the track was narrowing. We carried on in this way, making faster time where the going was good, and picking our way with more caution through the narrow tracks made by the wild ponies through the heather. Wilfred certainly did know the way. I would never have found it without him. But I kept a sharp look out for anything that might serve to guide me if I had to cover the ground alone. The heath, dotted with patches of gorse and the occasional cluster of trees, was peaceful. The only sound was the dull thud of the ponies' hooves on the soft soil. The air was fresh and balmy. I would sleep well that night. Eventually we reached another wide, stony track, crossing our path, and turned on to this. About ten minutes later Wilfred reined up, turned in the saddle and pointed.

'There it is, sir! That white building down there. That's The Old Excise House.'

It had taken us just under three-quarters of an hour. The arrival of horsemen caused the housekeeper to come to the door. As she did, her husband came round the corner of the house and greeted my guide.

''Tis you, then, Wilf.'

''Tis me, Jacob,' Wilfred agreed.

Jacob then came to hold Firefly's bridle and I managed to dismount in fairly good order.

'Ben!' It was Lizzie, running from the house and, to the amusement of Wilf and Jacob, throwing her arms about me.

'I can't stay long,' I told her. 'But I was anxious to see you and let you know I've arrived.'

'But you'll stay to dinner, sir?' This question came from the housekeeper, who had followed Lizzie.

'Indeed, I can't, I am sorry.' I turned to Lizzie, whose face clearly showed her disappointment.

'We'll have the opportunity to talk tomorrow, I hope,' I said quietly. 'I am very anxious to hear your account of the dinner party.'

Lizzie was leading me into the house. 'Aunt Parry is waiting!' she whispered.

Mrs Parry was indeed awaiting us in the parlour, seated

in state as if to grant a royal audience. Her ankle was swathed in bandages and propped on a tapestry stool. '*At last*, Inspector Ross,' she said. 'We have been waiting for you *all day*!'

'Ben only came from London today—' Lizzie began in protest, her face reddening.

'I was obliged to stop for a while in Southampton and discuss the matter with the inspector there, who has been overseeing the inquiry,' I explained.

Mrs Parry accepted this grudgingly, but next declared, 'Well, I am very pleased to see you, Mr Ross, but it would have been very helpful if you had come *at once*, as soon as poor Sir Henry's body was discovered.'

Lizzie was now crimson with suppressed ire.

'If only it had been possible!' I said hastily. 'But there is an official procedure in these matters, and it must be followed. Until we received a request from the local police, asking for the assistance of the Yard, I couldn't come.'

From the corner of my eye I saw a gleam in my wife's eye and knew she meant mischief. 'Bessie wrote to me, explaining the coalhouse door has fallen off,' she said brightly.

This totally unexpected contribution to the conversation left Mrs Parry startled and speechless, as Lizzie had known it would.

'It did,' I agreed. 'But Biddle's Uncle Walter has come to mend it. Walter is apparently an excellent worker and can turn his hand to anything.'

'What on earth,' asked Mrs Parry with rising ire, 'has this to do with your investigation? Of what possible interest is a coalhouse door? Mr Ross, we are in fear of our lives here!'

'Has anyone else been attacked, since the death of Sir Henry?' I asked.

'No,' she conceded unwillingly. She flung out a plump arm clad in cerise silk and pointed at the window. 'But if a charming and hospitable gentleman like poor Sir Henry has been slaughtered in his bed, who else can be safe?'

These words did interest me. I'd heard that his peers had respected the deceased. That he had had some influential friends. That he had been successful in his business affairs. No one, so far, had suggested that Sir Henry had been charming. But Mrs Parry was a wealthy widow. Lizzie, in her letter informing me of the murder, had written that, at the dinner party, the late Sir Henry had been affable most of the time. He'd charmed Mrs Parry. Lizzie had added that he'd not troubled to charm herself. This did not make me think better of him. If anything, the reverse was true.

Fortunately at that moment a very pretty girl with a mass of red hair came in, carrying the tea tray. As tea was being dispensed I took the opportunity to ask Mrs Parry, 'You appear to have met with some mishap, ma'am?'

Conversation changed direction away from the murder, and was concentrated on Mrs Parry's unfortunate fall, in which she had sprained her ankle. Cold compresses, I was assured, were having a beneficial effect but walking, even with a stick, was difficult.

It was then time for me to leave and start back to the Acorn. Lizzie came to the door to say goodbye. 'I have so much to tell you!' she said in a low voice.

'We'll have an opportunity to talk soon, my dear,' I promised. 'Is Mrs Parry being very difficult?'

'The murder of Sir Henry has really frightened her. She'll feel happier now you are here.' After a second's pause, Lizzie added, 'And so will I.'

'The lady's ankle injury must make life difficult, I imagine,' I said. I had noticed as I'd entered the house that the stair to the first floor appeared narrow, steep and dark. 'How does she manage to get upstairs?'

'She doesn't!' said Lizzie frankly. 'She could only just manage to get up the stairs before she twisted the ankle. The staircase is narrow and she is rather wide. She can't manage it at all now. However, fortunately there is a small room on the ground floor. It's fitted out to be Mr Hammet's study, when the Hammets are in residence. I imagine it's his refuge. The smell of cigar smoke lingers in it. There is a bookcase in there and a writing desk, and a very large chesterfield sofa. I expect he takes a nap on it after his lunch. Anyway, a bed has been made up for Aunt Parry on the chesterfield, so she has no need to tackle the staircase.'

'That's lucky,' I remarked.

'It's not very lucky for poor Nugent. All Aunt Parry's clothes, personal necessities and so on, are upstairs in her bedroom, which means Nugent is running up and down the stairs all day long. And if it's not Nugent, then I am sent on the errand. I have reverted to being her companion, as I was before we married. Well, I knew, before we came, that there was no other reason she invited me.' Lizzie's voice echoed with suppressed resentment.

I was filled with guilt, because I had urged Lizzie to

accept Mrs Parry's offer. 'This has been something of an unlucky visit for all three of you, so far.'

My wife rallied and with splendid confidence replied: 'It will be all right now you are here, Ben.'

That only made me feel worse. Everyone expected me to solve this dreadful mystery with the utmost speed. Apart from Mrs Parry and my own wife, urging me on were Dunn, so that I could return to my proper place in London; Hughes, so that he might close the file; the coroner, because Sir Henry had been his friend; Mr Pelham the solicitor in London because he had the will to settle; Beresford, because he was the heir; Harcourt the land manager and all the staff employed by the late Sir Henry because their future employment was at stake.

'Beresford is coming to the inn tomorrow at breakfast-time to take me to Sir Henry's house and the scene of the tragedy. We'll talk at greater length, Lizzie. I hope to dine with you and Mrs Parry tomorrow evening. Is there anything you think I should know before I see Beresford?'

She hesitated. 'There was something of a strained atmosphere at dinner, between the three men.'

'Any idea why?'

'No. I think they may have been discussing something earlier, some cause for dispute. It's only a guess.'

'Did you like Sir Henry?' I asked, curious that she hadn't shared Mrs Parry's insistence on his charm.

'Not a bit!' said Lizzie briskly.

Wilfred and Jacob were waiting with the ponies a little way off, holding a bridle apiece. If I stayed talking seriously with Lizzie much longer, they would be curious.

'Your lady was very pleased to see you, sir!' called Wilfred to me as we set off back to the Acorn.

The sun was setting, reflected on the surface of the water to our right, lending the ripple of the waves a rosy hue. I wished it did not make me think of blood. We turned to ride inland. A few birds swooped overhead, making for their roosting places. The heath, which had appeared so pleasant a sight during our ride across it earlier, was now patterned with shadows and had taken on a slightly sinister aspect.

'I was very pleased to see her, Wilfred,' I told him.

He returned me his gummy grin, just visible in the shadows. There is a comradeship that comes with the setting sun. It is probably rooted in an ancient fear of being alone in the dark; and instinct to draw together against whatever dangers might be out there.

'Wilfred,' I asked him. 'Did you ever meet Sir Henry Meager?'

'Not meet,' he replied at once. 'He wouldn't have had any time for the likes of me. I never worked for him, neither. Saw him a few times, riding out. He was a fine figure of a gentleman.'

'But you knew of him by reputation?'

'Oh, I knew of that,' he agreed.

'Of what?' I asked.

'Why, sir, his reputation, like you said.'

'And what, Wilfred, as far as you heard it, was Sir Henry's reputation?'

Wilfred waited a moment before he replied. Then he said, his voice seeming to echo in the gloom as it floated across the shadowy heather so that it was almost as if an oracle spoke, 'As I heard it, sir, he was a regular terror! Very violent temper, by all accounts; and he would have his way in everything. But then, he was an important man hereabouts. Important gentlemen,' concluded Wilfred sagely, 'have their ways. Best not for the rest of us to question them.'

Chapter Eight

Inspector Ben Ross

MRS GARVEY had kept a dinner waiting for me: steak and kidney pudding in a suet crust. I enjoyed it very much, but a heavy meal after a busy day and two rides across the heath finally finished me off. I fell into my bed and slept undisturbed until awoken by a knock at the door and the arrival of Mrs Garvey with a pot of tea, followed by the potman, Jed, with a can of hot water.

'You did ask to be called, sir, on account of Mr Beresford coming to meet you this morning,' she said brightly.

I did not remember requesting an early-morning call; although it was a good thing she had woken me. I thanked her, sat up in bed and let out an unwary yelp of pain.

'Ah,' said the landlady wisely, 'that will be from riding over the heath with Wilfred. You take cabs and such in London, I dare say.'

She and the grinning potman departed. I gingerly got out bed; aware that I had muscular aches and pains where I hadn't been aware I had muscles. After I'd stretched a few times, drunk my tea and moved around a little, I was able

123

to shave using the hot water, dress and make my way down-stairs. There I was shown into the snug again – apparently reserved for my private use – and served up a generous platter of bacon and eggs. As I did my best to do justice to the breakfast, it suddenly occurred to me that *I* had not warned Mrs Garvey that Mr Beresford was coming. She had given me the letter, it was true. Possibly Beresford himself had told her he meant to arrive at breakfast-time, or she had it from Tizard. It was a reminder, right from the start, that it was going to be difficult to conduct my inquiries unobserved and without the surrounding countryside knowing.

I was expecting Beresford to arrive on horseback. But a clatter of hooves and rattle of wheels announced his arrival, driving himself in a pony and trap. I admit to feeling relief that I did not have to scramble back into the saddle again immediately. I got to my feet as Beresford entered the snug. He looked much as I remembered him, a little heavier perhaps, but otherwise unchanged: a tweed-clad country gentleman, clean-shaven but with curly hair, now greying a little. A black armband had been sewn around the right sleeve of his jacket.

'I am not too early?' he asked, after we had shaken hands and exchanged greetings. 'Tom Tizard told me you wanted to make an early start.'

'Not too early at all,' I assured him. I decided to tackle the matter of Tizard and the berlin at once. 'It was very good of Harcourt to send Tizard to meet me at Hythe,' I told him. 'He indicated the carriage would be at my disposal, but I shall be able to manage. I am able to hire a pony from the inn here.'

'Ah, yes,' said Beresford, suppressing a smile, 'you were out riding yesterday evening, I hear. But you will need a guide.'

'I hope,' I said firmly, 'to avail myself again of the assistance of Wilfred, Mrs Garvey's stableman, as I did last night.'

I was well aware that Wilfred, too, would report my movements, as it seemed he had already done, but it was the best I could do. Wilfred, at least, had not worked for the victim in this case.

'As you wish, of course,' Beresford said. 'Let me know if you change your mind.'

'You have married, Mr Beresford, since my last visit here,' I said now, getting a grip on the conversation. 'My congratulations, sir!'

'Thank you. My wife and I hope that you and Mrs Ross, and Mrs Parry, will dine with us tonight.'

This was embarrassing. 'You will forgive me,' I said, 'if I say that my wife and I, and Mrs Parry, will be delighted to accept your kind invitation, but not, perhaps, until my inquiries are settled. Please don't be offended. It is because I am here to investigate your uncle's death.'

Beresford nodded. 'I do understand you want a free hand in your investigations and also that, as my uncle's designated heir, I must be a suspect. Don't, please!' He raised a hand to forestall me. 'Don't deny it. Of course I am. I'm the one who benefits by his death.' He frowned thoughtfully. 'Could Mrs Ross and Mrs Parry take tea with my wife this afternoon? Would that be in order? Agnes is very anxious that I should ask.' He hesitated. 'With so much to do, if the ladies could come this afternoon, Agnes would very much appreciate it. Although the invitation is somewhat rushed, the days after that will be busy.'

'I understand,' I told him. 'This is a difficult time for you and your wife.'

'Yes, she is an orphan and has no close female relative who could come and stay. It's another reason why I would be very pleased if your wife and Mrs Parry could come. Agnes is bearing up well under the shock and the pressure, given the circumstances, but I think she needs another female to talk to.'

'A very good idea,' I agreed.

'I wonder, have you met Pelham, my uncle's solicitor?' Beresford asked suddenly. 'He takes care of the affairs of a number of well-known families in London, so you may have run into him.'

'Mr Pelham and I,' I told him, 'have met on a few occasions. I have not yet spoken to him with regard to the present matter.' I was rather proud of this speech. I could simply have said that Pelham and I were old foes.

'He is coming down tonight from London,' Beresford continued, 'in order to attend my uncle's funeral, although the date of that is still not fixed. Pelham believes we should wait until you – the police – agree the burial can go ahead. In case . . .' Here Beresford drew a deep breath. 'In case it is felt a postmortem examination is necessary. The cause of death is clear enough, so I hope that will not be so. Once the funeral has taken place there can be a formal reading of the will, even though the contents are no secret.'

'Where is Sir Henry's body now? At the undertaker's or still at the Hall?' I asked. The reply was unexpected.

'The servants at the Hall are all in such a state that we felt, Harcourt and I, that it was not wise to leave the body there. So, at the moment, the coffin is in a disused icehouse in the grounds of my place, Oakwood House.'

I must have looked as startled as I was at this unusual – although sensible enough – place to keep the body, if it had to be moved from the Hall. My surprise must have shown itself.

'The alternative,' explained Beresford, after a quick, sideways glance at me, 'would be to leave it at the under-taker's establishment. That's in Lymington. But the undertaker is uneasy at such an idea. It is not known how long my uncle's remains would be there and other clients – I mean the living relatives of other deceased persons – might be upset at the notion of their own dear departed lying in a small morgue alongside a murder victim.'

Beresford hesitated. 'Friends and family of the dead person often call to pay their respects at the side of the coffin. With someone as well-known as Sir Henry, a gentleman and a murdered one at that, the undertaker feared a queue would form at his door, all manner of folk wanting to "pay their respects". It could become, the man told me, akin to a gruesome sideshow at a carnival of curiosities.'

It was a good point. I knew from experience that crowds gather before a house where there has been a murder, or follow the coffin of a perfect stranger to all of them, if the death has been sensational enough.

'The icehouse sounds a very sensible place to lodge the coffin,' I told him in my 'official' voice. Privately, I thought it rather peculiar. 'As for the ladies, I am sure they will be delighted to take tea with Mrs Beresford.'

'Good, then I'll arrange it.' Beresford looked relieved. 'I am worried about my wife, frankly.'

I waited for him to say more, but he didn't. I do admit I was keen for the ladies to visit Oakwood House, because I wanted to hear what Agnes Beresford was thinking about it all. Lizzie would certainly bring me an excellent report. I was being duplicitous, I knew, but that's what an investigating officer is often called on to be.

'Now then,' Beresford went on, 'you will want to quiz me regarding this dreadful business, will you not? I am happy for you to do it here, but there is some risk we might be overheard, if only in part. I thought I might drive you to my uncle's house in the trap and we could talk on the way. When we get there, it is for you, naturally, to decide what you want to do next. If you wish to go and visit Mrs Ross during the day I can take you there, or Tizard. Just let us know.'

He spoke earnestly and I believed him to be sincere, but it was all dashed awkward. Like it or not, I would have to accept some help.

'Thank you,' I told him. 'I'll be glad to accept your offer.'

We bowled out of the inn yard in fine style and travelled some way with only a few words shouted between us. The rattle of the wheels made anything else impossible. I was wondering just how we were going to talk 'on the way' when Beresford settled the matter. He had clearly made his plan beforehand. The road ran through woodland here. Then, unexpectedly, a swathe of open land appeared to our left, cutting a wide drive between the trees. Beresford pulled the trap to a halt and turned to me.

'We can sit in the trap and talk; or walk between the trees,' he said, 'as you prefer.'

I elected to walk and talk. 'I should have said earlier that I am truly sorry for the sudden and shocking bereavement in your family,' I told him. 'Were you and Sir Henry close?'

'We were closely related, but not close in any other way,' Beresford told me frankly. 'Ross, I should explain to you about my family in general. It will perhaps make things easier to understand. I need to begin with my grandfather, Captain Sir Hector Meager. He was sent to sea at the age of eleven, together with his ten-year-old brother, also a Henry. Great-Uncle Henry died of fever in the West Indies and there is a monument to his memory in the churchyard here. Grandfather Hector survived to have a distinguished naval career.'

'You must be very proud of him,' I said.

'Well, he was a hero, I suppose,' said Beresford. 'It didn't make him a pleasant man or one easy to deal with, as I understand it. He couldn't abide any kind of opposition. His manner of dealing with it was to treat it as a sea battle: fire a broadside and blast the enemy out of the water. I knew him when I was a young child and I was terrified of him.'

'Eleven is young to be sent to sea,' I said. 'But I was

sent down a coalmine at the even younger age of six, to be a trapper. My job was to sit in the dark with the rats and open and close the doors controlling the flow of air through the mine, as required. Fortunately, that period of my life did not last long. But I think I understand what made your grandfather so difficult to deal with.'

'Oh, yes, there were good reasons for it, I don't doubt,' Beresford agreed. 'It was a brutal upbringing amid dreadful sights and experiences. But he survived, and his naval career allowed him to return home wealthy from his share of prize money, so he married. My uncle was born and baptised Henry, in memory of Hector's own younger brother, who had not survived.'

Beresford hesitated. 'Grandfather then suffered a second loss. Sadly, his wife died not long after the birth of their son. Hostilities had broken out again, so my grandfather returned to sea, leaving his motherless child in the care of a godparent. That the baby survived at all must be counted very lucky. My uncle did not meet his father until five years later, when the old seadog finally retired from the navy, having been given his baronetcy. He came home and remarried. My mother was the child of that second marriage. When she was growing up, her half-brother, my uncle, was away at school. She did not have a close relationship with him.'

'And your uncle could hardly have known his own father at all,' I remarked.

Beresford made a gesture of dismissal. 'It happens in naval families. As I said just now, I do remember my grandfather, since he had chosen a life ashore by then. He lived to a ripe old age. "Old Indestructible" he was nicknamed. My mother used to take me to visit him, not because she had great affection for the old fellow, but because he expected it. I wasn't sent away for my schooling because, believe it or not, I was considered delicate.'

Beresford paused to grin briefly. 'My grandfather had little time for such an opinion. He had little time for any kind of medical opinion. Given his own way, he would probably have packed me off to sea, as had been done for him. But my parents withstood the storm, and I remained at home.'

'Yet your grandfather didn't send his own son, your Uncle Henry, to sea?'

'No.' Beresford shook his head. 'He was a bad-tempered old fellow. But, perhaps mindful of the death of his own brother, he had no wish to risk the life of the only son he had. Besides, it was now a time of peace.' Beresford made a wry grimace. 'Little chance of prize money!' he said.

'When young Henry had finished his schooling, he was sent off to travel the Continent, on what was called "the grand tour". That's why you'll see so much bric-a-brac around the house. Marble busts, third-rate oil paintings, bits of ancient pottery. Uncle Henry had no interest in art. He brought those things back in order to show his father he'd visited all the expected sites, museums, galleries and so forth. "Old Indestructible" had no interest in art either, so was no judge.

'When Henry arrived back from his travels, it was to discover that my grandfather had found a girl he wanted him to marry. Now, I can't tell you the details because my mother did not tell me all of it. She did say Henry didn't agree with his father's choice. I fancy he wanted to marry someone else. But Old Indestructible wanted to see his son married before he himself died; and he knew he didn't have much longer. So Henry was married as his father wished. My grandfather died at long last aged ninety-one; and Henry inherited.'

He paused. 'I remember my Aunt Madeleine, his wife. She was a very sweet person. They were married only a short time and were childless.'

We had walked some way by now, and Beresford turned back. We began to retrace our steps towards where the pony and trap waited patiently in the distance.

'To conclude,' said Beresford in the manner of one summing up an argument, 'you will understand that, although I was designated as his heir early on, my Uncle Henry and I were not close.'

There was a point to clear up. 'Was the estate entailed? I mean, if your uncle had had children of his own . . .'

'But he did not!' said Beresford shortly. 'There is no entail attached to the estate. I do not inherit by default, as it were. It was my uncle's personal decision and his wish to bequeath it all to me.'

He obviously didn't want to say more about that. But I already had a lot to mull over. I was beginning to suspect that the roots of this murder lay in the past, rather than in any recent events. Was that what Beresford wanted me to think? He had taken care to give me a lengthy family history. I was also well aware, as a detective of some experience in these matters, that the more information a witness volunteers, the likelier it is there is something he does not want you to know. Had I just been enveloped in a smoke-screen designed to hide some very important fact from me?

'May I ask?' I said as we reached the trap. 'When this is all settled, do you and Mrs Beresford plan to move into the Hall?'

'Oh no,' he replied at once. 'Agnes and I discussed that at length, even before Uncle Henry died. I shall be glad of the income from the land. But I shall probably seek out a tenant for the house. It is a rambling old place and not a happy one. Unhappiness, you know, seems to seep into the bricks of a house like that.'

'You knew it well as a child, visiting with your mother,' I said. 'I understand the house is very old. Tell me, is there any kind of a hiding place in it? A priest's hole or a secret corridor?'

Beresford, about to climb up into the trap, burst out laughing. 'If there is, I never found it! Believe me, Ross; I searched that house high and low when I was a boy. I had read my share of adventure yarns and was determined that there must be something. A secret escape route perhaps, dating from the time of the Civil War. The house was besieged by a party of Cromwell's men. The Meager at the time, a Royalist, was eventually obliged to admit them. The Roundheads searched the place. They found nothing of interest and no hiding Royalist soldiers or incriminating documents, so moved off and left the owner in possession. But no, I didn't find a secret tunnel; and I know of no tradition of there ever being one. It is an English country house of early period. That is all.'

He paused. 'And a damned inconvenient place to live in, believe you me! Freezing cold in winter no matter how many fires are lit. It was so dark indoors at noon, when I was a boy, it required candles or oil lamps in midsummer. Uncle Henry later paid a great deal of money to have gas pipes run out there. The cost of using the gas is such that my uncle then refused to have the gas mantles lit except in special circumstances, so oil lamps were again used as an economy measure. The gas mantles were lit in time for family and guests coming down to dinner, as when Mrs Ross and Mrs Parry came. No, no, Agnes and I will not be moving in.'

So, I thought, during much of the day the corridors and rooms of the house were gloomy. Anyone wishing to move around unobserved would not find it difficult if no noise were made: an invitation to intruders.

But, when I saw the Hall, I admit I was impressed. It was not as large as some houses of the period, but it had a sense of permanence about it. Storms might rage around it and Cromwell's Roundheads fire musket balls into its stout oak front door, but it would defy them all. As a home for 'Old Indestructible', it must have been perfect.

The estate manager, Harcourt, was waiting for us and came out on to the front steps to meet us. He was a handsome man just under six feet tall. To see him standing at the entry to the house, a stranger might have mistaken him for its owner. I judged his age to be about the same as Beresford's, possibly a year or two older, and thought he might prove a difficult customer.

However, he greeted me civilly as I came up to him.

But I noticed his eyes were wary. He was obviously ill at ease, for all the assurance of his stance. He had every good reason to be. His employer was dead, murdered, and his future must be uncertain. He had been at the fateful final dinner party. I was mindful of Lizzie's whispered warning that there had been tension between the three men that night. I guessed that, if there had been any argument, Beresford and Harcourt would join forces to prevent me from finding out what it had been about. Inquiry into Sir Henry's shocking death might be my business; but these two men would consider that private and business matters were not. It would be my duty to inform them otherwise. Nothing remains private in a murder case.

I decided to take the reins immediately in the inquiry. After all, I was not the usual sort of visitor, awaiting invitation.

'This is a shocking business and distressing to everyone, I am sure,' I began briskly. 'But I should like to see around the house and gain some idea of the layout. Particularly I am interested to learn where there are points of access and exit. I should like to meet the staff and speak to them all, possibly one at a time. I should like to speak to you again, Mr Beresford, about the evening of the murder; and to you, too, Mr Harcourt. I realise that Inspector Hughes has already spoken to everyone, but I should like to hear for myself about the evening of Sir Henry's death.'

'The staff are all gathered in the kitchen,' said Harcourt stiffly. 'They've all worked here for years and are very shocked. I should warn you that Warton, the butler, is particularly shaken. He is an elderly man and, frankly, somewhat unstable in his wits. Also the valet, Lynn, is in a bad way. He found the— body.'

The hesitation before he said the word 'body' was slight; but it was there. Harcourt, too, was shaken.

We made a slow and careful tour of the rooms. The main drawing room was oak-panelled and I glanced around it curiously. Beresford noticed and a faint smile touched his lips.

'I have tried each and every one of them over the years, Ross, and none of them move.' He then turned to Harcourt and added, 'The inspector is curious to know if there are any hidden passages or hidey-holes.'

Harcourt blinked and stared at me, startled. 'Good Lord, no!' he exclaimed.

We progressed from there to the library where the drawer of the desk was still open, its lock splintered. The box that had housed the pistols was open and the pair to the pistol Hughes had shown me still lay in it undisturbed. That was careless of Inspector Hughes. He should have removed both weapons when he came here at the outset of the investigation. Leaving a weapon lying around in an unlocked drawer in a house in which there had just been a murder is not good police work.

Beresford noticed my frown. 'The other pistol should be locked away safely,' he said. 'I hadn't realised it still lay here. I have a good strong safe, with a Chubb lock, at Oakwood House. I'll take it there when I leave.'

This was not ideal either. But I had no way of locking it up securely at the Acorn, and Beresford's safe was probably the best alternative. If Beresford were the heir, the pistol was in any case his property now.

I took my time over my tour, examining all the window catches, watched all the while by the other two. It was very annoying but I did not want to offend them so early by asking them both to leave me alone to make my search. It was when we came to Sir Henry's bedroom that they both stood back, by a common unspoken agreement, and let me go in alone.

Harcourt, stationed just outside the door, called, 'The doctor, when he came to examine the body and certify Sir Henry was dead, may have disturbed the bedclothes. I ordered the staff that nothing was to be touched – until the police had been. When Inspector Hughes came from Southampton, I don't think he moved anything. I am sure the housekeeper would like to remove the— the stained bed linen and clean generally.'

There was a smell of blood in the air, and a gruesome black stain on the pillow. Flies were crawling on it. 'Oh, tell her she may clear it all away,' I said sharply. 'Inspector Hughes ordered a photographer out here to make a record. There was no need to leave it in this state. Anyway, I have seen it now for myself.'

I wondered that Hughes had not told them to tidy and clean the room when he left the house. Perhaps he had assumed that, after the photographer had done his work, the staff would automatically clear everything away. My criticism had stung Harcourt, who had reddened.

'They are all very upset,' he said curtly. 'You are used to scenes of violent crime, Inspector Ross. The staff here are not.'

No, they weren't. The untouched state of the room should have brought home to me, forcefully, how very frightened they all must be. This room now held terrors for them. None of them wanted to be in it. I couldn't see Beresford, who had remained out of my line of sight in the corridor. He made no comment. Perhaps he thought I had criticised him personally, for not ordering the bed linen removed.

When I did finally meet the indoor staff in the cavernous kitchen, with its huge open grate and rows of gleaming brass pans on the wall, their terror was still apparent. Warton, the elderly butler, appeared so frail I urged him to sit down.

'Poor old fellow,' whispered Beresford to me. 'He began working here as a youngster, an under footman, when my grandfather was still alive.'

Lynn, the valet, was a younger man, but his nerves seemed also to be about to give way.

'Now then, Lynn,' I said encouragingly. 'You discovered the body, I understand. Don't be alarmed. Just tell me what you saw when you first entered the bedroom.'

'I walked in, sir, and saw him, saw Sir Henry! It was a dreadful sight, sir! The blood was everywhere and his brains. I nearly fainted. I have nightmares about it. I think I always shall.'

The wretched Lynn then burst into tears. Harcourt ordered him to 'pull himself together'.

The cook-housekeeper was a large lady who spoke in a whisper so faint as to be almost inaudible. The three house-maids clustered together like a huddle of rabbits faced by a particularly fierce fox. There was also the girl, Susan Bate, whom Hughes had mentioned as employed to wash the dishes. The orphanage waif, I thought. She had long dark hair beneath a mobcap and large brown eyes in an oval face with regular features. She would indeed have been pretty, but for a vacant stare and way of giggling from time to time. The sight of me seemed to set her off. The cook tapped her shoulder and ordered her to 'stop that!' and Susan subsided, repressing her mirth with some difficulty. The aged butler, Warton, seemed to be praying. I strongly suspected I would get no information of any value from any of them. Well, I'd been forewarned. Perhaps I'd do better with the outdoor staff, but I had no very high hopes. I revised my intention of speaking to them individually. I'd get nowhere.

'You are quite sure,' I asked the maids, 'that, when you went to dust and tidy the rooms in the morning, all the windows were fastened?'

The rabbits whispered as one, 'Yessir!'

I surveyed them all. 'None of you heard the shot? Or any unusual sound?'

'No, sir!' they all chorused.

Warton, the butler, who had been sitting dejectedly, his withered lips moving silently, suddenly cried out: 'The end of all things is nigh!' He began a rambling string of quotations, mostly from the Book of Revelations.

'Not *now*, Mr Warton!' commanded the cook in a stronger voice than I'd heard before.

'The end of all things!' wailed Warton. 'The four horsemen approach! The scarlet beast! The mother of harlots!'

'We don't want to know about that now, Mr Warton! It isn't respectable with poor Sir Henry barely cold!' The cook fairly shouted the words into his ear.

The skivvy, Susan, began to giggle again in her vacant way; and the maids all burst into tears.

It proved too much for the valet, Lynn, who crumpled in a faint on to the stone-flagged floor.

We left the rest of the staff to see to his needs, and Warton to resume his prophecy. The other three of us returned to the main part of the house. I told Beresford I should like to talk to him alone. I would talk to Harcourt afterwards. Harcourt said he'd go back to the kitchen to make sure Lynn was all right and Warton had calmed down. I turned to Beresford.

'It's such a fine day,' I said, 'that perhaps we might talk outside. I am curious to walk round the exterior of the building.'

'As you wish,' Beresford said courteously. But his manner was less relaxed than it had been during our drive here. The sight of the murder room had unnerved him, too.

We began our circuit of the house. I kept an eye on the exterior as we walked, noting any sheltered areas where an entry might be made undetected. As is the way of old gardens, many shrubs had grown to vigorous bushes above head height. The trees, planted perhaps during the Restoration period, were mighty giants. I was still far from convinced that entry had not been made at some point during the night of the murder. That a window catch had not been forced proved nothing. All that was needed was a friend within the house to open and close the window as the intruder required. But who? Warton the butler could be discounted, I thought. Lynn, the valet, also. What possible reason could they have? Could anyone have?

'Tell me about the last time you saw Sir Henry,' I invited my companion.

'Certainly!' he said briskly, and I knew I was in for another well-rehearsed speech, such as he'd delivered earlier as we walked between the trees.

'It was my uncle's habit to dine at six thirty. That may seem early to you, but he was old-fashioned in his ways. To serve dinner late would not suit the staff, either. My wife and I drove over in the trap at around four that afternoon. That was at my uncle's suggestion. Your wife and Mrs Parry were to arrive later to dine. But he wished to discuss a little estate business beforehand, with Harcourt present. As I was— as I *am* his heir, he was anxious I should be up to date in everything.'

Beresford paused and turned to me. 'I never wished this inheritance,' he said with a note of passion in his voice I had not heard before from him. 'As I warned you, and now you've seen for yourself, the house is a museum piece. The installation of the gas lighting only came about, in my opinion, in order to keep up with other gentlemen's residences in the area. Like a lot of very thrifty people, my uncle did not want to have the reputation of a pinchpenny. Agnes and I could never live here. Even less so, now that this has happened.'

'Did you let your uncle know how you felt about that?

Did he expect that you would move into the house at some future date, when you inherited?'

'That was his wish, of course,' Beresford said shortly.

'And you had let him know, perhaps, how you and your wife felt about it?'

'Oh, yes, I told him, made it absolutely clear. But he wasn't Old Indestructible's son for nothing. He meant to have his way, even when he would no longer be alive to enforce it!' Beresford broke off in some embarrassment. 'That is not a seemly way to speak since he is so recently deceased. Also, considering the way he died. But it is how it was.'

'And this was discussed at the meeting you had before the arrival of your dinner guests?'

'What?' Beresford sounded startled. 'Oh, no, not at all. Only general estate business.'

'Because Robert Harcourt was present?'

'Because it didn't arise!' Beresford said firmly.

Was that true? I wondered. I was not to be put in my place so easily. 'Is Harcourt aware you don't want to live in the house yourself?'

'He's aware of it. It will make no difference to him. I should like him to remain as estate manager. It is only the house that will be surplus to my requirements, shall I say? Letting it to a tenant will take care of that.'

'If you can find a tenant,' I said mildly, 'since you stress how inconvenient the house is.'

'If the rent is low enough, someone will be found, I dare say.' Beresford was uncomfortable at my continued questions about the house. His normal controlled manner had almost completely disappeared.

That was a signal to me that, somehow, I was asking the right questions, not the wrong ones.

'And this caused some dispute during the meeting before the dinner party?'

'No! I have already told you, Ross, the future of the house was not discussed then.'

'Then the meeting about estate business was amicable?'

He stared at me. 'Yes, why should it not be?'

'Why indeed?' I said pleasantly. But I had rattled him badly. There had been an argument, as Lizzie had shrewdly guessed, though I was not to be told its subject. Well, well, I could wait.

We had reached the back of the house and the stable yard. Tizard was there, standing over a sweating stable boy who was washing down the exterior of the berlin. Lounging against the wall of the carriage house to watch, hands in pockets, was a fellow with dark curly hair and an air about him that I recognised from his equivalent on the streets of London. This is someone who respects no man, and probably no woman, experience told me. He is not a habitual criminal, like a thief or a cracksman, but he is the sort who is always in trouble, nevertheless. He is what is generally called in London a 'bully-boy'.

'Who is that fellow?' I asked Beresford. 'He looks like a groom but hasn't the manner of one. Nor is he doing any work.'

Beresford appeared relieved to have the subject changed. 'Oh, that is Davy Evans,' he said. 'He lends a hand sometimes. He doesn't work here regularly, or anywhere else on a regular basis. But he takes jobs where he can find them.'

'Is he the fellow who drove the dogcart that fetched the ladies' baggage from the railway station? My wife mentioned him.'

'That's Davy,' agreed Beresford. 'Have you finished questioning me for the moment, Ross? I need to go back to my own home and take care of matters there.'

'I won't detain you any longer, Mr Beresford,' I told him. I was wondering how I was going to get back to the Acorn, and if I would have to eat my words and travel there in the damp berlin.

Beresford looked relieved. 'I suggest Tizard drives you back to the inn when you are ready. I will leave the trap here, as I understand you don't like the berlin, and the dogcart is an uncomfortable affair. I will borrow a saddle-horse from the stables. Tizard!'

Tom Tizard crossed the ancient cobbles of the yard in his limping gait and waited for his orders. He ignored me.

'Saddle up a horse for me, would you? Perhaps, later, when the inspector is ready to leave, you will drive him to the Acorn in my trap,' Beresford ordered.

'Right you are, sir,' said Tizard. 'Davy!' he called across the yard. 'Saddle up the bay mare for Mr Beresford.'

Davy Evans detached himself from the wall, raised a hand to signify acquiescence and went into the tack room, whence he emerged, carrying a saddle and bridle.

I wondered, when all this was over, whether Beresford would be content to allow Davy Evans to loiter about the place at will, as now. I left Beresford in the stable yard and retraced my steps to the front of the house; here I found Harcourt waiting for me on the front steps, his hands clasped behind his back and a meditative frown on his face.

'How are things in the kitchen?' I asked him.

'Warton has stopped ranting about the end of the world, so that is something. Lynn has come to his senses.' Harcourt paused. 'Or some semblance of them, at any rate. He wishes to know whether it will be in order for him to leave? He will need to seek a new place and cannot do it from here.'

'While the murder of his previous employer remains unsolved, I do not see how he can do it anywhere,' I pointed out. 'It is hardly a recommendation.'

A smile touched Harcourt's features. 'That's true. He has a mother living in Winchester and would like to go there. He feels he will recover in her house from the shock of his experience, finding Sir Henry's body.'

'Lynn can go wherever he likes,' I told him. 'But not until I have finished here. I cannot start losing witnesses when I have hardly begun my inquiries.'

'I'll tell him he has to stay for the time being,' Harcourt said.

The thud of a horse's hooves interrupted us. Beresford appeared from the direction of the stable yard riding the bay mare. A suede leather bag hung from his saddle, the contents making awkward angles in the suede. I guessed the bag contained the pistol in its box. He raised an arm in farewell salute but did not halt for a final word. Well, I would be seeing him again.

Harcourt and I watched him reach the far end of the drive and disappear from our sight.

Harcourt said suddenly, 'That lawyer fellow from London, Pelham, will be coming down from London, I understand.'

'So Mr Beresford told me. But you will have seen Pelham yourself recently. I believe he came only a matter of weeks ago, when Sir Henry signed a new will.'

'I saw him, certainly,' Harcourt agreed. 'I had no direct dealings with him.'

There was some movement in the hallway of the house behind us. I glanced back and saw that Warton, apparently recovered from his disorder in the kitchen, had entered the hall and stood looking towards us with deep mistrust on his wrinkled features. Perhaps he thinks I am not to be trusted with the teaspoons, I thought wryly. I certainly didn't think the old chap might want to talk to me, especially after the scene in the kitchen.

By common unspoken consent, Harcourt and I moved away from the main entrance and began to walk slowly down the drive with its great elms standing like troops at attention on either side.

When a case is over, there is always a review of how it was handled. Were there missed opportunities? Misunderstandings? Overlooked clues? Readers of newspapers (and of popular fiction) do so like to read about clues. They always think they might have done better than the professional police officer. Did I miss something on that first visit to the Hall? Perhaps I did. Would it have made any difference in the long term? That's much more difficult to know and missed moments trouble the sleep of the detective years afterwards. But one cannot brood about these things. Deal with the situation at the time: that is all any of us can do.

I glanced at Harcourt walking beside me with a slight scowl on his face. He must be a worried man with all this on his plate, besides running the estate. The scene in the kitchen must also have been embarrassing to him, although he was not responsible for the indoor staff. I must not waste time in conjectures. I should get on with the business that had brought me.

'How much,' I asked him, 'do you – and other members of the staff – know about the will?'

'We are none of us in Mr Pelham's confidence now,' retorted Harcourt brusquely, 'as we were none of us in Sir Henry's, except, in my case, in matters concerning the estate.'

'But you know – knew beforehand – that Mr Beresford is the main beneficiary?'

'He inherits, that's generally known,' agreed Harcourt. 'Sir Henry told the ladies, Mrs Parry and your wife, at the dinner party, that Beresford would be his heir. There was no secret about it.'

'Tell *me*,' I invited him, 'about that last day, the day of the dinner party, since you mention the event. You were a guest that evening.'

'I was invited,' Harcourt's voice corrected me. 'It avoided an odd number at table. I was as much invited, you might say, as the chairs around the table were.'

I was astonished at the bitterness in his voice.

'Tell me,' I said, 'and please understand that what you say need not reach the ears of Mr Beresford. Tell me, did you have a good working relationship with Sir Henry?'

Ann Granger

'I tried to be conscientious in my duties,' returned Harcourt in a stony voice. 'I believe Sir Henry was satisfied.'

'How did it come about that you became his estate manager?'

We had reached the end of the avenue and turned to walk back towards the house. 'He intended it, from my youth,' said Harcourt. 'He paid for my education for that purpose.'

Whatever answer I might have expected, it had not been that. 'He paid for your schooling? Was he a friend of your parents?' I exclaimed.

'No, he was my father.' Harcourt spoke quite calmly.

I was left speechless for the moment. He turned and looked at me with a gleam in his dark eyes. 'Didn't expect that, did you, Inspector Ross?' he asked, but not unpleasantly.

'No, I did not,' I confessed, wondering if this could be true and, if so, what role, if any, it played in the murder. 'Is this— is it generally known?'

'Oh, yes,' said Harcourt briskly. 'They all know it. Though, of course, no one talks of it. However, in the course of your inquiries someone may see fit to tell you, so you need not be worried about mentioning it to my cousin (on the wrong side of the blanket) Beresford.'

He walked on a few paces, then stopped and turned back. 'He may even tell you himself, eventually, if he thinks it wise.'

It was an extraordinary claim. I wondered that Beresford hadn't told me something of it already, during our walk through the trees earlier. But he'd stated firmly that his uncle and aunt had had no children. Well, now it seemed that there had been no children born in wedlock. Was this connected with Beresford's casual remark that, before he married his wife, Henry Meager had wanted to 'marry someone else'? I had been right to suspect that in telling me so much of his family history, Beresford had carefully concealed the most interesting fact. Always supposing, of course, that Harcourt spoke the truth.

I glanced at the man; but he wasn't looking at me. Having delivered his startling statement, he stared straight ahead. I did fancy, however, that a faint smile was on his lips. He had 'put the cat among the pigeons', as the old saying went, and it gave him satisfaction to know that he'd done so. He must know I would inquire into the evidence of this, sooner or later. Had he told me in order to confuse me? Delay me? Send me haring off down the wrong track? He wouldn't be the first to lay a false trail for the hard-pressed detective to untangle.

Chapter Nine

> *The business is not finished. If this detective*
> *from London, and his clever wife, are putting*
> *their noses into everything, so be it.*
> *I have taken account of that.*
> *It will make no difference to my plans.*

Elizabeth Martin Ross

FORTUNATELY THE bookshelf in the little study down-stairs, which had been converted into Mrs Parry's bedroom, contained a few novels. Among them was *The Tenant of Wildfell Hall* by Anne Brontë.

'I have not read it, though I have heard of it,' said Mrs Parry, eyeing the volume with distrust. 'I have heard that it is in questionable taste.'

'I think there is no reason why you should hesitate to read it, Aunt Parry,' I told her. 'I have read it.'

'Is it sentimental?' asked Mrs Parry. 'I cannot abide sentimental novels. I was brought up by a clergyman father to avoid such works of fiction. He believed them injurious to moral fibre.'

It was the first time I had heard Aunt Parry speak in this way, although I knew she was a parson's daughter

'*The Tenant of Wildfell Hall* is in no way a sentimental novel,' I assured her. 'And the author was also a clergyman's daughter.'

'Well, my ankle must be rested for another day or two, so I must read something, I suppose,' she conceded. 'I shall sit in the garden in that little arbour, and attempt it.'

Since she could not leave the house and grounds on account of the damaged ankle, Mrs Parry had taken over the little arbour which I had marked out for my own private retreat. Well, she might choose to sit there; but I didn't have to sit there with her.

'I thought I might take a walk up on the heath,' I told her. I had no wish to return to the village and the suspicious glances of the people there. Their earlier welcome would have evaporated in the light of events.

'As you wish, Elizabeth,' she said sulkily. 'But take care to avoid an accident such as I had. It would not do for both of us to be incapacitated.'

Walking out of the gate a little later, equipped for my walk with balmorals and the trusty stick, I encountered Jacob Dennis, for his part armed once more with a metal bucket and a spade.

'Is it for bait you dig down there on the foreshore, Mr Dennis?' I asked him.

'Aye, ma'am,' he agreed, squinting up at me. His hunch-back stance appeared to be natural to him, but I didn't know whether he had been born with this slight deformity of the spine or whether a lifetime crouched over a spade, digging either on the shore or in the garden, had left him so.

'Where do you fish?'

'Davy and I take the boat out. 'Tis Davy's boat,' he added.

'Davy Evans?'

'Aye, ma'am. 'Tis a sailing boat and Davy handles her well. We can go out and find plenty of fish.'

So that was the source of the fresh fish that appeared regularly at our dinner table here. But a sailing boat cost money and I was surprised Davy owned one. He appeared to have no regular income. Odd jobs provided by Sir Henry and others would not have paid for the boat. Clearly Davy had some other source of earnings.

I told him I was going to the heath to walk. He directed me to a quick way to reach it and we parted.

By the time I reached the heath my annoyance with Mrs Parry had faded away. I even began to feel sympathy for her. She had planned this holiday with such confidence and, so far, little had gone right for her. I reproached myself for being such a grump. It is because Ben is so near and yet I can't be with him or talk to him, I thought.

But now, none of this seemed to trouble me any more. Here, on the warm, almost windless day, the flat expanse of heather, gorse and occasional clumps of trees or bushes spread out as far as I could see. I appeared to be quite alone. I couldn't even see a pony or two. I set out to walk along one of the narrow tracks, my feet making hardly any sound. After I had gone quite a way, my eye was caught by a glitter to my left. Curious, I left the path and picked my way towards it.

It was a small irregularly shaped pond, probably originating in an accumulation of rainwater in a dip in the ground. Over time, the original large puddle had grown and become this pond, surrounded by bushes and a small tree or two. The earth around the edge was soft and marked with deep narrow holes. The free-roaming ponies and cattle knew of this place and came here to drink, leaving the imprint of their hooves like calling cards. I wondered whether anything lived in the water. I was peering into its depths when the shadowy image of a face appeared in it, staring up at me.

I gave a cry of alarm, starting back and colliding with someone who was standing behind me and had been looking over my shoulder. I was so convinced that I had been completely alone that I turned in anger and not a little fear, ready to confront this intruder who had crept up on me. I found myself looking at Cora Dawlish.

'Where did you spring from?' I demanded. It seemed impossible that I hadn't seen her. The landscape was open. There were few places of concealment and yet here she was, in her black clothes and jet beads, with a plaited straw bonnet on her head. It was old-fashioned in style, with a wide brim and high crown, such as might have been worn in the days of the Regency. It was tied on with faded blue ribbons. Had she been following me? She must have been doing so, I decided. The only reason I had not seen her must be because her approaching footsteps had been silent on the dusty track.

'I walk on the heath, as you're doing,' she replied. 'There are plants growing here that are of use to me.' She indicated the pocket of a large black apron swathed around her waist. I could see various pieces of greenery in it, including sprigs of heather.

'I wish you had called out to let me know you were near,' I told her, still discomfited. 'You startled me.'

'You are from the city,' she said, unmoved by my discomfort, 'or you would have known. A countrywoman would know another living being was nearby. You would have heard my breath, the rustle of my skirts. In the city, folk become blind and deaf. There is noise all around them and they hear nothing. The scene is always changing and they see nothing.'

'You have lived in the city at some time,' I said quietly. My anger had gone and that surprised me, because I should have taken the opportunity to tell her to stop spreading superstitious rumours about me. But I had assumed she and her sister had always lived in the village. That she could ever have lived in a big town or city startled me.

'A long time ago,' she confirmed. 'How does the lady's ankle?'

'Oh, quite well, making good progress. But she cannot walk on it yet.'

'I can make a poultice that can help with the inflammation,' she offered.

This also surprised me. Was she trying to make amends for her previous behaviour?

'Thank you,' I said awkwardly. 'But I don't think I could persuade her to use it.'

'As you wish,' she said.

'I should be getting back,' I told her. I turned away and was about to step briskly forward when she grabbed my arm, preventing me.

'Stop!' she ordered.

My former anger returned, flaring up. 'What—?' I began. But the protest died in my throat as something moved on the ground directly at my feet.

It was a snake, patterned with black diamonds in scaly beauty. It moved quickly, in a zigzag progress, across the narrow path I had been about to take, and slithered into the heather.

'You must learn to use your eyes, truth-seeker's wife,' said Cora, the old, familiar mocking note back in her voice now. 'It is an adder. When the day is warm they come out to bask in the sun. You almost stepped on it.'

'I didn't see it. Thank you,' I said awkwardly. 'You are right. I am a city dweller.'

She nodded. 'If you must step on one, step on its head,' she advised me. 'If you step on its tail, it will turn and bite.' A gleam entered her dark eyes. 'The same is true for some human beings,' she said. 'Strike first and strike true, or you will feel their fangs.'

'Yes,' I agreed awkwardly. Suddenly, I wanted nothing so much as to be away from her. 'I must go!'

I walked off, keeping my eyes on the ground now. After a few steps I looked back to see what she did, if she watched me. There was no sign of her. The open landscape was empty of any life.

Where had she gone? She had disappeared as

mysteriously as she had appeared by the pond in the first place. There were precious few hiding places here, just a bush or two. The old superstitious panic seized me. I crushed it ruthlessly, as she had warned me to do with a snake. She was not far away and I must be able to see her. She could *not* disappear. I continued to scrutinise the scene intently, and my eye caught a faint movement a little above the ground, on the edge of the pond. Something nodded. It was the wide brim of Cora's straw bonnet. She had found a dry, adder-free spot, and sat down, that was all. My eyes had been seeking a standing figure. Not seeing what I'd expected, I'd panicked. Yet I had only to lower my line of sight to locate her. It seemed she must always outwit me.

'One day,' I said aloud, but quietly, 'I will outwit you.'

Inspector Ben Ross

'Did you see the ruined tower while you and Mr Beresford took your walk around the house?' Harcourt asked me unexpectedly.

I realised I had been standing in silence, staring at him, as my brain wrestled to fit his extraordinary claim to be the murdered man's son into the pattern of what I already knew.

'No,' I replied automatically.

'It's what they called a folly. Every gentleman's grounds had one when there was a great fancy for Gothic mysteries. It is this way. It is in a sorry state, I'm afraid, but still a good place to sit and talk.' He gestured, stretching out his arm to point into a small clump of trees, and set off. I followed.

The trees were fewer in number than they appeared. They had been planted in a circle. At the centre was an open space in which stood a stone tower, with an open Gothic arch set into the façade, and narrow slits above for the use of archers who had never manned it. It was roofless, and appeared to have no purpose. Ivy had crept up the walls to several feet above head level. At the time it was constructed I dare say it appeared romantic. Young people would have made lovers' trysts here. Young ladies would have been instructed by their tutors to sketch it. Picnic gatherings would have taken place in it. There would have been none of this in the Old Indestructible's time, or in his son's. To me, the tower now looked sad and forgotten.

'What do you think of it?' asked Harcourt. I suspected he was suppressing a smile. It wasn't on his face but I could hear it in his voice.

'It's not to my taste,' I told him. 'But I'm a practical man.'

'It is a little better inside,' he told me, and led me under the Gothic arch.

There was no internal structure, any upper floor or stairs to the level of the arrow slits above. But there were signs that an upper floor might once have existed or been intended. The first few stone steps of a staircase clung to one wall; and overhead a stout beam ran from one side of the structure to the other, though this might have been installed as a brace for the outer walls. At any rate, the tower was an empty shell, the floor paved with stone flags. A marble bench ran around the walls. I looked up to the open sky and few tree branches nodding overhead, and thought it was freakish fancy; but it wasn't unpleasant.

'Was there ever an upper floor?' I asked Harcourt.

He shook his head. 'Never, to my knowledge. I don't think one was intended. The whole thing is meant to indicate mystery. Well, now we have a real mystery, but centred on the house, not here.' Harcourt gestured to the circular marble bench, indicating I should sit down.

When we were seated he said nothing, perhaps waiting for me to make some further comment. I decided I would take the initiative anyway, and speak first.

'My education was also paid for by a well-wisher,' I told him. 'Otherwise, I should be toiling in a coalmine even now. I don't suppose my benefactor, a local doctor, expected that I would eventually marry his daughter, but that is what happened. Although a great deal occurred between. But you claim Sir Henry was your father. Forgive me if I ask about your mother; and why you believe this to be the case.'

'My mother was French,' Harcourt began.

He showed no reluctance to talk about his origins. I fancied he was almost eager. That was something else I'd found in those making similar claims. They want the listener to believe it, either because they themselves believe it, or because it is part of a role they are playing.

'Sir Henry went travelling on the Continent as a young man,' Harcourt was saying, 'even though the consequences of war and political upheaval had made this difficult. He was accompanied on his travels by a battle-hardened ex-seaman, known to his father, Sir Hector Meager, from his time at sea. This fellow's duties were partly as manservant but chiefly as bodyguard. During his travels Henry met my mother. Her name was Isabelle. She had been orphaned and lived with an elderly female relative. Henry fell in love, proposed marriage and was accepted. The old lady, who was my mother's guardian, did not object. There was a problem, however, in that my father was not yet quite twenty, so underage. He could not marry without his father's permission. He persuaded the old lady that if he took her young charge to England, to meet his father, permission would be forthcoming and the couple would be married.'

'What about the ex-seaman?' I asked. 'Wasn't he supposed to be keeping an eye on the young man; and stepping in to prevent any embarrassing misunderstandings?'

'The old seadog had proved efficient at protecting his charge against assault or robbery. But preventing the young gentleman from engaging himself to be married had not been part of his duties. Or not as explained to him before leaving England.' Harcourt paused. 'In fairness to my father, I must say he did try to keep his word to my mother and her guardian, but he was not allowed to.'

'I imagine,' I said, 'and forgive me if I am anticipating you, but I suspect the problem was Sir Henry's father, Old Indestructible. The couple turned up on his doorstep and didn't get the reception young Henry had hoped for. Old Indestructible refused to give his consent to his son marrying anyone, other than someone his father had approved beforehand. Am I right? The old man also told him that, if Henry had any idea of waiting until he reached the age of majority, twenty-one, and then persisted in going ahead and marrying to disoblige his father, he'd cut Henry out of his inheritance. I am guessing all this, of course.'

'I see you are a very good investigating officer and have it all worked out,' said Harcourt drily. 'Quite so! Old Indestructible was furious. In the first place, his son had not consulted him before he entered into a contract with my mother. Secondly, his son was not yet twenty-one, so still under the age of consent, as you so rightly pointed out. He could not marry without his father's permission and that gave Sir Hector the whip hand. Lastly, but importantly, the old fellow had his eye on a different bride for his son. He refused outright to accept my mother, and put the matter immediately in the hands of his lawyers. They obtained a court ruling that any promises made by my father to Isabelle were without any validity in English law.

'At this point, my mother spoke up in her own defence. She declared she had taken Henry's word as the word of an English gentleman, and so had her elderly guardian. She expected my grandfather, also an English gentleman and a former officer, to understand that, and not oppose it.

'It cut no ice with the old man, of course, but he admired spirit and he wished to avoid scandal. He wanted no obstacle to his son's marriage to Miss Madeleine, the girl he'd chosen. Therefore, though he remained adamant that he would never agree to any marriage, he was prepared to settle a substantial sum on Isabelle, on the understanding that this was an act of generosity, done purely out of good will. She must sign a document acknowledging this, and declaring that she would make no further claims.

'My mother's first reaction was a refusal to be bought off. But my father knew Old Indestructible and his ways and realised his whole future was in jeopardy. He risked being cut off with a shilling, as the old saying went. Besides, there was a further complication in that my mother was now with child. Henry would find himself without a penny to support a young family.

'He persuaded my mother to accept my grandfather's offer. She realised that, now Henry had given in to his father's wish, there was no hope of their ever being married. The money was used to purchase a small house near the harbour in Lymington for my mother, and an annuity.

'All the same, things would have been very difficult for my mother. But a wealthy childless widower, a ship's chandler by the name of Harcourt, saw her, fell in love, and proposed marriage. He was prepared to accept the child my mother carried and raise it as his own. She agreed. At my baptism, her husband's name was entered in the parish register as father of the infant. So, you see, a very civilised solution was arrived at.' The bitterness in Harcourt's voice could not be hidden.

This was indeed an added complication. In the eyes of the public, and in law, Harcourt wasn't illegitimate. Harcourt's mother had been married when he was born, I thought. Her elderly husband's name stood in the baptismal register as the father. What prompted Harcourt's extraordinary claim? What did it achieve, other than to besmirch his mother's reputation? There was a lot about all this that I didn't know; and would find very difficult to discover.

'And Sir Henry later married the girl his father had chosen?' I guessed.

'Oh, yes, in due course he did; and a miserable marriage it was, so I understand. Not the fault of the lady, of course. But Sir Henry resented the wife forced on him. He— he was neither a good nor a faithful husband. His own father lived another twelve years, gradually getting madder and madder.'

'And Mr and Mrs Harcourt – and you?'

'The arrangement worked very well, in the circumstances. But by the time Old Indestructible died, those circumstances had changed. Harcourt, my mother's husband and – on paper – my father, had also died. He was a nice old fellow but he had speculated foolishly and left very little. My mother had been reduced to taking in paid lodgers. Worried for my future, she contacted Sir Henry to ask for his help. He was now, on the recent death of his father, in possession of his inheritance, so agreed to pay for my schooling. Also, when the time came, he promised he'd see that I entered a suitable profession. I was sent off to school and stayed there until I was old enough to earn a living. When I had only been at school for six months I was called into the headmaster's study to be told my mother had died. She had already been buried. I had only the memory of our parting as I left for the school. I do wonder if, when she hugged me for that last time, she knew she wouldn't see me again.'

Harcourt broke off suddenly and muttered, 'You will excuse me!'

He stood up and hurried out of the tower. My first thought was that he had been overcome by emotion when talking of his mother. But though I couldn't now see him, I could hear him. He was coughing, in an uncontrollable deep-seated fit, suggesting to me some problem with the lungs. The sound brought back an old memory to me, from my youth in the Derbyshire coalfield. Some of the miners coughed in that way, putting it down to the coal dust getting into the lungs. They had the appearance of strong men but few reached great age.

Harcourt had returned. His face was flushed but in other ways he appeared unaffected. He retook his seat and made no further excuse for his brief absence. On my part, I made no comment.

'As it happened,' Harcourt picked up his story, 'at the same time as I finished my schooling, the bursar of the school concerned found himself in need of a clerk. I took up the post; and remained there for another couple of years, book-keeping. Then Sir Henry appeared in my life again, to offer me a position assisting his then estate manager. In due course, when that agent retired, I took over. I have been here ever since. Of course, they all know who I am; because the old people hereabouts remember the drama when young Henry returned home with a French lady on his arm.'

'But did Sir Henry ever openly acknowledge you as his son?' I asked curiously.

'No, never!' Harcourt snapped. He drew a deep breath and regained his self-control. 'In fact, I think he resented me. Perhaps he regretted he had given me the job of running the estate, which kept me so close. I reminded him of a time he now chose to forget.' Harcourt turned to look me full in the face. 'I did not kill him,' he said.

'So tell me, please, about the final argument on the evening of the dinner party. Please, don't deny that there was a, shall we say, "lively" discussion before my wife and Mrs Parry arrived to dine. I believe there was.'

'Does Beresford say so?' Harcourt appeared surprised.

'No,' I admitted, 'he says only estate business was discussed.'

'So you have another informant?' Harcourt frowned, puzzled.

'That reply tells me I am right. There was a dispute.'

'But you won't tell me who that person is?' he challenged.

'My job here, Mr Harcourt, is to ask questions, not to answer them. I have reason to suspect Sir Henry's will was mentioned during that last meeting.'

He didn't like that. He drummed the fingers of his left hand on the marble seat, and eyed me with a mix of caution and annoyance.

'Very well,' he agreed at last, reluctantly. 'It was mentioned, of course, because he had just signed a new will. The main part of that was unchanged, Beresford was – and is – his heir. It was the legacies to members of the household that had to be brought up to date.'

'And you, Mr Harcourt? Do you know if you are mentioned in this will?'

Harcourt hesitated before replying. Then he said, 'Sir Henry's man of law is a fellow called Pelham, with an office in London.'

Ann Granger

'You should perhaps know I have met Mr Pelham in the past,' I said. 'In connection with other matters.'

'Then you will know that he is a clever man. He knew of my relationship to his client. He had suggested to Sir Henry that I be left a reasonable legacy, as his estate manager. It should not be a sum that would attract comment. But it should be fairly generous. I believe Pelham's argument was that, provided I were left a respectable sum, I would not be in a position to— make trouble. It would also be a condition of the bequest that I cease, in Pelham's words, "to make unsubstantiated claims of being Sir Henry's natural son."'

An almost savage scowl crossed Harcourt's face as he told me this. He paused and regained his self-control. The scowl faded but grim determination remained.

'I told Sir Henry I would decline any such legacy. I would not be "looked after" like any other long-time servant. Nor would I deny the truth of my parentage, even if Sir Henry chose to do so.' He gave a brief, mirthless smile. 'They were both astonished when I said I wouldn't take the money. Pelham thought I was trying to beat up the price; that I believed I was worth more. There was a very unpleasant scene. I thought I was going to be dismissed. But Pelham calmed Meager down. To turn me out would be to give me a free hand to tell my tale to anyone who cared to listen.'

Harcourt drew a deep breath. 'You are right. The matter was raised again at our last meeting, just before the dinner party. Pelham was back in London, of course, and it was intended to discuss only estate business. That led to plans for the future. Pelham had convinced Sir Henry I could be bought in time.

'Beresford probably thought so too, though I think my claim of kinship worried him less. He didn't care about it, frankly, and made it clear at that last meeting before the dinner party. It made no difference to him, he said. As to my birth, it was written in the register of baptisms that Edward Harcourt was my father. Beresford himself was the designated heir, son of Sir Henry's sister, and that was that. I could remain as estate manager if I wanted, when the time came. Or not, as I pleased.'

Checkmate! I thought to myself, as I looked at Harcourt's flushed features. Beresford was a clever fellow. He had handled the situation far better than Sir Henry or Pelham. But, in effect, for Harcourt to have been told to keep quiet and stop making a fuss, as one might say to a child? Oh, that must have enraged Harcourt at the time.

The man himself got his emotion under control now. 'I think eventually I got it into Meager's head that I didn't want *more money*. I wanted *nothing*! But he sulked, to put it mildly. If he'd lived to meet Pelham again, I am sure the lawyer would have persuaded the old chap I was playing some deep game. Of course that next meeting never came.' Harcourt's mouth twisted into a wry grimace. 'Fate plays strange tricks, doesn't it?'

I waited. Eventually, Harcourt turned to me and said in a cold voice, 'Meager's view was that I'd insulted him, you see. He said that I was ungrateful. He had "always looked after" me.'

Harcourt leaned back against the stone blocks of the

wall and stared ahead of him through the Gothic arch of the entry, towards the fringe of trees beyond. When he spoke, the impression I got was not that he spoke to me, but to the ghost of the late Sir Henry Meager.

'All those years at school,' he said. 'After the death of my mother, I had no one. Oh, the school fees were paid, but I never had so much as a letter from Sir Henry, or from anyone on his behalf, not even whoever his solicitor was at that time. Most of the boys had families or guardians who took an interest of some sort. They received letters from time to time. Occasionally the luckier ones received visits from a parent. I had no one, no family, and no guardian that I knew of. I suppose Sir Henry filled the role, but if so, no one took the trouble to explain it to me. No one, Inspector Ross.'

Harcourt turned back to me. 'He paid my fees, and he took me into his estate office, where I eventually became estate manager. He considered he'd done his duty. Most people, I dare say, would agree that he had. *But he wanted my gratitude, Inspector Ross. That he would never have.*'

'Because you hated him?' I suggested quietly.

'I suppose I did,' he agreed, as if we spoke of trivial matters. 'Yes, I dare say I did. And I wasn't the only one, because someone hated him enough to blow out his brains for him.' Harcourt smiled without humour. 'But I was not the person whose finger was on the trigger.'

Chapter Ten

Elizabeth Martin Ross

IT WAS as well that I decided to return to the house and not linger on the heath. When I arrived back, it was to find Aunt Parry in some agitation.

'Thank goodness you have come back, Elizabeth! It was very inconsiderate of you to wander off in that way.'

'I did not "wander off"!' I protested. 'I told you I was going to walk on the heath.'

'And while you have been gone,' continued Aunt Parry, ignoring my defence, 'a message has come from Mrs Beresford at Oakwood House. A groom rode over with it and has just left. We are invited to take tea with her this afternoon. She will send a carriage for us. I have been practising walking with the stick and I am sure my ankle will hold out.'

'That is kind of her at this time of mourning for her family,' I said. To be honest, I was surprised. 'She must be very much occupied with necessary arrangements.'

'I dare say it is because she is embarrassed,' retorted Aunt Parry frankly. 'After all, it was not to become involved in scandal and murder that I came here. But yes, yes, it is good of her. What will you wear, Elizabeth? Mrs Beresford will be in mourning, of course. We must do our best.'

I had feared we might have to travel in the berlin again. But the carriage sent for us that afternoon was a landau with a smart coachman. We were taken in style to Oakwood House. That, and the prospect of an outing, had put Mrs Parry in a very good humour. I, on the other hand, was apprehensive. Mrs Parry could, on occasion, be what is called 'a loose cannon'.

As expected, Agnes Beresford was in full mourning. She wore a long-sleeved gown of black taffeta, with a ruche at the hem, and a short train, the bodice trimmed with black velvet. On her head was a cap of black lace. The gown and cap must have been in her wardrobe from an earlier sad occasion, or held in reserve against sudden need, because there had been no time, since Sir Henry's death, to have them made.

Although the death had not actually taken place here, the house itself was also observing conventions. The curtains were drawn; mirrors were veiled. Even the piano was draped in a black shawl. But at least the curtains in the drawing room, into which we were shown, were not fully closed, only partly so. The room was therefore shadowy, but not so gloomy we could not see. Agnes, in her black gown, was of a piece with it. She was very pale. When she stood to greet us, it was as though we had entered the Underworld, to be welcomed in by some antique draped spectre. I couldn't help but feel embarrassed at being there, although we'd been invited.

'It is very good of you to ask us to take tea,' I said awkwardly. 'Both Mrs Parry and I are deeply conscious of what a sad and difficult time this must be.'

'You have my most sincere condolences,' said Aunt Parry, perfectly at ease. 'Sir Henry was a charming man and must be much missed.'

Agnes replied somewhat mechanically, 'Yes, of course. Thank you.' She then looked at the waiting butler and added, 'You may bring tea, Tompkins.'

She turned back to us. 'Please don't feel you are intruding. Andrew is so busy with everything and I am left sitting here. I am quite desperate for company.'

She gestured at the chairs and we all sat down. I had been wondering quite how the conversation would progress once the opening exchanges had taken place, but Agnes was so eager to speak that I believed she had spoken the truth. She was deeply shocked and anxious to unburden herself. Yet, somehow, I sensed a curious absence of grief. She seemed more to be frightened than distraught.

She continued now: 'I am very pleased to welcome you both here; and deeply appreciate that you have taken the trouble to come.' She hesitated again. 'You see,' she burst out suddenly, 'the only other company I have here when Andrew is away, is *him*!' She pointed at the window.

We both turned to look at the window but no face peered in at us.

'Who is he?' asked Mrs Parry cautiously.

'Why, Sir Henry! He is lying in his coffin in the old icehouse, out there in the grounds, until we can bury him in the churchyard, in the family plot. Of course, we are told not to believe in ghosts. But I do feel most strongly that he wanders about out there. I even feel that sometimes he is in the house. He cannot rest, I believe, until his killer is found.'

So that, I thought, explains why the house is in full mourning. Sir Henry did not die here, but he is dwelling here in death. I felt a rush of anger towards Andrew Beresford. Had he not considered the effect on his young wife of being left here alone with the servants and a body in the icehouse? No wonder the curtains were all drawn. Agnes feared to see Sir Henry's ghastly countenance, with bloodstains, looking in on her.

'It's not pleasant to have Sir Henry's remains so near,' I said. 'But I urge you not to give way to your imagination, although I perfectly understand it.'

'It is not just my imagination, you know,' Agnes answered energetically. 'Things have been happening.'

'What kind of things?' I asked.

Agnes hesitated. 'You will think me foolish.'

We assured her jointly that we would not.

'Well, there are the flowers. You see my piano over there? I have not played since Sir Henry died because I did not think it would be seemly, not with him lying . . . lying out there. And also because,' she hesitated. 'Because I had a ridiculous fear that, if I did begin to play, I'd turn and see him standing behind me, listening. He liked to hear me play, you see.'

'You do play beautifully, my dear Mrs Beresford,' Aunt Parry assured her.

'I begin to think I shall never play another note,' said Agnes despondently.

'What about the flowers?' I asked, impatient to know what had happened.

'Well, I came down here the morning Sir Henry was discovered dead in his bed – that is to say, the morning after the dinner party – and there was a white rose lying on the piano. Of course, we did not then know what had happened at the Hall during the night. I thought Andrew had placed it there, because we have roses like them in the garden. But when I thanked him, he denied it. We asked the servants but none of them could explain it. Then Robert Harcourt came with the dreadful news. Andrew rushed off to the Hall and, well, he has hardly been at home since.

'Yesterday, it happened again, only this time the rose was pink. Again I asked the servants; and again they couldn't tell me how it got there. I didn't like to mention it to Andrew because he has so much to worry him just now. But this morning there was something else on the piano, a small painted fan, the kind a lady might take to the theatre. I had never seen it before. The servants swear none of them placed it there. I didn't quiz them any further because, if they thought Sir Henry was trying to contact someone here, they would all leave at once. After he denied knowledge of the first rose, I haven't dared tell Andrew about the rest, because he'd be so upset.'

'Well, I suppose there are more things in heaven and earth . . .' mused Mrs Parry tactlessly. 'Perhaps you should ask the vicar to call and carry out some sort of ceremony?'

I glared at her. She flushed and fell silent.

'He's called already, to express sympathy and discuss the funeral, when we can hold it. I didn't tell him about any of this – the flowers on the piano,' added Agnes in despair. 'How can I? It's sounds so – so improbable. You are the only two people I've been able to talk to about it.'

'It's quite unnecessary to involve the vicar!' I said briskly. 'These are malicious tricks, Mrs Beresford, and the joker is alive, not dead. I do believe you should tell Mr Beresford. Perhaps I should tell my husband.'

Agnes turned to me and was speaking again, more calmly. 'Tell Inspector Ross, if you think he should know, but please ask him not to tell Andrew . . .'

'I can't guarantee that he will not. But I will explain how you feel about this.'

Agnes smiled nervously. 'Mrs Ross, both Andrew and I are greatly relieved that Inspector Ross has come to take charge of the investigations. Please tell him so. The inspector who came before – his name was Hughes and he came from Southampton – was very courteous and thorough, but— I felt he was ill at ease. That may have been because we are all under suspicion, or he made us feel so. Also, if I may be frank?'

Mrs Parry and I assured her she could be quite frank.

'Inspector Hughes seemed somewhat out of his depth. I don't intend any criticism of him; I'm sure he's done his best. But my husband is already acquainted with Inspector Ross and respects him. We are indeed all of us "out of our depth". To have someone here who already knows us gives us all confidence.'

'You cannot do better than have Inspector Ross investigate!' stated Mrs Parry, in a surprisingly enthusiastic tribute.

I wasn't quite sure what to say next. But the tea arrived at that moment and there was a natural interruption during which tea was poured and cake handed out.

Agnes then began to speak again. 'Things are very awkward, due to the manner of Sir Henry's death. The family solicitor, Mr Pelham, is travelling down from London today. I understand Mr Ross knows him?'

I replied cautiously that I believed Ben had had dealings before with Mr Pelham but I had never met him.

'He is a rather frightening man,' said Agnes frankly. 'He never smiles. I suppose the matters in which he deals are serious and one ought not to expect to be light-hearted in his manner. And now, of course, he is dealing with the death of a client and the bereaved family.'

She paused and looked a little flushed as if embarrassed. I thought I understood. This was not the usual kind of bereaved family. So far I had not heard a word of regret spoken. Agnes had not liked her husband's uncle, so much had been clear to me on the evening of the dinner party. But even if the deceased had not been popular, it is usual to find something good to say. Shakespeare had Mark Antony find something to say about Caesar, after all. Agnes was clearly struggling and eventually gave up the attempt. Her nature was to be honest. She couldn't find anything good; but she would say nothing bad. When she began to speak again, it was in a practical tone.

'Due to the manner of Sir Henry's death, as I was saying, final settlement of the will may be delayed. Mr Pelham wrote to say there should be no funeral until the police give their permission for it, or the coroner, one or

175

the other. Pelham will discuss all that with Andrew when he arrives.'

'He will be staying in this house?' asked Mrs Parry.

'Oh, no!' Agnes told her quickly. 'We offered him hospitality, naturally. But he declined. He felt in the circumstances he should stay independently of any of the persons mentioned in the will. Also he has some other business to transact, in Southampton. That has nothing to do with us. He has therefore taken a room at the Acorn Inn, where, I believe, Inspector Ross is staying?'

Oh, my goodness! I thought. *I don't think Ben knows that.*

Agnes burst out suddenly, 'We cannot imagine who could have done such a thing!'

She did not have to say the word 'murder' for us to take her meaning.

'It will turn out to be some vagabond,' declared Mrs Parry firmly. My earlier glare at her had only quenched her temporarily. She was back on form. 'Depend upon it, my dear Mrs Beresford, it will be some rogue who broke into the house with intent to steal.'

'Perhaps,' said Agnes doubtfully.

'Forgive me,' I said hesitantly, 'but it is absolutely certain nothing was taken from the house?'

'Nothing has been taken,' Agnes confirmed. 'There is no sign that anyone searched the Hall, other than in the library, where the drawer to the desk was forced open . . .' Her voice tailed away.

'And the wretch saw the pistol!' Mrs Parry made a dramatic gesture, as of someone seizing something and pointing it across the room.

Agnes flinched and I thought that I might, after all, murder Aunt Parry one day.

'He would have seen *both* pistols,' I began loudly. 'But he appears only to have taken *one*. I don't think a burglar—'

'Of course he was a burglar! He meant to search the house and took the one pistol to protect himself, should he be confronted,' insisted Aunt Parry, overriding anything I might want to say. 'Tragically, that is just what happened. In the course of his search, seeking valuables, he entered Sir Henry's bedroom. Sir Henry awoke and the miscreant fired. But for that, the intruder would have returned to the library, helped himself to the other pistol and anything else that took his eye. Has the silver all been accounted for?'

'There was no sign of anyone breaking in,' said Agnes, in a very small voice. She had become, if possible, even paler. 'The silver is all there. Warton, the butler, made a most thorough check. He has been in charge of the silver for many years and would have noticed if even the smallest item were missing.'

Mrs Parry had an answer to that. 'When he had shot poor Sir Henry, the wretch panicked. He did not want to be weighed down with booty or caught with any in his possession. He was forced to leave everyone and flee.'

'But how did he get in without any sign of a forced window or door?' Agnes protested.

'Oh, these burglar fellows are very clever,' said Mrs Parry. 'They know all the tricks. Why, where I live in Marylebone, there have been some quite audacious burglaries from time to time. And that is in town, with a regular police patrol going past the house. On consideration, I feel the villain who killed Sir Henry was a professional house-breaker, not just a wandering tramp. A quiet country house would present no obstacle to a determined thief. The whole neighbourhood should be on the alert!'

I decided Mrs Parry must be stopped in her speculations. It was enough that the Beresfords had Sir Henry's death to contend with, to say nothing of his restless spirit roaming the grounds, without poor Agnes being further frightened out of her wits at the thought of a ruthless burglar next turning his attention to Oakwood House.

'He left the firearm behind at the scene of his crime,' I said firmly. 'Whoever he is, and wherever he is now, at least we have no reason to believe him armed.'

But Mrs Parry was now well wedded to her theory of the burglar. 'He left the pistol because of its distinctive type. He could not risk being found with it, or attempting to sell it. What we shall find, mark my words, is that this may even be the work of a gang. It is the beginning of the season in London and country houses all over the place are standing empty, but for a notional staff. They are sitting targets. These rogues have but to go around them all, one by one, and help themselves. The wretches could be camped out on the heath.'

'If it was only a burglar . . .' said Agnes unexpectedly. 'Somehow that would be not so bad. Dreadful, but— nothing to do with any of us.'

That was what she feared, I decided. That somehow responsibility for the murder would be laid at the door of this house. But why? There was no sign that the Beresfords were in need of money. What motive could Andrew Beresford have?

There was an awkward pause and then we began to talk of other things. It was as if we all three of us were anxious to ignore what had happened. The conversation became tea-table chatter of a desperate normality. Mrs Parry repeated her abhorrence of seaside resorts served by the railway, because it brought hordes of *hoi polloi* to these towns. I told our hostess that Mrs Dennis had received a postcard from Italy from the Hammets. Agnes revealed that she and her husband had travelled to Italy on their wedding journey. Mrs Parry recalled, with a sentimental sigh, that she and her late husband, my godfather, had travelled to Scotland. I confessed that Ben and I had not made any wedding journey because Ben had been busy with work at Scotland Yard. But we had promised ourselves a really good holiday somewhere, as soon as it was practical. The more we prattled, the more it seemed the ghost of Sir Henry intruded, as if it stood in the corner of the room and watched us with a sardonic twist of the lips. We were all trying to close him out; but he would not be excluded. I thought to myself that, when Mrs Parry and I left, poor Agnes Beresford would be alone here with that spectral presence, until her husband returned from the business that delayed him.

As we were leaving, Agnes suddenly seized my hand. 'My dear Mrs Ross, I cannot thank you enough for coming, and Mrs Parry also. It has been such a relief just to be able to talk to someone.'

We were driven back to The Old Excise House in the

landau. Halfway there, Mrs Parry leaned towards me and spoke just loudly enough for me to hear; but not to allow the coachman to catch an imprudent word.

'I am surprised Mrs Beresford did not find something kind to say about poor Sir Henry. I suppose it is the shock of it all; to say nothing of the coffin being on the premises. Although when my late father, as part of his duties, visited the family of a deceased parishioner, it was quite usual to find the coffin set out on the dining-room table, so that neighbours could come and pay their respects.'

'If Sir Henry's coffin had been brought into the house, I think Mrs Beresford would have quitted it until after the funeral,' I said. 'She is worried enough about his lying in the icehouse.'

'All very strange,' mused Mrs Parry. 'Somehow a little disrespectful, I must say.'

'What do you make of the roses and the fan, left on the piano?" I asked her.

'Oh, there will be some simple explanation,' Mrs Parry assured me. 'I am afraid Mrs Beresford is not in full command of her imagination at the moment.' She paused and added, 'Mr Ross is coming to dine with us this evening, is he not?'

'Yes,' I said. 'He's riding over from the inn on a hired pony.'

'I shall tell him my ideas,' said Mrs Parry with satisfaction. 'He will be very interested to hear what I have to say. My theory of a gang of thieves explains everything!'

It might do so, I thought, but that does not mean it is correct. But I didn't say so.

Inspector Ben Ross

Harcourt and I returned to the house where I requested that the pony and trap be made ready. I wanted to return to the inn, write up my notes, and think about what I'd learned. This whole house rattles with secrets, I thought. I must find time to talk to Lizzie this evening, before dinner, and without Mrs Parry's presence.

'Worked out who's responsible, have you, Inspector?' asked Tizard over his shoulder. He shook the reins and whistled to the pony.

'Not yet. But I will,' I called back above the rattle of the wheels and the thud of the pony's hooves.

'People here will be expecting a quick result,' warned Tizard. 'You being an expert in these matters, and come all the way down from London. They're all frightened out of their wits. Well, it's a bad business, no mistake. You can't blame anyone here for wondering what might happen next.'

It occurred to me that the coachman might have opened this conversation for some particular reason. 'Have you anything to tell me now that we're alone, Tizard?'

The coachman thought this over and took his time replying. 'No, can't say as I have, Inspector Ross. It's a bad business. Sir Henry always treated me very fair.'

'Would you say he was a generous man?'

This question startled Tizard, who twisted on his seat to look at me in some surprise. 'Well, now,' he said. 'He was a rich one, to be sure. 'Tis true he could be a little careful with the pennies. But I wouldn't say that was a fault.'

'He seems to have made use of that fellow, Evans,' I said next. 'I wonder he didn't employ him full time as a groom.'

'Oh, Davy wouldn't have liked that,' Tizard retorted. 'A very independent sort of chap, is Davy. He is very good with the horses, though. Handles a boat well, too.'

'Perhaps he should have joined the navy?' I suggested.

'Taking orders all day long?' Tizard gave a bark of laughter. 'Davy wouldn't like that.'

And that, somehow, put an end to the conversation. But one thing had emerged from it. My standing had risen a notch or two in Tizard's estimation. It hadn't risen to the dizzy heights where he would address me as 'sir'. But at least, now, I was addressed as 'Inspector'.

We rattled into the yard of the Acorn Inn just as an empty hired fly was leaving. Another guest and accompanying luggage had been delivered. Jed, the potman, was carrying indoors a black portmanteau that looked expensive. Now, then, I wondered, who is here?

I soon found out. Mrs Garvey greeted me with excitement. 'There you are, Inspector Ross! There is a new gentleman arrived and he had been asking about you. I put him in the snug.'

Ah, the snug. It had been set aside for my refuge but now I was to share it with another. Mrs Garvey preceded me to the door, tapped at it and opened it.

'Inspector Ross has returned, sir.'

'Is he there?' asked a dry, familiar voice. My heart sank. I was indeed to have no privacy in this investigation. The portmanteau I'd seen belonged to Pelham, the solicitor, and the fellow was apparently staying at the Acorn.

'I am here, Mr Pelham!' I called, and walked into the room.

Behind me, Mrs Garvey, called out to ask if we required a pot of tea. I told her yes, bring tea, because it seemed the quickest way to get rid of her.

Pelham, tall, thin black-clad crow that he was, rose to his feet and greeted me with a formal nod. We exchanged a handshake lacking in any warmth. His palm was dry and cold, though it was a warm day. His extraordinarily pale face showed no emotion. It occurred to me that, if he'd not already had an occupation, he would have done very well as a professional mourner.

'You have had a good journey from London, Mr Pelham?' I asked as we seated ourselves.

'Yes,' said Pelham. 'I came on an early train. I had business in Southampton. Afterwards, I crossed to Hythe on the ferry and hired the fly at the livery stable there to come on here. It was straightforward.'

He waited, his slate-blue eyes fixed on my face. They were as expressionless and unnerving as those of a china doll. I realised I was expected to give an account of my day. Well now, I thought. You will not learn anything from me that you cannot find out from others. You would not discuss your legal business with me. I have no intention of taking you into my confidence regarding police business.

'I have been to see the scene of the crime,' I told him.

'A dreadful affair,' said Pelham. 'Sir Henry was a very distinguished gentleman, well known in the district.'

'I'm sure he was,' I agreed. 'I understand he was a magistrate.'

'Naturally. Are the staff all still there?'

I nodded. 'I have told them they must have police permission before they disperse about the country. Tell me, sir, while in Southampton did you have time to call on Inspector Hughes there?'

Pelham removed a pince-nez from his waistcoat pocket and began to polish it methodically with a silk handkerchief, surely carried for that purpose.

'I called to present my compliments,' he said. 'Since it is probable I shall meet Inspector Hughes again. He tells me the investigation has been handed fully over to you.'

I almost chuckled but managed to keep a straight face. Pelham had got nowhere with Hughes.

A knock at the door heralded Mrs Garvey with the tea tray. There was silence until she had left again.

'My understanding,' said Pelham, 'is that your wife and another lady are staying in the area, for the sea air.'

'Indeed they are.'

'And that they dined with Sir Henry on the evening before the dreadful event.'

'They did. They are both very shocked.'

Well, Mrs Parry was shocked. Lizzie was also, of course, but in addition I knew my wife's busy brain would be assembling the details and looking for those little inconsistencies that often open the door to a solution.

'Has Mrs Ross, or the other lady . . .'

'Mrs Parry,' I supplied as he paused. He probably already knew the lady's name but he was playing his cards carefully.

'Quite so. A family member, I understand?'

'The late Mr Parry was my wife's godfather.'

Pelham did a rapid mental calculation. 'Then Mrs Parry must be considerably older than your wife.'

'I have never presumed to ask the lady's age,' I said.

A flush appeared on Pelham's pale cheeks.

I continued, 'However, I should point out that she was the late Mr Parry's second wife, and younger than him at the time of their marriage. She is, of course, a few years older than my wife.'

'Ah.' Pelham nodded as he slid that piece of information into place, as if it were a piece of a Chinese puzzle box. He had suppressed his show of irritation.

'I wonder,' he asked, pouring tea in his cup with studied concentration, 'whether either lady noticed anything unusual during dinner that night?'

'I have seen my wife since I arrived, but only to speak briefly. I have not yet had the opportunity to discuss the evening in detail with her, or with Mrs Parry. I hope to do so this evening. They are both important witnesses, whether they noticed anything amiss or whether they didn't. If neither of them did, that might also be significant.' I allowed myself a polite smile. 'Sometimes the absence of information tells its own story. I dare say you have come across similar situations in your profession.'

Pelham fixed me with a sharp look, the first expression to enter those disconcerting pale orbs. 'I would greatly appreciate being kept informed of your progress, Inspector.'

'I will make sure to let you know anything I feel you should be aware of,' I told him. *Touché!*

I stood up. 'And now I must leave you to your tea, Mr Pelham. I have work to do.'

Pelham didn't so far forget himself as to scowl. But he gave me a look of intense dislike. It was a mutual feeling.

I didn't know where Pelham would be dining that night. If it were to be at the inn, it would be without my company. For my part, I was glad I hadn't to fend off his questions for a whole evening. I requested that Firefly be saddled so that I could ride to The Old Excise House. 'I shall be able to find my way,' I told Mrs Garvey. 'Please don't trouble Wilfred.'

Nevertheless, when I went out to the stable, both Firefly and the other pony were saddled up, and Wilfred was waiting, clearly intending to escort me.

'There is really no need, Wilfred,' I told him, stifling my annoyance. 'I made good note of the way there and back.'

'Ah, now,' said Wilfred with a sage nod of the head. 'I dare say you did, sir, being the observant gentleman that you are. But that was in daylight. Returning back here late, by moonlight, you won't recognise the heath. None of the landmarks you're depending on will be visible or else they will look quite different. The moon plays tricks, sir! Why, it will be a whole different world out there.'

There was some truth in this, although I suspected that if I didn't know the way, Firefly would take me back to his stable without my guidance. 'I don't want to inconvenience you, Wilfred,' I said firmly.

'Bless you, that's no inconvenience, sir! Truth of the matter is, I've got family living in the village. So, while you're dining with your ladies, I'll ride on down to their cottage and pay my visits, and get my supper there. Then

I'll come back later, and ride back here with you.' He treated me to his gap-toothed grin.

I knew I'd been outmanoeuvred, but there was nothing I could do without outright argument. With both Pelham and Wilfred to fend off, I was between the proverbial rock and a hard place. I therefore accepted with good grace and we set off. I concentrated my mind on the next task ahead of me, finding some way of detaching Lizzie from Mrs Parry for a while. I wanted to talk to her alone.

Mrs Parry, as it turned out, gave me less trouble than Wilfred. 'I have been too quick to use the ankle again,' she announced as I entered the parlour. 'I shall have to rest it again for a day or two.'

'I am very sorry to hear that, ma'am,' I told her. 'Perhaps we should fetch the doctor to attend to it.'

'Oh, no!' She waved away the suggestion. 'Rest and a few more cold packs should do it.'

'I had been hoping,' I told her, 'to take a walk on the shore here, before the light fades. But if you are unable . . .'

'Oh, my dear man! You must take your walk. You have come principally to see Elizabeth, I am sure?' She gave me a playful look. I thought I preferred Pelham's disapproval. 'Fill your lungs with sea air!' ordered Mrs Parry, still smiling at me. 'Then, when you come back, we can have dinner and a really good discussion of all this.'

Lizzie and I accordingly made our way down the steps to the beach below. As she took my arm, I asked, 'Mrs Parry seems in very good humour for someone who has both twisted her ankle and finds herself in the midst of a murder inquiry. What exactly does she mean by "discussion", I wonder.'

'You should beware!' replied my wife in a dramatic tone. 'Aunt Parry has taken it into her head to play detective. She has been waiting impatiently to tell you her theory regarding Sir Henry's death.'

I groaned. A witness who doesn't want to talk is a nuisance. But so is one who imagines he or she can solve the crime ahead of the police. They can be very difficult to detach from a cherished theory.

'I thought she disapproved of police work?'

'That was before we visited Agnes Beresford this afternoon. Now she is ready to explain the whole thing to you.'

'And name the killer?' I asked. 'Or is that too much to hope for?'

'Well, no,' Lizzie admitted. 'She hasn't quite managed that, yet. You see, she is convinced it is a housebreaker. That seems chiefly because there have been some burglaries in Dorset Square. It is not a petty thief, she insists. It is a skilled, professional thief. When you find him, it will be discovered that he is known to the police already.'

'Ah, well,' I said. 'She may be right. I don't think she is, myself. But as I haven't arrested anyone else, who am I to reject Mrs Parry's theory? My poor Lizzie, is she driving you right out of your mind?'

'Not quite. That weak ankle is proving a blessing. She can't go everywhere with me.'

'And how did you find Mrs Beresford?' I asked with real interest. 'Is she coping well?'

Lizzie stopped and looked up at me with such a serious

expression that I felt a pang of foreboding. 'There is something I need to tell you about,' she began, 'only Agnes Beresford is anxious her husband should not know of it, because he has so much to worry him just now. Obviously, she is very lonely at Oakwood House. And did you know, Ben? Sir Henry is there. I mean his body in his coffin is in a little icehouse in the grounds. I am seriously displeased with Beresford.'

'The undertaker in Lymington does not want to keep it on his premises,' I replied promptly. 'He claims it would be bad for his business. And the staff at the Hall are having a collective nervous breakdown, so it couldn't be left there. Beresford has a disused icehouse. I suppose it seemed the only solution.'

Lizzie clearly didn't think so. Her face reddened and her eyes sparkled with anger. These were not good signs, but she did look very handsome just then. She drew in a deep breath and then burst out with her tale.

'Andrew Beresford clearly loves his wife, but he's obviously very busy with the practical side of all this. I don't care what you say, or whether the Hall staff are in hysterics, or the undertaker making a fuss, the body should be somewhere else. Preferably in the churchyard, buried. Agnes is a sweet person. She is also very, very frightened.'

'Of something or of someone?'

'Someone who is playing wicked tricks and trying to distress her.' Lizzie recounted the incidents of the roses and the painted fan left on the piano at Oakwood House.

'That's very strange,' I agreed, 'and, as you say, a very unpleasant thing to have done by someone. But I won't mention it to Beresford, if his wife doesn't wish me to. I strongly recommend that she tell him herself. I understand she doesn't want to worry him but, in his shoes, I would certainly prefer my wife to confide in me. Was there anything more?'

Lizzie frowned a little as she considered her reply. 'I think,' she said at last, 'Agnes is afraid of what might happen next.'

'Hm,' I murmured. 'She has reason to think there may be another crime?'

'She doesn't know what to expect and is living in dread. I suppose it wouldn't be surprising if Mrs Parry were right in her theory of gangs of violent thieves roaming the heath. She hardly talks of anything else. But, actually, although that would be a very worrying thought, I believe Agnes might find it preferable to the alternative. She admitted to us she is afraid the culprit may turn out to be someone near to the family. Not Andrew, obviously. But someone they know; and that must be a constant worry. Just to believe that among the people you meet regularly one must be a murderer.' Lizzie glanced up at me again. 'You've spoken with Beresford by now. What do you feel? Does he fear the same thing?'

'From my talk with him,' I told her, 'I had the impression that, unlike some heirs, he was not in any hurry to come into his inheritance. He is frank that he will appreciate the income from land. He and his wife are very much set against moving into his uncle's house, however. He says it is because of its many inconveniences. However, it may be something else worries him. I wouldn't have described him as being afraid. But he is a worried man.'

Lizzie asked, 'Does he believe it possible that the killer, whoever he is, will next turn his attentions to Oakwood House?'

'And Beresford may be his next victim? Is that what Agnes Beresford fears? We don't know, that is the truth of it. Otherwise, Beresford's much occupied with settling the affairs of the estate, so that he can seek a tenant for the house itself. That is his intention. Until we solve the question of his uncle's murder, however, all that must hang in the balance. There will be long conversations with Pelham, I fancy.'

'It is a very old-fashioned house, full of dark nooks and corners and a great deal of family antiques, portraits and so on,' mused Lizzie. 'I don't think I would care to live there. But furniture, curtains, carpets, decoration can be all changed; and the house does have the benefit of gas lighting. I wish we had it here at The Old Excise House.'

'I gather Sir Henry was loath to use the gas lighting. It cost a good deal to have it installed and he seems to have regretted the outlay. The gas mantles were specially lit for your dinner party, so Harcourt tells me. I also toured the house today and agree, it's a strange place with more hiding places than may be obvious.'

'A secret passage?' cried Lizzie in excitement. 'Where? How do you get into it?'

'I'm sorry I can't promise you that. Everyone is anxious to deny the existence of any such thing. That could be because there's none or because the secret is lost. Or, indeed, because no one wants to tell me where it is.' I hesitated. 'I can tell you, in strictest confidence, that Mr Harcourt claims to be Sir Henry's illegitimate son.'

'*Mr Harcourt!*' Lizzie stared up at me, open-mouthed. 'Well, I suppose that might explain why his manner was a little strange at dinner. My goodness, is it true?'

'Ah, that's the thing! It's not exactly a secret. Harcourt told me everyone knew of it. But Beresford, in recounting his family history to me, made no mention of it. So, for the time being, keep it to yourself, my dear.'

'Goodness, yes,' said Lizzie. She mulled over the information for a moment and declared triumphantly: 'It's that portrait, you know! I mean the one of Sir Henry's father, the old naval hero, as a young man. There is a definite likeness to Harcourt in it.'

'That sort of thing is easy to imagine after the fact,' I warned her. 'Did the resemblance strike you before I told you of Harcourt's claim?'

'Something struck me. I didn't think of Harcourt immediately,' Lizzie confessed, and frowned. 'No, not Harcourt, I think it reminded me of someone else, but I can't place who. I won't tell anyone what you've told me. And we mustn't let Aunt Parry know of it because I shall never hear the last of it.'

'Of course,' I warned her, 'because Harcourt believes it to be the case, that doesn't mean it's true. He has come to believe it himself largely because Sir Henry paid his school fees, as far as I can make out. It's more likely Sir Henry paid the school fees as a charitable act, because he thought the boy a bright lad: and possibly the mother was an old friend. Gossip can become entrenched in people's minds after a long time. At no time, that I've yet heard, did Sir Henry ever openly recognise Harcourt as his son, or show any intention to do so before he died.'

'I wonder how much, if anything, Agnes knows of all this,' Lizzie mused.

'I'd be surprised if Beresford has told her scandalous and unproven stories about his uncle.' Ben spoke firmly. 'All that's certain is that Sir Henry intended to leave small amounts to his household retainers. However, taking account of the fact that Harcourt was estate manager, he would receive a little more than the others. Harcourt, far from feeling grateful, seems to have taken offence. He would not be treated as if he were no different from the household servants, other than by degree of responsibility. I believe that to be the cause of the quarrel you suspect had taken place before you and Mrs Parry arrived for dinner.'

I squeezed her hand. 'So, dearest Lizzie, tell me everything that has happened since you and she arrived here. Everything, mind! Don't leave out a thing. I'll make up my mind if it's important or not. I want a complete picture.'

Chapter Eleven

Elizabeth Martin Ross

OBEYING BEN'S instruction, I began with our arrival and told Ben everything that had happened before Mrs Parry and I visited Agnes that afternoon. This time I described my walks to the village and my meeting with the Dawlish sisters, including the one with Cora on the heath.

'Oddly enough,' I told him, 'in offering one of her herbal poultices to dress Mrs Parry's ankle, I had the strange feeling she was attempting to make some reparation for all she said earlier and even making some kind of apology. Perhaps that's too strong a word. It may be that she is worried. She did say, at our first meeting, that my reappearance would bring death to the community. I felt at the time that was malicious mockery. But now that a death has actually occurred, and the victim is someone of importance locally, she is awkwardly placed. She may wish to placate me; or distance herself from the whole affair.'

'She may wish to avoid any suggestion she knew Sir Henry was going to die!' Ben suggested. 'That may certainly worry her a lot.'

'If you were to say any such thing to her, she would reply she foresaw it in the tea leaves, or some such nonsense. She believes herself to be a witch.'

'She told you this herself?' Ben asked sharply.

'Actually, no, she didn't,' I admitted. 'Her sister, Tibby Dawlish, told me that she was. Cora herself promptly said she "helped people". She did not describe herself as a witch.'

'Then she was wise to rephrase what her sister had rashly claimed, especially when speaking to a police officer's wife. If Cora Dawlish has been getting money from people using her supposed talents, for want of a better description, then that would be an offence. She might well find herself before the magistrates, even before the judge at the Assizes. We don't burn witches nowadays; or admit, in law, that they can make magic. But we don't tolerate fraudulent attempts to extort money from the superstitious, either.'

'Somehow,' I told Ben, 'I don't think Cora Dawlish is knowingly fraudulent.'

Ben smiled. 'Cora Dawlish may or may not believe she has special powers, just as Harcourt may believe he is Meager's son. They could both be deluded. They may have persuaded themselves of the fact because they want to be more important than they are. It is not unknown.'

'I understand what you are saying,' I assured him. 'It could just be an attempt to give herself some standing in their community. The two sisters live in that tiny cottage, never go anywhere, and would be of no importance to anyone otherwise. Of course, *I* don't believe the old woman is a witch. As you say, we cannot know that Harcourt was

Sir Henry's son, even if Harcourt believes it. Poor man, I feel quite sorry for him.'

'Then don't be. He has had a very good position as estate manager and I believe Beresford wants to keep him on, when he takes over.'

'Harcourt may not want to stay on, if he believes Andrew Beresford is his cousin!' I protested.

'Why not?' asked Ben. 'Odder things have happened. But tell me about that dinner party.'

I gave Ben as good an account as I could of the dinner party and my impression that there had been a dispute.

But talking of eating recalled me to the time. The sun was setting. 'Oh!' I exclaimed. 'Dinner! Aunt Parry will be waiting.'

Meals played an important role in Aunt Parry's day and she was waiting impatiently for our return. Mrs Dennis's excellent cooking put her back in good humour. When we retired to the parlour afterwards, she settled herself with Ben's aid, with her ankle propped up once more on the footstool, and declared, 'I have been giving much thought to your problem, Mr Ross.'

'So Lizzie tells me,' said Ben.

Aunt Parry cast me a suspicious look. 'Has Elizabeth already explained my theory?'

'Oh, no,' I hastened to deny. 'I only told him that you were taking an interest.'

'Well, there is little else to take one's interest hereabouts,' replied Aunt Parry, 'although we spent a most pleasant afternoon with Mrs Beresford, as you will know, Mr Ross.

Now then.' Her manner became brisk. 'This brings us to the murder of Sir Henry: a shocking and tragic business. But it occupies the brain and I have been thinking who might be responsible for poor Sir Henry's dreadful death. It is clear to me that the killer was a professional housebreaker, who has travelled down from London for the purpose of marauding about the district, robbing the wealthy.'

'It may well turn out so,' Ben agreed.

I thought he sounded a little too bland not to arouse Aunt Parry's suspicions, but she was too swept up in her theory to notice that he seemed less than impressed.

'It is more than probable that there is a gang of them. They will have been hiding out on the heath. Of course, with Sir Henry murdered, they may have fled. But what happened must be this. One or more of them found a way into his home and first found the pistol. Then, armed with it, they began to search upstairs. Poor Sir Henry awoke and saw them. They had no hesitation in using the pistol to silence him.'

She sat back and smiled graciously upon us, but also with the expectancy of voiced agreement.

'It is certainly to be considered, ma'am,' said Ben.

Mrs Parry frowned and opened her mouth. Luckily, at that point Mrs Dennis came in to announce, 'There is no need for any hurry, Mr Ross, sir. I've just come to let you know that Wilf Dawlish is sitting in the kitchen, talking with Jacob, and is ready for when you'll need him to guide you back to the Acorn.'

'*Dawlish!*' Ben and I exclaimed in one voice.

Inspector Ben Ross

It was late when Wilfred and I set off back to the inn. The
moon seemed curiously bright, suspended above us like a
silver penny. A 'poacher's moon', they called that, I thought.
It disguised and distorted, but did not totally conceal.
Shadows lent everything an unearthly look, both veiled yet
visible. Dark shapes, like paper figures cut out to play a
role on the stage of a toy theatre, loomed up and then
vanished abruptly. Even though I discounted Mrs Parry's
belief in a gang of desperate housebreakers come down
from London, I still found myself scanning the heath for
signs of campfires. I knew that, even if I saw a red glow,
it wouldn't mark the encampment of a gang of desperadoes
from London. I didn't for one moment believe Mrs Parry
was right. If for no other reason, that was because with
the London Season at hand, every kind of thief, whether
operating solo or in a gang, was heading towards London,
not away from the capital. I had not said this to Mrs Parry
because I did not want her worrying that her own house
in Dorset Square was being ransacked even as we sat at
dinner here. No, Agnes Beresford's fears were well founded.
The motive for Sir Henry's death was homegrown. Nor
did I discount the mystery of who had left the roses and
the fan on Agnes's piano. There was still malice lurking
here. But one point seemed to have escaped Mrs Parry.
Robbers wouldn't bother with playing unkind tricks. The
story of the flowers and fan made me more certain that
the murder had nothing to do with a burglary gone awry.
It was connected with the Beresfords and Meagers, who,

after all, had been linked by kinship into one unhappy family.

As for a fire, that might mark where gypsies had halted for the night. They had a reputation for petty pilfering, but of a trivial kind. I doubted they would have broken into an occupied house with the attendant risks.

We had other company, Wilfred and I, riding across the heath. From time to time, bulky shapes moved among the patches of gorse and bramble, figures of fantasy in the purple night: the ponies. If I had not noticed them, then Firefly let me know of their presence, throwing up his head and occasionally blowing gustily through his nostrils. Sometimes an answering call would come from the near distance, a soft whinny or snicker. Once, a dark shape that was not a pony leaped out from a clump of trees, bounded across our path and was gone. Firefly threw up his head, startled into executing a complicated set of dance steps. I grabbed at his mane to steady myself as he bounced around, and was nearly thrown.

'Deer,' called Wilfred to me. 'They grow bold at night and come out into the open. Otherwise you don't see them much around here, being shy beasts. Just stroke the pony's neck, sir, that will calm him.'

William the Conqueror had decreed this area a royal hunting preserve, I remembered being told at school. Out there somewhere, the Conqueror's son, also William and nicknamed 'Rufus' for his red beard, had been slain. Sir Walter Tyrrell, a hunting companion, had loosed an arrow to kill a stag. But it had been deflected by an oak tree and struck the king. Even as a schoolboy, I'd thought this unlikely. So, accident or murder? Sir Walter had not waited to explain. He had fled the scene and taken ship for France immediately. No one knew the truth, only that the king was dead, and his brother, Henry, claimed the English throne. Henry had also been hunting that day and was known to be a man of violent temper. Inheritance, I thought, the cause of so much trouble in families since Cain slew Abel.

Up to that point, Wilfred and I had been riding in silence. I'd sensed a certain apprehension in my companion. Now that he'd spoken, I decided it was the moment to make my bid for information.

'Dawlish is your surname, Wilfred?'

'Yessir!' came the answer through the gloom, smartly spoken. He had reckoned on my finding out his surname sooner or later and had been waiting for me to ask questions.

'These family members you have been visiting tonight, they wouldn't be two elderly sisters called Tibby and Cora?'

'That's right, sir,' agreed Wilfred, a little too promptly. 'I saw a few others in the family, too.'

'Tell me about Tibby and Cora.'

'Oh, well, sir,' began Wilfred, again too quickly.

I have listened to enough alibis to recognise the onset of a prepared speech and knew I was in for one now.

'A really funny old couple, they are. They ought to be an act on the stage, in the music halls, they really did. They make you laugh.'

They hadn't made Lizzie laugh. 'They have the reputation of being wise women,' I said, 'or so I understand.'

'Why, whoever told you that, Mr Ross? They're nothing but a pair of foolish old biddies.'

'One of them has the reputation of being something of a witch, I gather.'

'What, one of the aunties?' exclaimed Wilfred. I had to concede he was a good actor. I couldn't make out his features, but his voice rang with sincerity. 'Bless you, sir, no! Nothing of the sort.'

'Aunt Tibby told my wife so. She said her sister, Cora, was a witch.'

'No, sir, never! Oh, she might have said it to your good lady. But it was her joke. No, no, nothing like that. I told you, they're a comical pair. They might say all sorts of things, but you don't want to pay any attention. And Aunt Tibby, well, she's not quite right in the head, you know.'

I made no comment on that. I wanted to worry Wilfred. He couldn't see my face to judge whether or not I'd bought his explanation. We rode on for a while in silence.

'I was at Sir Henry's house earlier in the day,' I said at last, switching to a new subject.

'Oh, up at the Hall, were you?' Wilfred knew that already but, like a good draughts player, he was moving his pieces with care.

'There was a fellow hanging around the stables there, by the name of Davy Evans.'

'Oh, I dare say,' returned Wilfred after a pause. Studying the draughts board, I thought. Wondering where I am going next. Ready to outmanoeuvre me. He continued, 'He's usually looking for jobs of work and he's good with horses.'

'Did you see him tonight?' I asked next.

'No, I didn't see anything of Davy.'

'Yet I understand he lodges with your aunties, Tibby and Cora.'

Wilfred didn't know who had told me this, so was uncertain whether to confirm or deny it. 'Sometimes,' he said at last. 'I fancy he comes and goes. That's Davy's way. Don't see him for days on end and then he turns up. He's maybe been working on a farm or been out fishing in his boat.'

'Or poaching?' I asked casually.

'I don't know about that,' returned Wilfred, now very uneasy. 'I never heard it said. He causes no trouble, Davy, but he's what they call a free spirit.'

I'd have called him a ne'er-do-well. At the beginning of the century, when smugglers landed their goods on the beaches at the Forest's edge, Davy would've been there among them. It was to control the activities of Davy Evans and his kind in this part of the country that The Old Excise House had been built.

'So, is Davy kin to you, by any chance?'

'Not directly,' Wilfred said firmly. 'He's more of what you'd call a connection. He's an Evans; and they don't live in the village.'

Time to abandon this game of draughts and outmanoeuvre Wilfred in something else: his persistent shadowing of my activities.

'I shall be going across to Southampton tomorrow,' I called out to him. 'So I'll need Firefly again in the morning to ride to Hythe. I don't need any guide to find my way there. I'll leave the pony at the livery stables in Hythe, take the ferry across, come back when I've finished, collect Firefly and ride him home.'

'Right you are, sir,' called Wilfred. He sounded relieved. In Southampton he could not be expected to keep track of me. I was proving more troublesome than expected.

'You don't know if the other gentleman staying at the inn needs the animal?'

'The lawyer fellow?' asked Wilfred, with the country-man's reserve regarding professional persons.

'Yes, Mr Pelham.'

'He won't need either of the ponies,' said Wilfred with confidence. 'Mr Beresford will be sending the trap for him.' He paused and added, 'Anyway, I don't see Lawyer Pelham riding one of Mrs Garvey's ponies. Would be beneath his dignity, most likely.'

'I'm inclined to agree with you, Wilfred,' I told him. With this exchange we arrived back at the Acorn in a spirit of harmony.

Chapter Twelve

Inspector Ben Ross

IT WAS common courtesy, as well as advisable, to keep Inspector Hughes informed of my progress, or lack of it, regarding the murder of Sir Henry Meager. I had informed Mrs Garvey, when Wilfred and I returned the previous evening, that I'd be hiring Firefly for the whole of the following day. (I insisted I would not need Wilfred.) As I was telling her this, it was going through my mind that I'd almost certainly have to argue the increasing costs of hiring the pony with Superintendent Dunn on my return to London. If Dunn knew that I had been offered the use of the berlin and Tizard to drive me, *gratis*, the extra expense would not go down well.

Mrs Garvey said, 'Right you are, sir!' She accompanied the words with a beaming smile. She was doing very nicely out of all of this. She continued, 'Mr Pelham, the legal gentleman, is in the snug.'

Whether this was a warning or not, I didn't know. 'Alone?' I asked.

'Yes, sir, I do believe he's working on some papers.'

So Pelham had commandeered the snug as his office. This annoyed me. First come, first served. I had developed proprietorial feelings regarding the snug and was quite surprised to find myself feeling so cross about the matter. Then again, I didn't like Pelham. After a moment's struggle, I decided it would not only be polite to put my head into the room and bid Pelham goodnight but also prudent to appear to satisfy his request to be kept informed. I had nothing I wished to tell him regarding the case, of course, nor had he any business to pester me for constant detail. But if you have a dog of uncertain temper following you about, you throw him a scrap of food from time to time. This time Pelham would have to be satisfied with a little information regarding my travel plans.

I rapped at the door and walked in. Pelham sat at the little table with an oil lamp burning. He looked up with a cross expression as I appeared, then forced something like a smile; it was more of a grimace. It put me in mind of a stone gargoyle at the end of a waterspout.

'I won't disturb you, Mr Pelham,' I said. 'I only come to bid you goodnight, and to let you know I shall be going over to Southampton tomorrow. I like to keep in touch with Inspector Hughes there. Have you still some legal business to conduct hereabouts, or will you be returning to Town?'

'I shall stay a day or two longer,' returned Pelham unwillingly, 'to see how things turn out, and consult with my client, Beresford. Did you spend a pleasant evening, Inspector?'

'Yes, thank you. I had the pleasure of dining with my

wife and Mrs Parry. We had an excellent meal. Mr Beresford will send the trap for you in the morning, I dare say.'

'Yes!' snapped Pelham. Again came the gargoyle grimace masquerading as a smile. 'I am not so intrepid as you are, Inspector Ross, riding around the countryside at night.'

'There is a beautiful moon,' I told him. 'It is nearly as clear as day out there.'

Pelham didn't snarl, but he'd have liked to.

I begged a carrot of the cook the following morning, as I felt I owed something to Firefly. He had to work a lot harder on my account. I fancied he recognised me when I came out to his stable; he snickered a welcome, or it might just be that he'd seen the carrot. The ferry across to Southampton was packed that morning and I was lucky to find myself a spot on deck, wedged between two solidly built countrywomen with large baskets balanced on their laps.

Hughes greeted me with a friendly grin and said, 'I've been wondering how you were getting on. Found a likely suspect yet?'

'I have been opening up a tangled mess of old scandal,' I replied. 'As to whether it has brought me nearer to naming a culprit, no, it hasn't. But I am convinced the roots of the matter go back a long, long way.'

'It's to do with the will, then?' asked Hughes. 'Well, it nearly always is, when the gentry take to murdering one another.'

'Very probably. I can't say for sure. There is a solicitor by the name of Pelham who has come down from London.

He handled the late Sir Henry's affairs and he appears to deal with Andrew Beresford's also. He's lodging, as I am, at the Acorn. Also, I've met him before, in London. This is his second visit to the area in recent times. He was down a month or so ago to revise Sir Henry's will.'

'He called on me a day or so ago to let me know he'd returned, but I was busy and had little time to spare him. Got your money on anyone at all?' Hughes leaned back in his chair and squinted at me.

'At the moment, the estate manager, Robert Harcourt, would appear to be the frontrunner. I am not naming him as a murderer, far from it, or not yet, anyway. But he could have a motive.'

'Met him, too,' said Hughes. 'Why have you got your eye on him, then?'

'There is bad feeling there. Harcourt claims to be the late Sir Henry's son, born out of wedlock and never acknowledged. Mind you, when I say "out of wedlock", I don't mean his mother was not married. She was, but not to Sir Henry. Her acquaintance with Sir Henry, however, dated from before her marriage. I warned you it was a tangled mess!' I told Hughes the tale, as Harcourt had recounted it to me.

'What the better classes get up to, eh? Well, Harcourt could never prove it,' said Hughes, when I'd finished. 'If he's thinking of challenging the will, he'll have the devil of a job.' He shook his head gloomily.

'The strange thing,' I replied, 'is that he's not complaining he's been *cut out* of the will. My understanding is that he *has refused to be included* in it, because of the wording of any legacy left to him. He was treated, in his view, as one of the servants.'

'And he wants this will to include some written acknowledgment of his paternity?' Hughes retorted shrewdly.

'He didn't say that. You may well be right, though.'

Hughes shook his head. 'Sir Henry wouldn't do that, I reckon. Even if it were true, apart from anything else, think of the scandal. Who else knows of Harcourt's claim to be Meager's son?'

'He says everyone knows it.'

'Which could mean that nobody does, other than himself – or what he's decided himself is the case.' Hughes drummed his fingers on his desk in a way that reminded me of Dunn, who had the same habit when thinking. 'Suppose,' Hughes went on suddenly, 'I were to put a possible sequence of events to you? Your case, of course,' he added hurriedly. 'But I made the initial inquiries, visited the scene of the crime, and it doesn't go out of my mind. It seemed such a— such a personal sort of a crime. There was hatred in it.'

'How so?' I was interested, because the murder had struck me in the same way. It had not been the result of a random housebreaking, even if Mrs Parry was convinced it was so.

'From the feel of it, you know?' Hughes smiled. 'Anyway, it has to be more interesting than the robbery at a wholesale fruit importer's warehouse, which I've got on my desk at the moment.'

'What kind of fruit? I asked automatically. A detective always wants precise information, and his response to news of a robbery is to ask what's been taken, even if he's not on the case.

'What they call tropical,' Hughes replied. 'Bananas, pineapples, that sort of thing.'

'Then the costermongers in London will be selling it from their barrows while we sit here,' I replied. 'With town houses being opened up by the wealthy, the fashionable dinner parties have begun. Your missing tropical fruits will form the centrepiece of every dessert course.'

'Never saw such a thing as a pineapple when I was a boy,' said Hughes moodily. 'Apples, that was fruit to us. Mam made apple pies and very good they were.'

'Tell me your theory about the murder,' I invited him.

'How's this, then?' asked Hughes, his soft Welsh lilt becoming gradually more noticeable as he began to tell a story. Or perhaps he was still thinking of his mother's apple pies. 'Meager had recently revised his will. His solicitor had come down from London just for that purpose. Beresford was understood to be the main beneficiary. But there were other legacies and someone wanted to know the details. Now then.' Hughes leaned forward, his hands clasped on the desk and his dark eyes glowing with enthusiasm. 'It was known in the household, and possibly outside of it, that Meager kept some private papers locked in the drawer in the library, along with the pair of pistols. Someone gets the idea into his head that a copy of the will is kept there. That person is desperate to see it, because he has an interest. He slips into the house. He breaks open the drawer of the desk. Perhaps he finds the will, reads it, and the legacy he hoped for is not there. Or, in view of what you've just told me, Harcourt might have broken in, hoping that Sir Henry had, after all, acknowledged him as a son. And he discovered he hadn't. Or the will isn't there; and the intruder suspects it might be kept by Sir Henry upstairs in a safe in his bedroom. Whatever the reason, the fellow takes one of the pistols, and makes his way upstairs to Sir Henry's room. He either shoots the victim in anger as he lies in bed or he starts to search the room and disturbs the sleeping man, who sits up in bed and demands to know what the devil he's doing there. Intruder panics, fires, throws the pistol down on the bed and flees.'

Hughes sat back. 'What do you think, Ross?'

'I think that either scenario would fit the facts, as we know them at the moment,' I said cautiously. 'And it would point a finger at Harcourt in an obvious sort of way.' But I didn't think Hughes had supplied the answer. There was something else, something I'd so far missed.

'You don't accept it?' Hughes asked.

'There is something else I should perhaps tell you.' I recounted the story of the roses and the painted fan. 'I can't see Harcourt doing that. Apart from anything else, frightening Agnes Beresford would avail him nothing. Unless, of course, he is trying to throw the police off the scent.'

'Laying a false trail, eh?' Hughes thought it over and then heaved a sigh. 'Well, your case now, as I said. I'll stick to my tropical fruit. Unless there is something I can do to help you?'

He was itching to help me. He had been called to the

crime initially and then it had been taken from him and passed to a London man. I sympathised, and there was something he could do, as it happened.

'Among the servants,' I said, 'there is a skivvy, Susan Bate. She is on the list you gave me. She's a little touched.' I tapped my head. 'Giggles a lot.'

'Ah, yes, I remember her.' Hughes nodded. 'Now that's a sad business, awful pity when a pretty girl like that doesn't have all her wits. Still, she's employed, or has been until this murder.'

'You mentioned to me,' I said, 'when we originally spoke of the staff, that the skivvy had come to the Hall from an orphanage.'

'So she did,' replied Hughes promptly. 'I don't have to look that up, because it's stuck in my mind. She didn't come from the workhouse, you see. She hadn't been brought up on the parish. She came from a private orphanage run by nuns, in Winchester.'

'Winchester!' I exclaimed, startled. 'That's a long way off. Of course, I understand it's Hampshire's county capital, but it's a long way to go to find a girl to wash your dishes.' I was startled for another reason too. I had heard the city of Winchester mentioned recently, but where?

'Want me to look into it?' asked Hughes, raising an eyebrow.

'If you could find a moment, I know you're busy . . .'

'No trouble at all,' he returned. 'Wonderful thing, the telegraph system. I'll just send a telegram to the police at Winchester; ask them to make inquiries at the convent. I'll let you know what comes of it.'

'I'm very obliged,' I told him. 'I could send the telegram myself, but I fancy it would come better from you. They will know you.'

'Any particular reason why you're interested in her?'

'Oh,' I returned as vaguely as I dared. 'Just crossed my mind that the late Sir Henry Meager might have fathered more than one illegitimate child, not only Harcourt, if Harcourt is indeed his son.'

'Ah, now,' said Hughes. 'It's the way of the world, I dare say. But I don't think that unfortunate child would take a pistol and shoot the man in question. Bit beyond her, that.'

'Quite,' I agreed. 'But someone else might do it on her behalf. Oh,' I added as casually as I could. 'The other pistol, the pair to the murder weapon that you have here, had remained at the Hall. I saw it when I walked round the place. Beresford has now taken possession of it and it is locked in his safe at his house. I had nowhere secure for it at the inn.'

Hughes flushed. 'It shouldn't have been left at the Hall,' he admitted. 'But Beresford shouldn't have it either. Do you want me to send a constable to take possession of it and bring it here?'

'A good idea,' I said approvingly. 'However it would need tact. Beresford might simply reply that the pistol is his property now.'

'That pistol and the murder weapon make a pair and were kept in a case together. As such, they are both evidence, even if only one of them fired the fatal shot,' Hughes replied firmly. 'Now then, Ross, I am the first to admit the pair of pistols should not have been parted. But I'll sort it out without offending the gentleman in question.'

'I am sure you will,' I soothed him.

'Anything else?' asked Hughes after a moment's silence. 'Because I'm getting a bit hungry myself and I fancy you must be, having started out so early. There's an excellent chophouse nearby.'

We duly repaired to the chophouse and made a very good meal.

It was late afternoon when I collected Firefly from the livery stable in Hythe. He'd spent his day resting up after I'd ridden him there that morning, so he was fresh. Also some equine instinct told him he was on his way home, which meant we set off back to the Acorn at a good clip. Thus all was going well until we got there. The one thing I wasn't looking forward to was avoiding Pelham's questions. The solicitor wasn't there, however, but a dogcart was. It was drawn up before the door. Standing at the head of the pony harnessed to it was a lad I recognised. I'd last seen him washing the berlin carriage in the stable yard at the Hall. When he saw me arrive atop Firefly, he raised an arm to attract my attention. At the same time Wilfred appeared and took Firefly's bridle. Both the lad and Wilfred were obviously bursting to give me some news; and nothing led me to suppose it would be good. Bad news travels fast.

'What's wrong?' I asked resignedly.

'Joe here,' said Wilfred, indicating the boy by the dogcart, 'is waiting to drive you to the Hall, sir. It's a pity you have to go in the dogcart. It'll rattle your bones a bit.

But when Tom Tizard came with the berlin, you were in Southampton. So Lawyer Pelham took the berlin and has gone ahead of you to the Hall.'

'Just tell me what's happened!' I snapped. Confound Pelham. I couldn't get rid of him.

'Mr Harcourt's gone missing, sir!' called Joe.

'How so, missing?' I asked sharply. 'Has he packed his bags and decamped?'

Was Harcourt indeed our man? Had he lost his nerve and fled?

'No, no, sir, nothing like that.' Wilfred gave Joe a severe look. He considered himself senior to a stableboy and if a dramatic tale was to be told Wilfred meant to be the one to tell it.

'He set out on his regular visit to the tenant farmers, riding round from one to the other to find out if all was in order, and nothing causing any problem. Apart, of course, from Sir Henry being murdered. They'll all be very worried what that will mean to them. He took a horse from the stables at the Hall, and it came home without him. They're all out looking for him, lest he's had a serious accident . . .'

I didn't wait to hear any more. The light was beginning to fade. 'Right, Joe!' I ordered. 'Drive me to the Hall and tell me as we go along everything that's happened.'

I was glad I had eaten a good luncheon with Hughes. I suspected it was going to be very late before I got a chance to dine.

The first person I saw on arrival at the Hall was Pelham. Black-clad and pale-faced as always, he was standing at the front entrance to the house, as if waiting expressly for me. I didn't doubt that was exactly what he was doing; and I shouldn't have been surprised. Nevertheless, it was still disagreeable to find myself outmanoeuvred. I had not wanted to tell him anything new. Now he was in the position of being more informed than I was. He was probably enjoying his revenge.

Joe pulled up and I scrambled down from the dogcart, wincing. Wilfred had been right to warn me it would be a bumpy ride. I felt as though I been put in a sack and shaken up and down vigorously by a giant, so that all my joints had become loose. At least my obvious physical discomfort served to hide my annoyance.

'Ah, Inspector Ross,' Pelham greeted me, with a suave grimace. I wouldn't have called it a smile. I didn't think I'd ever seen Pelham smile. But he reeked of satisfaction and came as near to showing it as I'd ever seen. 'Such a pity you had chosen to go over to Southampton today.' He was almost purring. 'That boy will have told you that Mr Harcourt's horse came home without him earlier today—'

I was not about to allow Pelham to lecture me. 'Any news of Harcourt himself?' I interrupted him.

'Indeed there is, and it is bad news.'

And never did bad news have a smugger messenger. My heart sank.

'He was found on a track running through some woods. Clearly he had been thrown.'

'You don't know the circumstances? He is still unconscious?' I knew I asked the question more in hope than in expectation.

'He is dead,' said Pelham simply. 'His body was brought back on a cart and is laid out in one of the bedrooms upstairs here. Dr Wilson, a local practitioner, was called to confirm death. He is still here and talking with Mr Beresford.'

'The body should not have been moved,' I snapped.

'It could hardly be left lying where it was on the muddy ground.' Pelham's tones were now icy. 'Particularly as we did not know whether you would return tonight from Southampton.'

'No, no, of course not,' I admitted. He was right. Riding accidents were common enough and I had no cause to treat this as a criminal matter. But I didn't like another death following so quickly after a murder; particularly when it was the death of the only suspect who might be said to have had a motive. Now I had to look elsewhere and had almost nothing to guide me.

'Mr Beresford and the doctor are waiting to see if you would arrive before nightfall. The doctor is anxious to return home. He has other patients.' Pelham spoke reproachfully.

I heartily disliked the way Pelham spoke of my absence in Southampton as if it had been some avoidable dereliction of duty; and not just the unfortunate coincidence it was. 'I'd be obliged if you'd take me to them,' I said.

'This way, Mr Ross,' said Pelham, invisible frost closing on his words as they reached the air.

If I didn't like the way Pelham treated me then he didn't like being treated as the butler. Incidentally, where was the butler? Quoting scripture again in the kitchen? Were the maids in a fresh bout of hysterical weeping? Had the wretched valet, Lynn, passed out again? Lynn . . . Something tugged at my memory, but I hadn't time to identify it now.

Indoors, gathering gloom had necessitated the lighting of the gas mantles, which burned brightly. Beresford must have ordered it. The frugal ghost of the late Sir Henry was probably scowling at this needless expense. No doubt he would have ordered oil lamps lit in such circumstances. Both Beresford and the doctor were in the dining room, seated at the table, a bottle of brandy and two glasses before them. There was a third used but empty glass nearby, so Pelham had evidently had a drink to restore his nerves.

As I entered Beresford jumped to his feet with every sign of relief. 'Thank God!' he exclaimed. 'I was afraid you might stay overnight in Southampton.' He indicated a stocky young man with a weather-beaten countenance and short-cropped hair. A country doctor, who rode round visiting his housebound patients, I thought, and calling on those important enough to summon his presence, not find their way to him. 'Dr Wilson,' Beresford said.

I shook the doctor's hand. 'I understand,' I said, 'that the body is upstairs. I should like to view it.'

'Of course, this way . . .'

Beresford set off and the doctor and I followed. I was glad Pelham did not attempt to tag along. He must have seen the body already and once was enough for him. As we three left the room I saw Pelham, from the corner of my eye, seat himself at the table and reach for the brandy.

Harcourt's corpse was laid out on a bed in a small back

bedroom. They had removed his coat and his riding boots, but it was otherwise clothed, other than that the shirt had been unbuttoned and the cravat removed. The coat had been folded neatly and hung over the back of a chair. The boots were also lined up beside the chair. The effect was exactly as though their owner were only taking a nap and, on waking, would get up and put them on again.

My first emotion was one of pity. Harcourt had believed, rightly or wrongly, that he was entitled to be in this house. Not as a dinner guest, called in to make up the numbers, or just to discuss estate business. No, Harcourt had believed himself a member of the family. Now, in death, he lay on a bed here. I wondered if he had ever been upstairs in life. If he had shot Sir Henry, then the answer would be yes, at least once. But I did not now believe he'd shot Meager, if only because as long as Sir Henry remained alive Harcourt's greatest wish, to be acknowledged, still flickered in his hopes. That wish, to be known as a gentleman's son, if not exactly a gentleman himself, might yet turn out to play a part in what had happened here; even if I couldn't yet see how.

'Cause of death?' I asked the doctor. I knew my voice to sound cold, monotonous, a policeman doing his duty.

'Broken neck, clear enough.' Wilson hesitated. 'There is a mark on the forehead. I understand a large stone lay near the head where he was found.'

'Had his neck not been broken, could such a blow have killed him?' I asked.

Wilson hesitated. 'It might have done. I could not be sure. It would require a post-mortem examination to determine whether the skull is cracked. For myself, I am satisfied the broken neck killed him.' He still looked awkward. 'The mark on the forehead, where it struck the stone, is clear to see. But there is no bruising. Look for yourself.'

I bent over the corpse again and studied the pale face. There was a mark, sure enough, in the form of broken skin only and a smear of mud. There was no purple bruise. There was, or had been, no significant bleeding. I asked quietly, 'Tell me, doctor, in your opinion, is it possible that contact was inflicted after death?'

'I think so,' Wilson replied, also quietly.

But Beresford had overheard us. He chose to interpret my question as a criticism. 'It was not easy to remove him from where he lay. We had to carry him on a hurdle through the trees, and then load him onto a cart. The journey back was over rough ground. The— the body might have received some knocks then.'

'Yes, yes, of course!' I soothed him. But that was not what I had been thinking.

'Thank you, doctor,' I told the medical man.

'Am I still required?' he replied. 'I have an evening surgery and must get back.'

I told him I didn't need him at the moment and thanked him again. He took himself off.

When I turned back Beresford was standing by the bedside, staring down morosely at Harcourt's body. He looked very shaken.

'Poor fellow,' he said. 'He could be difficult on occasion. But he was an excellent estate manager.'

'Were you aware he claimed to be an illegitimate son of your late uncle?' It was a question I had to ask and now was probably the best time to ask it. Beresford would not have the time to manage his reaction. He'd just answer. Witnesses often complain that an officer has questioned them immediately after a shocking event. They believe their feelings should have been respected before the law badgered them. No, the time to ask the questions is before they've had time to consider the best replies.

'Oh, yes, I know he did,' Beresford said frankly, and in fairness to the man, I think he would not have tried to deny it. But he looked straight at me and added: 'Don't ask me if he really was. I have no idea. One could not have asked Uncle Henry. Had he wanted to, my uncle could have said he'd fathered Mrs Harcourt's child. But what would that have done? Other than cast a shadow on mother and child and cause deep embarrassment to the lady's husband, Mr Harcourt senior? He was a decent old fellow, by all accounts, and content to have his name recorded in the baptismal register as father of the infant.'

'Can you tell me the sequence of today's events?'

Beresford was visibly happier to discuss this topic, but said, 'May we not leave the poor fellow here in peace? I don't think discussing it over his body is quite the thing.'

'Pelham will still be downstairs, I suppose?' I knew the answer to that, at least. Of course he was.

'He's waiting for you to be finished; and then Tizard will drive you both back to the Acorn in the berlin.' Beresford had read my mind and gave me a slightly sardonic look. 'You won't shake him off,' he said. 'I know from my own experience that he has the sticking quality of a limpet. But he is an excellent solicitor.'

'I have no doubt of that. Before we rejoin him,' I asked hesitantly, 'I wonder if I might take a look at your grandfather's portrait. My wife has told me about it.'

Beresford raised his eyebrows but only asked, 'Which one? There are two, one of him as a young man, one in old age.'

'Perhaps the earlier one first, then the later one.'

'Of course.'

'Here we are,' Beresford spoke a few minutes after. 'My grandfather Captain Hector Meager. He had not been given his baronetcy at that time.'

Standing before the portrait of Old Indestructible in his youth I could only be impressed. There he was, preserved for generations to admire, in his naval uniform, the wind blowing his Byronic curls and the foam-tipped waves in the background throwing spray into the air.

'He had just been promoted to the rank of captain,' Beresford told me. 'The portrait was commissioned to mark the occasion.'

'He was young to have been given his own command!' I exclaimed.

'We were at war,' said Beresford. 'The loss of naval officers and crew was great. My grandfather's older brother, also named Henry and in the navy, did not survive, though it was fever that took him. Admiral Nelson had been but twenty when he was made captain. My grandfather had to wait until he was twenty-four.' Beresford turned away from the painting and led me to another, that of his grandfather in old age.

'Still a fine-looking old gentleman,' I remarked. 'But looks very fierce.'

'He was very fierce,' agreed Beresford. 'I was only a small boy when I was taken to see him and he terrified me. I don't suppose he meant to. He just didn't know any other way.' He turned to look me directly in the face. 'Well, what do you think, Ross? Do you see poor Robert Harcourt there?'

'Do I think Harcourt looks – looked – like his claimed grandfather? I couldn't swear to it. Possibly, there is a likeness. But then, you see, I am a detective and I require proof. A chance resemblance isn't proof he was Sir Hector Meager's grandson, and consequently Sir Henry's son, even if poor Harcourt believed he was. Did he claim his mother told him the truth of his parentage?'

'If she did, she never made the claim in writing. If you ask me what I think, then I believe that Harcourt took it into his head he was my Uncle Henry's son, because Henry paid his school fees. I am ready to believe there was an old love affair between my uncle and the lady who later became Mrs Harcourt. My Uncle Henry liked a pretty woman and, yes, he had brought the lady from France when he was young. It doesn't make him Robert's father. But Harcourt brooded over it for years and the idea became fixed.'

Beresford indicated the general direction of the study. 'I think we'll leave Pelham to the brandy in the dining room. He arrived after the body was found, anyway. I sent for you when it was realised Harcourt was missing. As you were not at the Acorn, Pelham, according to Tizard, commandeered the berlin and ordered Tom to drive him immediately to the Hall.'

I was increasingly seriously annoyed with Pelham. His business was with the will, not with the investigation into Sir Henry Meager's death. Clearly Beresford was also annoyed by the solicitor's interest in the investigation.

'Before we are disturbed, then . . .' I said. 'Let us go into the study.'

The last time I had been in this room, it had been to examine the desk with the forced drawer, in which the pair of pistols had been kept. The drawer still stood open but now it was empty.

Seeing me looking at it, Beresford said, 'The pistol that is pair to the murder weapon is now locked in the safe I have at my house.'

'Good,' I said. 'It is possible Inspector Hughes at Southampton may send a constable to take charge of it. He feels the pistol and its companion together form evidence.'

'Oh, well, if that's what Hughes wants.' Beresford spoke rapidly. Perhaps he feared Pelham might appear at any moment, and was more worried about that than the pistol. Good, it would save argument when Hughes's constable arrived to collect it. He went on in the same rapid way.

'As for the sequence of today's events, which you will want to know. That, at least, is not in question. I understand that Robert Harcourt requested yesterday that a horse be saddled ready for him at ten this morning. His intention was to visit the tenant farmers and calm their nerves. The murder has caused something of a panic in the countryside.

They all live in lonely farmhouses and the thought of break-in and violence frightens them. Also, Sir Henry was their landlord. Harcourt wanted to reassure them all personally that the investigation was in good hands and they need have no fears.'

I was grateful for his confidence in my powers of detection, but I said nothing.

'He had been gone a little over an hour. It was about a quarter to twelve when the horse arrived back in the stable yard, riderless, lathered up and behaving wildly. I have this information from Tom Tizard, who then took it upon himself to organise a search, and also sent word to me. Tom is a shrewd old fellow, and keeps his head. I came here with a couple of my men and we also joined the hunt. I decided on the probable route Harcourt would have taken. We followed it, calling at each farm and establishing that Harcourt had been there and left. We now had a good idea of the way he would have taken to return to the Hall, after the final visit. This way includes a path through woodland. It's a narrow path, not much used and uneven. The trees and undergrowth crowd in on either side. We had just begun to ride along it in single file when Davy Evans, a local man, came running towards us. He had come across the body.'

'What was Evans doing on that path?' I asked sharply.

'He had been here at the Hall, helping in the stables. He does it often. Uncle Henry was pleased to tolerate his coming and going. I don't know why he didn't just employ him as a groom. I honestly think it is because Evans likes his independence, and it amused Uncle to let him have it;

or it saved money on regular wages. My uncle could count the pennies, as I may have mentioned before. But Evans was on hand, so Tizard had enlisted his help to search. When we encountered him, he was coming down the path from the opposite direction.'

I frowned. 'Would that not have meant he was coming away from the direction of the Hall, towards that of the farm you'd just left?'

'Yes. He must have heard us coming. He was on foot. The horse he'd borrowed from the stables here had been left tethered near the scene.'

I did not like the involvement of Davy Evans in this at all. But if he had been working in the stable yard while Harcourt had been on his visit to the farms, then he had an alibi, if there had been any mischief.

'Is Evans still about the place? I need to speak to him,' I said.

'I had told him to stay until you came,' Beresford admitted. 'But then we learned you had gone to Southampton, so I wasn't sure when that might be. I told Evans he could go.' He frowned. 'He rode off on the horse he'd been riding earlier, when he found the body. That was a liberty. I shall speak to him about it!'

New times were coming for Davy, I thought. The easy way he'd come and gone at the Hall in Sir Henry's day was over.

'How did the body look? Lying on his back or on his face?' I wished I'd seen Harcourt's body at the scene for myself.

'He lay mainly on his side but with upper arm and

shoulder turned down towards the path. But his head was tilted backwards and I didn't like the angle of it. It wasn't natural. I feared he had broken his neck. At any rate, although I saw he was dead, I tried for a pulse and there was none.'

'What about this large stone or rock that lay by the head?'

'Yes, I saw that. I originally thought, on first seeing him, that his head might have struck it as he fell and that had caused the skull to flip back quickly and snap his neck. I am not a medical man. It's how it looked to me.' Beresford's voice was strained. 'But now the doctor has declared the injury to be post-mortem. You thought so at once.'

'I have seen numerous injuries and quite a few dead bodies,' I said to Beresford. 'And there was no blood, even in a small amount.'

He muttered, 'Of course, quite so.'

It was how it would look to anyone, I thought. Beresford could be excused assuming, on first sight of the body, that was what had happened. But there was something about that tiny, bloodless injury that made me uneasy. I was already very worried by this new death following so quickly on the earlier one.

'I shall have to visit the scene myself,' I continued. 'But it has grown rather dark.'

'Under the trees where the path runs it will be impossible, this late, to see much, even with lanterns,' Beresford said. 'But I ordered the area secured. There are barriers at both the entrance and exit from the path to prevent anyone using it. And I sent out word to the farms that no one is to go near the woods. I don't think anyone will. They will all be too terrified.'

'Hm,' I murmured. Having the area so secure also meant that if anyone wanted to tamper with the scene, they could do so without fear of being disturbed. 'I will come early tomorrow,' I said. 'Perhaps Tom Tizard could fetch me from the Acorn at around nine? And now perhaps I should go back to the inn before it gets any darker. Would Mr Pelham be ready to leave, do you think?'

'I'm sure he is.' Beresford moved to the bell to ring for the butler.

Warton appeared so quickly he must have been loitering in the hall. He appeared reasonably sensible and was not promising us the end of the world. Beresford asked him to tell Tizard to bring the berlin round to the front of the house.

'Yes, sir,' said Warton. But he still lingered and seemed to have something on his mind. Were we, after all, to hear more from Revelations? 'I beg your pardon, Mr Beresford, but Tizard asks if, before the two gentlemen leave, both yourself and the police inspector could go out to the stable. There is something there he feels you should see.'

'Tonight?' asked Beresford, frowning.

'Tizard is most anxious, sir. It concerns the horse Mr Harcourt was riding this morning. Tizard fears there may been have foul play, sir.'

Chapter Thirteen

Inspector Ben Ross

TIZARD AND the boy, Joe, were waiting in the stable yard, both carrying lanterns.

'What's wrong, Tom?' Beresford asked sharply.

'There is something you should see, sir, and the inspector, too.' Tizard turned and led the way into the stable block. It was in the form of a large brick barn with the stalls in a row along the wall. It was warm and stuffy and smelled strongly of horse. At our entry, all the horses came to the front of their stalls, ears pricked, curious to watch what we would do. They moved restlessly, stamping their hooves, snorting, aware that something was amiss. The horse Tizard wanted us to see was in the last stall on the right.

'This is Whisper, gentlemen; she's the mare Mr Harcourt took out this morning. She's calm enough now but a little wary of strangers.' Tizard nodded towards me.

Whisper tossed her head and fixed us with rolling eyes. Joe, the stableboy, slipped into the stall and spoke to her soothingly, running his hand down her neck.

'She's all right with Joe,' said Tizard. 'He looks after her.'

'She seems to have scratches on her withers and neck,' I said. 'That would be from trees or undergrowth?'

'She does, sir, but that's not what I wanted to show you. Just hold her steady, Joe. I want the gentlemen to look at her front legs.' He held the lantern so that the light fell on the animal's lower legs. 'See there, sir?' he asked Beresford.

I wasn't sure what I was supposed to see but also peered at the places Tizard indicated. There were clearly marks and they looked to my untutored eye like cuts, rather than the scratches on the animal's neck.

'Good grief!' gasped Beresford. 'Wire!'

'Yessir, wire right enough. All right, Joe.' Tizard nodded at the stableboy, who released his grip on Whisper's leg. The mare stamped her feet and began to move restlessly again. Joe stroked her neck and she quietened.

'Who the devil is responsible for that? I'll have no wire fencing on my land and Sir Henry allowed none on his!' Beresford spoke with controlled fury.

'No more he did, sir, lest any rider should set his horse at a hedge to jump it. Neither horse nor rider can see the wire, and it brings them both down.' This explanation was addressed to me.

'Do I understand this rightly?' I asked Beresford. 'Harcourt's fall came about because someone had fixed wire across the path he would take through the wood, about a foot above the ground? Was there any sign of wire when you saw the body, Mr Beresford?'

'No, dammit! I'd not have missed that. It's a miracle the horse wasn't injured, as well as Harcourt.'

'A word!' I said to Beresford and walked out of the stable. Beresford followed and waited with me in the yard. 'Forgive me asking you more questions about your discovery of the body. But if you could think, sir, and be certain before you answer,' I asked. *'Are you sure there was no sign of any wire, or there having been any wire, when Evans led you to the body?'*

'No, confound it! I told you, I'd not have overlooked that. The horse must have had a crashing fall and, as Tizard says, it's amazing that the animal wasn't injured. She could have broken a leg as easily as poor Harcourt broke his neck. The horse could've broken *her* neck, come to that.'

'So,' I continued, 'whoever set the trap did so calculating that either on his way to that last farm, or on his way back from it – depending in which order Harcourt visited the farms – Harcourt would use that track. The wire was set; and the person who set it must have hidden in the trees and waited. Harcourt came through – how fast do you think he would have been going?'

'Probably at a canter.'

'Fast enough to have no time to spot the trap. Down go horse and rider. The horse scrambles up and bolts away from the scene. Harcourt is left lying dead on the path. The trap-setter hastily removes the wire and makes off. I need to see the spot, Beresford, but it's too late and too dark now. Can Tizard fetch me even earlier from the Acorn, say around eight, tomorrow morning?'

Beresford nodded. 'Of course. He can bring you here

and I'll be here waiting with horses saddled for both of us. We can ride out to the place.'

'I want Davy Evans to be there also. He found the body, and there are questions I'll need to ask him.'

'He did. I'll arrange it. I'll send someone to find Evans at first light.' Beresford hesitated. 'My whole attention was on Harcourt, lying in the path. I saw the rock that's been mentioned, though it seems not to have played any part in what happened. I didn't examine the area in detail. But, now I think about it, the bushes growing by the path were crushed and damaged. The mare must have fallen against them, landed among them. It broke her fall and saved her from serious injury, if so. Poor Harcourt wasn't so lucky. He came off and hit the surface of the path. But we'll check all that tomorrow.'

I did not discount the importance of the rock; but I needed to see the place Harcourt had died for myself, and think the whole thing through. And Evans, too, I needed to talk to him. Of all the people who might have discovered the body, I disliked it being Davy Evans. Oh, yes, I understood the explanation, but I still didn't like it. Evans had been working as a groom that day at the Hall. He'd done so before, so that wasn't strange. But it gave him an alibi and somehow that irked me. Often, in my past experience, the innocent often can't produce an alibi, simply because they have no reason to provide themselves with one.

On the other hand, I've heard some wonderful alibis from crooks in my time. And if ever you have it in mind to commit a murder in, say, St John's Wood, then make sure half a dozen witnesses will swear you were playing cards with them in Bow at the time.

What time had Evans arrived at the Hall that morning and begun work? Why had Sir Henry allowed the fellow to come and go in that casual way, helping out when needed or being called upon for a single job – like taking the dogcart to Southampton to bring back the luggage for Lizzie and Mrs Parry? I thought I had an idea why that was so. But I couldn't prove it; that was the trouble.

'I'd like to go back to the inn now,' I said, 'and take Mr Pelham with me, unless you have further need of him.'

'Tizard!' shouted Beresford and the coachman appeared in the stable doorway. 'Put the horses to the berlin. The gentlemen wish to return to the Acorn.'

To me he added more quietly, 'Take Pelham with you, by all means. His hanging about the place is beginning to annoy me. I suppose he's anxious as to the progress of the investigation into my uncle's death. After all, if you were to decide I killed him, it would rule me out as heir. I didn't kill him, by the way. He was a man it was difficult to feel much affection for, but he was always decent to me.'

He paused. 'Harcourt's belief he was my cousin could be irritating, too. Not that he referred to it when talking to me. But I realised he told others, as he told you. It made things awkward. Poor fellow, he is lying dead in this house, so I won't say more against him. But you should know that, although it is true that I wanted him to remain as estate manager here, I would have made it a condition of his staying that he spoke no more to anyone of this— delusion of his.'

'It's awkward to talk about him at this moment,' I agreed. 'But given this "delusion", as you call it, would it not be better if Harcourt had not remained here to run the estate for you?'

'And have him go elsewhere and take the story with him?' Beresford shook his head. 'No. At least here people were aware of it and, like all old news, it had lost its interest for them.'

Perhaps so, I thought. All the same, Harcourt was dead: and the accusation had died with him. That, at least, Beresford could not regret.

A little later, Pelham and I set off. Carriage lamps were fixed to the berlin to light our way, but it was gloomy within. Pelham, seated opposite me and wearing his customary black coat, was a shadowy figure with a pale oval marking his face. I sensed, rather than saw, that he studied me. I waited for him to speak, as I knew he would, if I didn't volunteer any information. There was a question he was bursting to ask. He asked it now, unable to wait until we reached the Acorn.

'There was something of interest to be seen in the stables, I take it?' His voice echoed in the darkness, the individual words hard to catch against the background rattle and scrape of the wheels.

'There was, sir,' I said. 'But I am not yet ready to discuss it, you understand. It's a matter that has to be thought over.'

'Quite,' said Pelham; and if he was displeased, his voice was as it always was, dry and unemotional. I wondered whether the fellow ever sounded pleased about anything.

I did not alert him to the fact that the berlin would be coming back to the inn in the morning to collect me; I didn't want him tagging along. To make sure he did not, when we descended at the inn door I whispered to Tizard, who held the carriage door as I climbed down, 'Say nothing!'

'Sir!' replied Tizard simply. He'd understood. 'Goodnight to you both, gentlemen.'

It was the first time Tizard had addressed me as 'sir'. I was climbing the ladder in his esteem.

Pelham must have been longing to question me again about what I'd been shown in the stables but he accepted it would be in vain, so he only bid me 'Goodnight!' in a very grumpy voice; and stalked off upstairs to his bed.

I remained in the study for a little, a jumble of thoughts running through my brain. Then I began to think again of the tale of William Rufus, slain by a rogue arrow. What brought that scrap of history back to mind now? I asked myself. The answer came to me. It was because Harcourt's body had been brought back to the Hall on a cart. The body of William Rufus had been abandoned by all his companions, left lying where it fell. The dead king had been brought to Winchester on a charcoal burner's cart. That body, too, must have received a few knocks along the way, together with a liberal staining of charcoal. So, if the broken skin on Harcourt's forehead were due to a jolting cart, well, that would be feasible. Beresford thought so. But I didn't believe it.

Elizabeth Martin Ross

The tragic news of poor Robert Harcourt's death did not reach The Old Excise House until late that day, and unfortunately reached it while I wasn't there. The day itself had been uneventful for Mrs Parry and only mildly eventful for myself. She complained about her ankle and said she would rest and finish *The Tenant of Wildfell Hall*. I walked along the shoreline and thought long and hard about all that had happened since we arrived. One conclusion I arrived at was a worrying one.

On my return I wrote a letter for Agnes Beresford. The letter was to thank Agnes for her hospitality and to offer that of The Old Excise House in return. If she would like to come, we should be delighted to see her. In any case, I thought, a letter would be a friendly word and poor Agnes needed friends just now. Also, she needed to be away from Oakwood House for an hour or two. In my opinion it was stupid beyond belief for Andrew Beresford to have ordered the coffin to be stored, pro tem, in the disused icehouse. I liked and respected him. But because he would not have fancies about ghosts himself it had not entered his head that his wife might do so.

I could not dismiss altogether her fear that Sir Henry's ghost wandered about the grounds as due only to an overactive imagination. But, I had thought to myself that morning, what if Agnes's belief was founded on more than superstition or nerves? Of course, I did not believe for one moment that Sir Henry stalked the grounds of Oakwood House, wrapped in his burial shroud. Rather, some ill-natured person might like to scare Agnes while her husband was away from the house. In addition, there was the mystery of the roses and the fan left on the piano. That was an act directed at Agnes herself, not at her husband.

Agnes struck me as a complete innocent in all this. Nevertheless she was Beresford's wife and he was Sir Henry's heir. Someone had committed murder. That someone was still out there, undiscovered. Was the next target to be Beresford himself? Was someone lurking in the grounds of Oakwood House with murder in mind? Was the first part of the plan to frighten Agnes Beresford away from the house, perhaps to stay with a friend? She was an orphan, but she could not be friendless. I would have offered to spend the day with Agnes at Oakwood House, if that would help her. But Mrs Parry, though inconvenienced by the twisted ankle when it came to taking any exercise, would have insisted on struggling to her feet and accompanying me to Oakwood House in the Beresfords' landau if it were sent for us. Agnes needed a friendly presence, not Mrs Parry with her theories of desperate villains lurking on the heath. Nor, come to think of it, with her suggestion that the vicar might be called in to drive away any ill-intentioned spirit. Possibly the vicar might not be very keen on the idea, either.

It was now past four o'clock in the afternoon but the light would be good for another three hours. I could walk down to the village and post my letter.

'But we are about to take tea!' complained Mrs Parry. 'What a very odd idea to walk to the village now, and just to post a letter. If the letter must go today, why not give it to that girl, Jessie? She can run down to the village with it.'

'To be honest, Aunt Parry,' I told her, 'we made an excellent luncheon and I am sure Mrs Dennis will produce a generous dinner. I think I will go without a meal in between today.'

'Really?' asked Mrs Parry doubtfully. 'I never miss a cup of tea and just a little slice of cake at this time of day.'

'I think I need the walk,' I said firmly.

'But you walked this morning, Elizabeth, all along the beach here. I was quite concerned that you were gone so long, scrambling your way across the pebbles. You might have had the misfortune to turn an ankle as I did.'

Her last pronouncement, just as I was leaving, was: 'You know, Elizabeth, you can be very thoughtless about the feelings of others!'

I pinned up my skirts to avoid the brambles and set off down the pathway to the village. It seemed very quiet everywhere. Not even the birds were chirping. Perhaps, with the evening coming on, they were preparing to roost. I did feel a little guilty at refusing to stay and take tea with Aunt Parry, but I was finding her company rather wearing. I was no longer her paid companion, as I had once briefly been, and I was entitled to time of my own.

Automatically, as I emerged from the shaded path into the open and reached the Dawlish sisters' cottage, I looked for the pair of them, expecting to see them both seated in their usual place. But only one of them sat there, Cora.

She watched me approach with sharp little eyes in her round, rather doughy, face. She did not smile.

'Good afternoon, Miss Cora,' I said to her.

Her reply was unexpected and far less civil. 'Well, truth-seeker's wife, so now your man has more work on his hands,' she retorted in her dour way. If, during our meeting on the heath, I had sensed her mood to be conciliatory, that had quite vanished now.

'How so?' I asked.

Now a smile touched her lips, but it was not a pleasant one. 'Death follows you about, it seems to me.'

My heart sank. 'Who has died?' I asked. As I spoke I was searching my brain for a possible answer.

'Mr Harcourt,' she said. 'Thrown from his horse this morning and broken his neck.'

This was not an answer I could have expected. It was so shocking I was truly horrified and reluctant to believe it. 'Who told you of this?' I asked sharply.

She looked sullen. 'Davy Evans came by and told us, half an hour ago. It was Davy found him. Harcourt rode out from the Hall this morning and the mare came home without him. Tom Tizard started the search for him, and Mr Beresford from Oakwood House came to take over. But it was Davy found him.'

I looked towards the cottage door, firmly shut. 'Is Evans here now?' I asked. 'I would like to speak to him, if he is.'

'He has ridden back to the Hall,' she replied. 'They are all waiting for your husband, the truth-seeker himself. But he has gone over to Southampton. Maybe he is back now and someone will have fetched him from the Acorn.'

I was now really angry. Cora Dawlish knew where to find my husband, indeed had a very good knowledge of his movements, whereas I did not. Cora and her sister seemed to know everything. In fact I suspected the pair of them knew a great deal more about everyone's business than they chose to tell. That is the base of their power, I thought. No wonder the villagers are in awe of them.

'I am on my way to the post office,' I said. 'Good day to you, Miss Cora.'

The village, when I reached it, seemed to be deserted, but for a few urchins loitering around the pump. Doors and windows were all fast shut. Not a face looked out as I walked by. The sense of fear was almost palpable. I posted my letter in the box, and turned to go when something flew past me and rattled along the ground. I looked down just in time to see a pebble come to rest.

I turned angrily, even as a second missile came hurtling towards me. I managed to jump aside and avoid it. The urchins round the pump had formed up in a little phalanx, facing me. Among them I recognised the tousle-headed lad in the overlarge hand-me-downs whom I'd previously seen holding the bridle of Harcourt's horse. He seemed to be the ringleader, although he was now empty-handed. Others had armed themselves with stones, as I saw from clenched fists. Well, those young hooligans were mistaken if they thought me an easy target. I strode wrathfully towards them. Their bravado crumbled in an instant; and they scattered in every direction, running between the buildings and vanishing like rats into crannies. Their tousle-headed ringleader ran faster than the others. He'd seen the recognition in my face when I saw him.

Foiled in my vengeance, I could only turn back and

start off again. But a man in blue-and-red uniform had come out of the post office. I recognised Charlie, the postman, who had brought letters to The Old Excise House.

'Born to be hung!' said Charlie cheerfully, shaking his head. Presumably he meant the children. 'Not harmed, Mrs Ross, I hope?'

'Their aim was poor,' I replied angrily. 'But their intention was at best ill-natured. At any rate, it was an assault. Where do I find the nearest constable?'

'Oh, now, you don't need to trouble old Gosling,' said Charlie placatingly. 'I'll take care of it for you. I'll speak to their parents. You'll have no more trouble of that sort.'

'I should not have been subjected to it in the first place!' I stormed. It wasn't Charlie's fault and he was trying to pour oil on troubled waters. But I was in no mood to settle for less than some sort of vengeance. 'And I've seen the ringleader before. He has hand-me-down clothes and fair hair.'

Charlie leaned towards me. 'If I might offer a word of advice, ma'am? Meaning it for the best, you understand? Let the matter go. I promise you, there will be no more trouble.'

My anger was subsiding. 'Very well, Charlie, I'll leave it in your hands,' I told him.

'That's it, ma'am. You do that.' He smiled and nodded, his dark little eyes twinkling in the way I remembered.

'Charlie!' I asked suspiciously. 'Your surname wouldn't be Dawlish, would it?'

He looked shocked. 'Bless you, ma'am, no! I've got nothing to do with that pair of old crows. It's what you mean to ask, isn't it? Whether I've got anything to do with the aunties, sitting up there on their bench, day in day out? You'll have passed them, I dare say, on your way down to the village and back.'

'It is. Everyone seems to be related to everyone else around here. Even Wilfred, the stableman at the Acorn, is a Dawlish.'

'Take no notice of those two old biddies,' said Charlie earnestly. 'They might scare some folk but not me. Bats in the belfry, that's what they've got.' He grinned and tapped his forehead meaningfully. 'And they're no kin of mine. As for Wilf Dawlish, he's a good fellow. He can't help his relatives, any more than anyone can. There are plenty of folk who've got someone in the family who is dotty.'

'And Davy Evans, who lodges with the sisters? Is he connected to that family?'

Charlie pursed his mouth. 'I wouldn't know anything about that. I stay away from Davy and, if I might be so bold, you and the other lady staying up at The Old Excise House might be advised to avoid him. By all accounts, Davy is a useful sort of chap, there's no denying it. But I wouldn't go buying any bottles of French brandy from him.'

Startled, I said firmly, 'I have no intention of buying any brandy from Davy or anyone else!' It was time to change the subject. 'You have heard the news of Mr Harcourt's riding accident, I dare say?'

'Yes, ma'am. 'Tis very sad.' Charlie shook his head mournfully. 'A fine man, Mr Harcourt.'

'News travels fast around here. Did you also hear it from Davy Evans?'

'No, ma'am, I fancy I heard it from Jacob Dennis.'

'Jacob Dennis!' I exclaimed. 'But he is at The Old Excise House, gardening.'

'He was down here in the Black Horse public house, less than an hour ago,' said Charlie. 'Very likely he's gone back home now.'

Then the news would have travelled ahead of me there and Mrs Parry would know all about it.

'I must get back, Charlie. I'm obliged to you over the matter of those hooligans.'

'You want me to send someone to walk with you, ma'am?'

But I had already set off making the best speed I could, although the return walk was uphill. I called back over my shoulder to say I needed no escort. When I reached the sisters' cottage, it was to see that Aunt Tibby had joined Aunt Cora. The pair of them sat there, watching me puff my way along. I fancied they were enjoying the sight. But my legs were aching and my feet sore.

I halted in front of them long enough to snap, 'I'd be obliged to you both if you'd stop telling everyone in the village I bring death with me. If you don't, I shall count it as slander and put the matter in the hands of the law.'

I did not wait for any reply but marched on. As I feared, when I got home I found Mrs Parry in a fine state of panic.

'Where have you been, Elizabeth! I have been worried quite out of my wits. I told you not to go wandering about

out there alone. But you would not take my advice. There is murderer on the loose and poor Mr Harcourt is dead.'

'I heard the news in the village but my understanding is that it was a tragic riding accident,' I replied.

'It makes no difference,' she retorted. 'He is dead, poor man, and I don't believe he would be if poor Sir Henry had not been killed first.'

'We have no evidence it has been anything other than a riding accident,' I maintained stubbornly. But, in truth, privately I was inclined to agree with her.

'We should go back to London!' declared Mrs Parry. 'I'll tell Nugent to pack.'

'You will return if you wish, of course,' I said. 'But I shall stay here while my husband is here.'

'But Inspector Ross is *not* here!' argued Mrs Parry. 'He's staying at that inn, what did you say it was called? The Acorn, that's it, and there is little protection he can give us from there. Why can't he come and stay here at The Old Excise House?'

'Because it would not be practical for him, Aunt Parry. He is here on official business.'

This argument did not impress Aunt Parry, who simmered in silence for a few moments before a new idea struck her. 'Perhaps we *all* should move to the inn.'

There was a moment while I quite enjoyed imagining the scene in which Aunt Parry and I, with Nugent and all our baggage, arrived to confront Ben at the Acorn. I dismissed it, but it had served to lighten my mood. I did my best to look stern.

'You would not be comfortable there, even if the inn

could accommodate us all, and I dare say it could not. At any rate, I shall stay here.'

'You were always a very difficult, headstrong girl when you were my companion,' stated Aunt Parry. 'And I am sorry to say that marriage has not improved your disposition.'

She sulked until we sat down to dinner. I realised that she was genuinely frightened, and felt a little guilty at being so unsympathetic. To make amends I offered to play cards for the rest of the evening, and she cheered up a little. A drawer in the little study proved to contain packs for Bezique. That was one of Aunt Parry's favourites and she beat me soundly.

Chapter Fourteen

Inspector Ben Ross

THE BERLIN rumbled to a halt before the Acorn at five minutes past eight the following morning. I had made my arrangements with Mrs Garvey the evening before, so I was ready; I dashed out of the door and leaped in before Pelham could realise what was happening and demand to accompany me. Even so, he had heard the rumble of wheels. I had a fleeting vision, as we rattled and creaked our way out of the inn yard, of Pelham in his shirt, leaning out of an upper window. The expression on his face was one I would cherish. It would not have surprised me if he had shaken his fist. When I returned later, he would be waiting for me and then we'd have some sparks flying.

Mrs Garvey had made me coffee. I drank it so fast I nearly scalded my throat. She'd also kindly put up a ham sandwich for my breakfast. I munched it as we lurched along the road to the Hall.

When I reached my destination I found there were four

horses saddled and ready, waiting for us. Beresford was grim-faced. Davy Evans was there as I'd requested, and skulked in the background. There was no other way to describe it. He avoided my eye and stared sullenly at the ground. I suspected he'd had a dressing down about taking the horse to ride off and spread the news. There was also a man I'd not seen before, having the appearance of a groom. He must be the man sent to fetch Evans to the Hall.

The horse made ready for me was a larger animal than Firefly and I felt a little apprehensive as I scrambled into the saddle.

'Don't worry, sir,' said young Joe, who held the animal's head. 'She's a quiet beast.'

'How long will it take us to get to the spot?' I called to Beresford.

'No more than fifteen or twenty minutes,' he called back.

I took that to mean he could have ridden there in fifteen minutes or less. Extra time was being allowed to take account of my limited equestrian skills. I was glad I'd done some riding about the countryside and was not a complete novice.

It did take us twenty minutes to reach the wood through which ran the path taken by the unfortunate Harcourt. I slid from the saddle and set off with Beresford towards the trees. I was aware of Davy Evans behind us, keeping his distance. A log barrier had been rolled across the entrance to the path through the copse, as Beresford had warned me. He now signalled to the groom to remove it and Evans came forward to help. In all this, Evans avoided my gaze; no doubt aware I had a close eye on him. The path was narrow and the trees and banks of bracken crowded in upon it on either side. Nettles poked up among the fronds. Foxgloves raised their heads in splashes of purplish pink; otherwise it was a gloomy tunnel into which we walked.

After two or three minutes, Beresford halted. 'Here!' he said briefly.

Even without his having spoken, I would have known this was the place. Just ahead of us, the bracken and foxgloves on one side had been crushed into a flattened carpet of vegetation. That was where the horse had landed when it had been brought down on its side. Immediately before us, and just before the damaged undergrowth, the path was churned and stamped by the boots of those who'd retrieved the body. The small rock, or large stone, mentioned by Beresford was still there. I picked it up, examined it carefully and set it down again. I turned to Evans, who had been watching uneasily.

'Show me exactly where the body lay,' I ordered him.

He came forward silently and pointed down at the ground.

'I need to know exactly,' I snapped. 'Get down and show me the position.'

He'd not expected that and he didn't like it. But he dropped to his knees and stretched out to show how the body had lain.

'All right,' I told him. He scrambled to his feet with

alacrity. But I hadn't finished with him yet. 'You saw no wire?'

'No, sir,' he said.

'Then we must search for where it was fixed.'

It did not take us long. The groom called out, 'Here, Mr Beresford, sir!'

He had located a sturdy sapling around the base of which, about ten inches above the ground, the bark was scored with incisions that resembled the cuts on the legs of the horse as I'd been shown them the previous evening. A search, on the exact opposite side of the path, revealed similar traces of wire around another young tree trunk. But of the wire itself there was no sign. We searched in the undergrowth around for several minutes in case whoever had removed it had simply tossed it away. But we had no luck. Our killer – and there was now no doubt we had a murder on our hands – was a careful planner.

'Now then, Evans,' I said to the fellow. 'Tell me again exactly why you took this path and what you saw.'

'We were sent out to search for Mr Harcourt, after his horse came home riderless,' Evans replied promptly. 'We knew where he'd been going. He was making a round of the tenant farmers. I knew the route the rest of the search party was taking, but I decided to go round in the opposite direction. I'd reckoned that, if he was visiting Honeywell Farm, Mr Harcourt would take this way through the wood, either going or coming back. So I came here – and I saw him.' He pointed at the path. 'Lying there dead, like I showed you.'

'On your way here, did you look out for him? He might have been walking home on foot, having been thrown for some reason.'

'Of course I looked out for him!' Evans raised his voice truculently. 'I didn't know then he was dead, did I? I kept a sharp lookout but didn't see him, nor any other living soul.'

'Then you entered this copse?' I prompted.

He drew in a deep breath. 'Yes, sir, like I told you.'

'And the very first thing you saw was . . . ?'

Evans paused and frowned. 'Hoofmarks,' he said. 'In the mud. It's generally pretty muddy, this path. The sun don't get through the branches and dry out the ground. The prints showed an animal going at some speed, so I went in very slow and saw there was something on the path ahead. I dismounted, hitched my horse to a branch and came along here on foot. There he was, Harcourt, stretched out dead, like I showed you. I knelt over him and checked he was a goner.'

He pointed to twin indentations, round in shape and side by side. 'There, that's where I knelt! Them's my knees made those holes in the mud. And them, over there, that's where I knelt just now, to get down and lie flat, as you told me to. Anyway, I thought to myself, do I go back straight away to the Hall and tell someone? But I knew Mr Beresford was out with the search party. So I reckoned, as I'd not seen him on my way there, he must be working his way round the circle the opposite way, and would be calling at Honeywell Farm last. I turned back to remount and ride on to Honeywell, but I heard voices and hoofbeats coming from that direction, towards me, and sure enough it was Mr Beresford and his party coming towards the wood. I ran out, waved to stop them and told them what I'd found. That's it!' he concluded defiantly.

'What about the large stone, or small rock, if you prefer, that lies by the body? '

Evans looked startled. 'What of it?'

'You saw it. It's that one, I fancy, lying there.' I pointed at it.

'Oh, aye, I saw that. Paid little attention to it. I suppose he might have hit his head on it.' Evans shrugged.

'There are no similar large stones around, just the one there. Why is that, do you think? The soil around here is peaty, not rocky.'

'No idea, sir.' Evans had regained his calm. 'But you do find an odd one like that, here and there, in the undergrowth.'

'And you saw no one else around at the time? You heard no one, in the undergrowth, or noticed any movement among the trees?'

'No, sir, not a living soul, nor beast, neither.'

'But this wood must be full of wildlife?'

'Aye, but it's shy. When men are moving around here, they make off.' Evans indicated the woodland and brambles around us. 'Do you hear or see anything now? You won't, because we're here.'

He not only sounded confident, but also slightly superior. I was a townie, ignorant of the ways of woodland creatures. I gave him a nod, which he took as dismissal. He looked relieved and turned to walk away.

Beresford, who had been watching and listening, now asked, 'Well?'

'The undergrowth must be searched for the wire. Obviously someone removed it from where it had been tied across the path, and removed it quickly. This may be the work of one pair of hands, but it's also possible there are two people involved: one who set the trap and a second one, hidden nearby, who scurried out and removed the wire immediately, before making off with it. Also, we must alert them at Honeywell Farm. If anyone, living or working there, comes across a tangle of discarded wire anywhere, they should let us know – or let you know – at once. Then you can send word to me. But we must find that wire. It is important evidence and the coroner will certainly ask if it's been found, and if not, why not. We must make every effort.'

'Do I leave the path open now? Or put back the barrier?' he asked. 'I can't promise someone won't move it. It will be an inconvenience to local people.'

'You can leave it open now. But we'll take that large stone with us.'

'Why are you so interested in that?' asked Beresford curiously.

I glanced around to ensure no one overheard us. 'Because we know this is no accident. We have clear evidence that the horse was brought down by wire. As for the stone, I suspect that was brought here, either by the person who set the wire; or by the accomplice who waited to remove it. Had Harcourt's horse been brought down and Harcourt thrown, but not killed, only lying dazed and possibly with other injuries, the setter of wire, or an accomplice hiding in the trees nearby, would have been ready to finish him off with a blow from this stone.'

'That is savagery,' said Beresford, clearly appalled.

'It is murder,' I said simply. 'Murder is a savage crime, however it is committed.'

Beresford scowled even more darkly and shook his head as if to dismiss this. It was a gesture familiar enough to me. There is a degree of wickedness in some crimes that is so offensive to decent people they cannot comprehend it. They reject it as impossible.

Beresford was still finding it hard to accept. 'But, see here, Ross! If the person who was responsible, or an accomplice, emerged from the undergrowth to check the body, as you suggest, and then that person found that Harcourt was dead, why strike the poor fellow's head with that stone? He was already dead, from the broken neck,' he protested.

'Yes, he was,' I agreed.

Beresford frowned. 'I admit I struggle to understand,' he said. 'Dr Wilson observed a place on Harcourt's head, here . . .' Beresford touched his temple. 'So did you, and it seemed to me you took a lot of interest in it. The skin was broken, but there was no blood or sign of bleeding. Nor is there on this stone. You and Wilson agreed the injury was inflicted after death. If so, it is inexplicable.'

'Well, sir, there is a great deal of anger and hatred in this murder, as there was in that of Sir Henry Meager. Harcourt lay dead. But it gave someone great personal satisfaction to strike his head with that rock.'

'Then that person is indeed a barbarian,' said Beresford quietly. 'It was vicious and unnecessary.'

'Oh, yes, Mr Beresford, it was certainly that. But it was also a mistake. It means now I know for sure what I already suspected: all this is about revenge.'

On my way back to the inn later in the day, I asked Tizard to stop at The Old Excise House. I didn't expect to be the bearer of the bad news, because I'd learned Evans had 'borrowed' the horse to ride off and spread it himself. Anyway, the word would have run round the countryside even without Evans. Bad news travels fast. Tizard seemed to cheer up at the thought of stopping off there. He would see the Dennises and be able to tell them his own version of it all.

Lizzie and Mrs Parry had certainly heard it. Lizzie came running out as I approached the door and asked breathlessly, 'You have found him, haven't you? I went down to the village yesterday morning and heard it from Cora Dawlish. When I returned, the news had got here ahead of me. Jacob Dennis walks down to the public house in the village for a pint at lunchtime and he brought it back. He really is dead, then, poor Harcourt?'

'Yes, Lizzie, he is dead. I wish I could also say it was a genuine riding accident, but I am afraid it was murder. There is clear evidence wire was stretched across the path to bring down the horse. I have been at the scene of the crime this morning. Now I have to go back to the Acorn Inn and tell Pelham. I believe Harcourt was named as a beneficiary in Sir Henry's will, although he had protested against it. Whether that resulted in the bequest to him being struck out, I don't know. I hope Pelham will tell me. Then I have to go across to Southampton and inform Hughes about all this.' I kissed her cheek. 'I am sorry, my dear, but I cannot stay longer.'

'Of course, but you will come in and speak to Mrs Parry? She must know you are here.'

'What sort of state is she in?' I asked suspiciously. I did not need to have to deal with Julia Parry in a state of hysterics, as well as everything else.

'She can be surprisingly sensible,' Lizzie told me. 'She is not a fool, you know. She is selfish and demanding and prejudiced in all manner of ways. But she recognises a real emergency.'

Indeed, Mrs Parry received me quite graciously. 'It is good of you to stop by and reassure us,' she said. 'We understand how busy you are. This is a sad and terrible business. Is it true that Mr Harcourt's horse was brought down by wire?'

'Yes, ma'am, it's true.'

'And the trap was set deliberately?'

'I am afraid it looks that way.'

'There will be an inquest?'

'Yes, ma'am, although I cannot say when. Within the next day or two, I expect.' I was about to add, 'Unless something more happens,' – but I bit back the words.

'I feel we should attend,' decreed Mrs Parry. 'I shall inquire of Mrs Dennis how transport can be arranged. Where will it take place?'

'I suspect it will be in Lymington.'

Tizard was holding court in his own version of an inquest in the kitchen. He was not pleased at being pried away from his audience by my insistence on returning at once to the Acorn. But I had questions of my own to face there, from Lawyer Pelham.

Chapter Fifteen

Inspector Ben Ross

PELHAM WAS waiting for me, sure enough, 'with a face that would have curdled milk', as my mother used to say.

'I have to go across to Southampton to see Inspector Hughes, Mr Pelham,' I told him briskly. 'I'd be obliged if you could wait until I return this evening before you quiz me. I may have something more I can tell you by then,' I added, to soften my tone.

'I trust you will not avoid me again!' snapped Pelham.

I rode Firefly to Hythe, left him at the livery stables there as before, and took the ferry across the water to Southampton.

'Well,' said Hughes, when he'd heard my tale. 'This is a complicated business and I am glad you are here to deal with it. I met Harcourt when I went across to the Hall on the day Meager's body was discovered. He struck me as a competent fellow. I'm sorry he's dead. I have a little news for you here, by the way. I have heard from the police in Winchester. I telegraphed them with your inquiry about the girl, Susan Bate, as I told you I would.'

'I am sorry to have troubled you with that,' I told him. 'It was only my curiosity.'

'Well, it's mine too, now,' said Hughes cheerfully. 'And don't apologise. You were following a sound instinct. The child was not abandoned to the parish, but was brought as an infant to a private orphanage run by nuns in Winchester, as I'd already told you. They don't take in just any baby or child, you understand. They have room for only fifteen at most. There has to be a reason for a new child being taken in; special family circumstances, for example. The, um, persons depositing a child generally make a generous donation to the place when they do so, and contribute to the orphanage from time to time while the child is in its care.'

'And someone did that when Susan Bate was brought there?' I asked in surprise.

'Indeed so. The sister in charge of the convent's records looked up the arrival of the infant thirteen years ago. She was but three months old at the time. She was brought to the convent by a lawyer, whose name is not recorded, on behalf of a family whose name is not recorded either. At least, it's not set down in the ledger shown to the officer making the inquiry. But that, I dare say, was to protect the identity of the mother. It is understood locally that the babies raised there are born to girls of good family. Those who have "made a mistake" and been deceived. It wouldn't surprise me if there were not a second set of records somewhere. But to see those would need a judge's authority. The nuns appear to have been very fond of the child, and taken particular pains with her, on account of the fact she was clearly slow. The doctor who attended the orphanage at the time thought it possible the birth had been a difficult one and the infant deprived of oxygen. But she was otherwise healthy and of pleasant temperament and, as she grew, showed willingness to do as bid. When she became old enough to leave the convent, another lawyer came and took her away. He had been asked to find a suitable girl to work in the kitchen as a general skivvy.'

Hughes leaned back in his chair and beamed at me. 'This is my moment, see?' he said. 'Now I shall surprise you!'

I thought I could guess what he was going to say, but I hadn't the heart to disappoint him. 'Go on,' I invited.

'The nun was able to tell the officer the name of the lawyer who took her away, and where she went. The lawyer's name was Pelham. He took her to work at a house in the county, belonging to Sir Henry Meager. The nun was rather impressed by that, my informant tells me.' Hughes smiled slightly. 'Make of it what you will.'

There was a silence during which I sought carefully for the right words. 'I cannot say I am altogether surprised,' I said at last.

'Think she is a by-blow of Meager's?' he asked.

'There is no way of knowing. But when I return this evening, Pelham will find that I have questions for him, as he is hoarding up questions for me.'

'Have you seen the girl? Does she look like a Meager?' asked Hughes.

'That would be difficult to say. The Meagers, going by their portraits, were a fierce-looking lot. I have seen Susan and she has a meek appearance and giggles a great deal. She does, however, have striking brown eyes and fine features.'

'Seems to me,' said Hughes, 'that if this fellow Harcourt was right and Meager was his natural father, then Meager might have quite a family scattered about the county.'

'He might,' I agreed. 'His valet, Lynn, has a mother in Winchester. It's been bothering me. Now I begin to wonder about him.'

'How old is he?' asked Hughes.

'Perhaps thirty or so, and of fair complexion, and a nervous disposition. He did find the body. That might account for his nerves. Even the strongest imagination wouldn't link him with the Meager family portraits in looks or disposition.'

'Want me to inquire?' asked Hughes.

'Thank you, but not at the moment. Things are complicated enough! I thank you again for the information regarding Susan Bate. Now I must get back to the inn. Pelham is waiting there for me and now I have questions for him.'

I had not eaten since the morning and on my return to the Acorn found that Pelham had delayed dining until I returned. So we dined together in the snug. This ought to have been awkward, but in the circumstances the privacy meant we could both relax. Also, I was tired. If Pelham wanted to talk, the sooner we got it over with, the better. Then I could retire to my bed and get some well-earned sleep.

But Pelham had another reason for wanting to talk that evening. 'I shall be leaving in the morning, to return to London,' he announced as we sat down at the table in the snug. He shook out his napkin and tucked one corner into his top waistcoat buttonhole. 'I have work to attend to there and cannot linger here indefinitely.'

Neither could I remain indefinitely, I thought but did not say aloud. I might also have said, but did not, that he'd had no reason to wait about here for as long as he had. But it was time to take the initiative.

'Susan Bate!' I said briskly.

Pelham was so startled that he dropped the soup spoon and splashed the liquid. 'What of her?' he asked. A fraction too late, he added, 'Do you refer to one of the servants at the Hall?'

'Yes, the girl who washes the dishes. I understand she came to the Hall from an orphanage run by nuns in Winchester, and that you yourself went there and fetched her.'

Pelham scowled. 'You should not have come by this information. I presume you have it from the convent. They are not at liberty to disclose information about the children in their care.'

'Oh, they were very discreet about the circumstances of the baby being brought to the convent thirteen years ago. The fact that she left there to take up the situation at the Hall can surely not be secret?'

'No,' muttered Pelham, 'not secret. There is no need for secrecy. I spoke of discretion. The convent should have shown more discretion.'

'Sir Henry lies dead, murdered, in a coffin kept for the time being in a disused icehouse on Mr Beresford's estate. This is not a family, it seems to me, which is much given to discretion. Was it at Sir Henry's orders that the infant Susan was handed over to the convent?'

'I cannot say,' returned Pelham. He'd had time to resume his usual implacable manner. 'I did not represent Sir Henry at that time. You speak of thirteen years ago.'

'Do you know whether Sir Henry gave money to the convent, over the years, perhaps?'

'Sir Henry was not an uncharitable man,' said Pelham stiffly.

'Nothing I have heard about him since I arrived here,' I pointed out, 'has suggested to me that he was a particularly charitable one! Everyone seems agreed he was careful about money.'

Pelham smiled thinly. 'Surely it is better to do good deeds quietly, not make a fanfare about them?'

I would get no further for the moment with this line or questioning. I changed it. 'What of the valet, Lynn? He has a mother in Winchester, I believe?'

Now Pelham looked genuinely astonished. 'What on earth do you suggest, Inspector Ross? As it happens, Sir Henry was in need of a valet. He asked us, as his solicitors, based in London, to inquire of the agencies there; those that find and place upper servants in gentlemen's households. We carried out this request. Lynn seemed a suitable candidate. We recommended him to Sir Henry. If Lynn has a mother in Winchester, I do assure you, Inspector, that it is news to me. It can only be coincidence. It could, of course, be a reason why Lynn was eager to accept the position. It would put him within visiting distance of his parent.'

This all made sense and I saw no reason to quibble with Pelham's account. In truth, I was quite relieved. Sir Henry's private life seemed already to be quite complicated enough.

We finished the soup in silence. We both needed time to think. Mrs Garvey arrived with roast duck, which put both Pelham and myself into a better mood.

'Now, then, Inspector,' the solicitor began in quite a relaxed tone. 'You have asked me several questions. May I not ask a few of you? Beginning with the death of Robert Harcourt, naturally. Are you now satisfied it was an accident?'

'Unfortunately, no, I am not. There is evidence the horse was brought down by a carefully set trap. But my investigation has barely begun.'

Pelham was moved enough to set down his knife and fork. 'I am very sorry to hear that. Harcourt was a capable man; and another murder is not what we need.'

'He told me he believed himself Sir Henry's natural son.' I wondered, as I spoke, whether Pelham would show surprise but he did not.

'That claim was entirely unsubstantiated.' Pelham sighed. 'When a wealthy man dies, Inspector, you would be surprised how many persons, of all kinds, turn up to make a claim on the estate.'

'I thought Harcourt had rejected the legacy Sir Henry had left him in the will?'

'Oh, no,' said Pelham. 'You misunderstand, Ross, or

have been misled. Harcourt made a fuss about the new will, but it was not on account of anything it contained. It was on account of something the will *did not*, would never, contain.'

'A declaration by Sir Henry that he was Harcourt's natural father?'

'Exactly. I cannot stress too greatly, Inspector, that Sir Henry never recognised Harcourt as his offspring in any way. As a young man, it's true, Sir Henry was acquainted with the late Mrs Harcourt, Robert's mother.'

'He brought her to his home from France,' I said. 'Or is that not true? He had promised her marriage.'

'He may gave brought her with him from France when he was a young fellow!' snapped Pelham. 'That, alone, does not make him Harcourt's parent. Wealthy young men, Inspector, sometimes use inappropriate language when strongly attracted to pretty girls. There is no evidence at all that he ever had any intention of marrying her, whatever he might have led her to believe at the time; or whatever she might have claimed. He would have known he needed parental consent; and it would be quite out of the question. She was a mistress, nothing more, and his own father, Captain Sir Hector Meager, very quickly got rid of her – found a husband for her. That was the end of the matter. I dare say the girl was well satisfied.

'Later, of course, and quite inadvisably, Sir Henry paid for the boy's education. I have already told you that Sir Henry was not uncharitable. Sadly, the boy, Robert, misunderstood the situation. He let his fancy run riot and the version of his parentage he imagined became fixed in his brain.' Pelham shook his head slowly. 'It is a not unfamiliar tale. Ask any solicitor.' He dabbed at his lips with the corner of his napkin.

'What happens now to any legacy made to Harcourt under the terms of Sir Henry's will?'

'We shall endeavour to trace any relatives of Harcourt himself, particularly in Lymington, where he was born. To track down his mother's family in France would be well nigh impossible. I understand she was an orphan when the young Henry Meager met her on his Continental tour.'

'He also told me she had been living with an elderly female relative at the time Henry Meager met her.'

'Yes, yes,' snapped Pelham. 'It may be true she was living with a female relative when Henry Meager met her. Or it may not. You are familiar with the term *entremetteuse*, Inspector Ross?'

'I have heard it,' I said. 'At best it means a matchmaker, and at worst a procuress, does it not?'

'Quite so. A wealthy young man travelling alone on the Continent, with no guardian but a retired seaman to keep him from physical harm, would be natural prey for such a person. As I say, it is unlikely there is anyone in France with a claim.'

'You do not have a romantic disposition, Mr Pelham,' I exclaimed.

For the first time in our acquaintance, the lawyer allowed himself a dry smile. 'I most certainly do not. I have been a family solicitor for too long. But there may be some Harcourt connections on the male side. I shall initiate inquiries in Lymington.'

'Mr Pelham,' I said. 'It seems strange to me that the details of a will are known before the person whose will it is has died. Everyone seems to know what was in Sir Henry's will, while he was still alive!'

'Not exactly. You seem to be under a considerable misunderstanding about the will, Inspector. The details were not known, only the general outline. Chiefly, our client, Sir Henry, wanted it made clear that Mr Beresford was his designated heir. In the absence of an entail on the estate, he wished, by making that public, to reassure his tenants that it would stay in the family. The thought of a stranger becoming their landlord would have caused some apprehension. But they all know Mr Beresford.'

Though I was not convinced, we were to discuss it no further. The clatter of hooves and rattle of wheels sounded from outside and a conveyance of some kind pulled up at the inn. We heard the potman, Jem, run out, shouting, and another voice I thought was that of Wilfred. Then a female voice, that of Mrs Garvey, joined the babble. It culminated in a blood-curdling scream from the landlady.

'What the deuce?' demanded Pelham, scowling.

The door to the snug was thrown open and Mrs Garvey herself appeared in great agitation. There was a look of something near to terror on her face. The figure of Beresford's groom, whom I'd encountered that morning, loomed up behind her. It was clear from his shaken expression that something very serious had happened.

'Oh, sirs!' cried Mrs Garvey. 'Begging your pardon for disturbing you as you eat. But Callan, Mr Beresford's groom, is here with awful news!'

Pelham and I both jumped to our feet. 'Not another murder?' I demanded.

'Oh, no, sir, not a murder, it is almost something worse! It *does* concern Sir Henry. He's been resurrected, sirs!'

Chapter Sixteen

Inspector Ben Ross

'*WHAT?*' PELHAM and I cried out together.

'You'd best come and see for yourself, gents,' said Callan hoarsely. 'I brought the trap on Mr Beresford's orders. He asks you come at once. He wants you both to— to witness it, sirs.'

This time there was no question of leaving Pelham behind. We both raced outside and scrambled into the trap that had been sent to fetch us. Callan drove us to Oakwood House at a reckless speed given the poor visibility; the wheels rumbling and bouncing over the road and the trap shaking so much, it seemed about to fall apart. Twice I feared we might overturn and Pelham was clinging on for dear life.

But we were not the only ones making a hasty way there. The countryside appeared to be alive with moving figures, afoot, on horse or pony, or in vehicles of various sorts, including country carts. All were converging on the same goal. As we neared Beresford's house we saw that a pink haze suffused the sky and illuminated all around it.

'It is a fire!' shouted Pelham, his fingers still gripping the side of the trap. 'Is it the house?'

'No, gents!' shouted back Callan over his shoulder. 'It's not the house. It's a bonfire on the shore!'

'You know the location, Ross?' yelled Pelham to me. 'How close is the house to the shore?'

'The gardens run down to the beach. There will be a gate in the outer garden wall, allowing access to it, and probably a path leading down!' I shouted back.

Our breakneck progress bought us into the stable yard of Oakwood House. We both scrambled down from the trap.

'This way, gents!' called Callan, beckoning to us to follow him.

I didn't need Callan to show me the way and broke into a run. Pelham had no intention of being left behind and panted along on my heels. We hastened across the gardens with others following behind us as the crowd converged on the target. We dodged onlookers and pushed aside those who got in our way. Then we were at the opened gate to the path that led down to the beach. We slithered down it and saw at last what had brought us and all the other spectators to this spot.

A bonfire had been built on the shore. Someone must have stockpiled wood and other inflammable material nearby and brought it out for this purpose. The stack was not so very high, but high enough. In the middle a pole had been fixed, long, straight and sturdy. I guessed it to be part of a former sailing ship's mast. The flames, yellow and red, crackled through the burning mass and licked at the base of the pole. Fanned by the strong breeze, they danced wildly around it. Above the fire, the air glowed cerise, and golden sparks erupted in showers across the night sky. All of it served to illuminate the thing that was at the centre of the devilish creation. Tied to the mast so that it stood upright atop the blaze was a human figure. I thought at first it was a dummy, but almost at once realised it was not. Beside me, Pelham was repeating, in tones of horror, 'No, no, surely not!'

Yet there was no mistaking Sir Henry Meager's white dead face staring out at us. Bound around the corpse's forehead was a silk kerchief, hiding the wound beneath, and giving the figure a piratical appearance. The effect was both gruesome and ludicrous. I have seen some terrible sights in my time as a police officer, but never anything as dreadful as this; and I pray I may never see another.

'Dear heaven!' Pelham was crying out. 'They have broken open the coffin and taken out the body. Who could have done this— this sacrilege?'

'The person who tied wire across the path Harcourt would take to ride back to the Hall,' I replied grimly.

Pelham was silent for a moment and then said steadily, 'Inspector Ross, I do believe there is a monster among us.'

For the first time I was in complete agreement with him.

Efforts were being made to quench the flames. At the sea's edge men were working hand pumps to send sprays of water, targeting the bonfire. As the seawater hit the flames, so a hissing could be heard, as if some huge serpent lived within the inferno, and clouds of steam mingled with the smoke. But the water achieved little, for the conflagration was well alight and would have to burn itself out. It seemed to me that, realising this, the operators of the hose carrying the water from the shore were aiming the jets at the figure, drenching the corpse in an attempt to save that from being consumed.

Still, all around me, people were crying out in horror and dismay. I saw a man who must be the local parson, with his hands clasped and head bent in prayer. There were women on their knees, some also praying and others wailing. Many just looked terrified. Yet none of them ran away. They all remained, kept there by the gruesome theatre of it all. With the crowd weaving and gesticulating before the blaze, and the praying women and parson, it was like being present at some cruel martyrdom.

In all this mayhem I searched desperately for Beresford. It wasn't easy to see him, but I glimpsed him at last, down by the water's edge, directing those who worked the pumps. Beresford had experience quenching the sporadic fires that broke out of the heath in high summer, I knew. If anyone could save the corpse was being consumed, it was he. I pushed my way through the crowd to reach him. As I did, I kept looking around me in the crowd for one face in particular. But Davy Evans, who previously had seemed to have the knack of turning up everywhere, was nowhere to be seen.

I managed to reach Beresford and called his name. He did not hear me the first time, so I had to bellow it again, in his ear. Now he glanced over his shoulder, saw me, and shouted: 'The icehouse was locked. The door was smashed in!'

'Where is Davy Evans?' I yelled.

'Not to be found!' Beresford broke off to direct the men with the hose to send the spray of water higher in the air. Then he turned back to me, his face blackened with grime and running with sweat. 'I sent a man to the cottage where he lives. He wasn't there! The old women he lives with said he had gone night fishing, in his boat.'

'Confound it!' I shouted. 'He has run for it. Can he make France in that boat of his?'

'The vessel is small but equipped with a sail and the wind is getting stronger by the minute!' Beresford panted. 'It's a long way but Evans is a skilled sailor. Or he may have arranged a rendez-vous with another vessel. Out there!' He flung a hand out towards the water. 'I believe Evans to be something of a small-time smuggler. It's never been completely eradicated hereabouts. A larger craft may wait out there to pick him up.'

'It's quite possible. Ne'er-do-wells like him generally have an escape route planned if they have to run for it!' I agreed.

I made my way back to Pelham, who stood watching, his pale features reddened by the glow of the fire. His normal self-possession had given way to shock. When I told him what Beresford had said, I had to repeat it twice. He seemed unable to take it in.

'Is the fellow Evans the most likely candidate for your murderer?' he asked at last. 'Did you suspect him before tonight?'

'I suspected a conspiracy, Mr Pelham; of which I am reasonably certain Davy Evans is a part. If it's true that he's run for it, then he's betrayed himself. Now we have to catch him! But by morning, if the wind favours him in the course he's set, he may well be in France. Who knows where he'll go next?'

It was getting very cold and I pulled my greatcoat about me.

Pelham, who missed nothing, observed, 'It is indeed unpleasantly cold and also, I fancy, damp.'

'Is it raining? I don't think so,' I said.

Callan, on his perch, had overheard our conversation. 'I don't think we're in for rain, gents. More likely a fog is coming up. We're on the shore here. Take a look about you.'

We did so. It was true that wisps of a semi-transparent white veil had begun to swirl around our heads. We were now too far from Oakwood House for this to be smoke from the bonfire. But its odour clung to our clothes, bringing the memory of Sir Henry's funeral pyre with us.

'That's sea mist, that is, gents,' Callan continued. 'I, for one, wouldn't care to be out there in a small sailing boat.' And he pointed with his whip in what must be the general direction of the English Channel.

We were all silent thereafter until we reached the Acorn. By now the mist had thickened to fog; and the inn put me in mind of a baroque painting in which figures recline on cotton-wool clouds. Its door lantern and lighted windows glowed dimly though the vapour, but made a welcome sight. We'd been heard. The door opened and Mrs Garvey, shawl clutched about her throat, peered anxiously into the haze.

Concerned at the worsening conditions, I called up to our driver after we'd descended, 'You'll be able to find your way back all right, Callan?'

'The horse knows his way home,' called down Callan. The trap clattered away.

Pelham and I turned to go into the inn. Quietly, Pelham said, 'God help him.'

He was not talking of Callan.

Chapter Seventeen

Elizabeth Martin Ross

ONCE AGAIN, bad news reached The Old Excise House in the early morning. I was awoken at six by a loud and unearthly wailing that seemed to be directly under my bed. I realised the noise was rising up from the kitchen and spreading through the gaps between the floorboards. I dressed hurriedly and went downstairs in time to collide with Aunt Parry, who had emerged from the former study now her bedroom. She was wrapped in a rose-pink silk peignoir and still wore her lace nightcap. Nugent came noisily down the stairs behind me and arrived breathless.

'Now what?' demanded Aunt Parry angrily. 'I never knew a household like it for servants yowling in the morning!'

'Whatever it is, it's taking place in the kitchen,' I said. 'I'll go and look.'

I hurried out as Nugent stepped forward to soothe her employer, and made my way to the kitchen where I found disorder reigned supreme.

Central to it was Jessie Dennis, who sat on the floor,

her skirts spread around her, her long red hair loose about her shoulders. She was wailing and held clenched fists in front of her as if she had been beating her breast. Her mother stooped over her, trying to haul her to her feet and berating her. But Jessie sagged in a dead weight and her mother had to abandon the attempt and could only stand by, scowling in rage and frustration. By the back door stood Jacob Dennis and a man I recognised as Wilfred Dawlish. His reason for being there at such an early hour must be because he had brought bad news. The two men stood close, side by side, united in ineffectual male dismay.

'You stupid girl! Stop that noise! You're well free of him. Good riddance to bad rubbish, that's what it is.' Mrs Dennis bent forward to grasp her daughter's shoulders and shook her violently.

'*I love him!*' howled Jessie.

'Love? What do you know about love? He's a bad lot, always was. If he's taken himself off and we never set eyes on him again, then you should thank your lucky stars! He was always a wastrel.'

Jessie managed to free herself from her parent's grip. Her upper half fell forward so that she folded like a collapsed puppet, her face buried in her skirts, her shoulders shaking with a new outburst of sobs.

This provided a moment when I could ask, 'What has happened?'

All present froze in a kind of *tableau vivant*. The two men and Mrs Dennis stared at me. Jessie remained in a heap on the floor, moaning.

'Oh, ma'am!' exclaimed Mrs Dennis. 'I didn't see you.

I beg your pardon! You see what you've done, you silly child,' she added, prodding her daughter with her foot. 'You've woken the ladies.' Turning back to me, Mrs Dennis added apprehensively, 'Mrs Parry is awake, too, is she, ma'am?'

'Yes, she is, but Nugent is with her. Will you please tell me what has happened?'

Wilf Dawlish edged towards the back door and escape. 'I'd best get back to the inn or Mrs Garvey will box my ears.'

'You stay here, Wilf!' snapped Jacob, seizing the stableman's arm. 'Don't leave me here alone with all this.'

'They're your womenfolk,' retorted Wilfred. 'You take care of it.'

I decided it was time I took charge of things. 'Before you leave, Wilfred,' I said loudly, 'am I to understand from all this that you have brought some bad news this morning?'

'Yes, ma'am,' said Wilfred unhappily. 'But I've got to go back to the inn. Your husband will very likely want the pony saddled up. Jacob here can tell you all about it.'

There was a movement behind me. Silence fell, even on the part of Jessie, who looked up and stared past me, silenced, mouth agape. I turned and saw that Mrs Parry had entered the kitchen and stood, like a vast rose-pink satin tent, dominating the scene.

'Lord bless us,' muttered Wilfred, 'I never seen nothing like that!' He had temporarily forgotten the urgent need to return to the inn, and remained, shaking his head in disbelief.

'*Well* . . .' demanded Mrs Parry, her voice echoing

around the kitchen like the clap of doom. 'Speak up! Did you not hear Mrs Ross's question?'

'Yes'm!' Wilfred made an awkward bow. 'I heard it and I was just wondering how best to tell it. There's been bad mischief done this past night, ladies. I'm sorry you have to learn of it from me. 'Tis the work of the devil, nothing less.'

'Davy never did it, I swear,' cried Jessie from the floor. 'And now I'll never see him again. He's gone!'

Mrs Parry turned a basilisk stare on the luckless Jessie. 'Have you some information to give us?'

'No, ma'am,' whispered Jessie.

'Then be quiet, and get to your feet. You are too old for childish tantrums.'

'Yes'm,' whispered Jessie and struggled awkwardly to her feet.

'Go outside and put your head under the pump!' ordered her mother.

Jessie turned and trailed to the back door where her father and Wilfred parted to allow her space to exit.

'A chair!' commanded Mrs Parry.

Mrs Dennis dragged forward a wooden chair and dusted the seat with her apron. Jacob was spurred into action and pulled out another chair for me. Wilfred stared longingly out of the back door, perhaps wondering if he could bolt for it.

'Speak!' Mrs Parry pointed a finger at him. 'You, there, the fellow from the inn!'

Wilfred came forward and made another awkward bow. 'It's like this, ma'am. I fear it will distress you and the other lady . . .' Wilfred made another of his peculiar jerky bows in my direction. 'But there has been mischief at Oakwood House.'

'Oakwood House?' Mrs Parry and I cried together.

I added anxiously, 'Are Mr and Mrs Beresford safe?'

'Yes,'m, they're safe, though very shocked, Mrs Beresford in particular. It concerns Sir Henry's body, you see.'

'His body? What about it?'

'Well, they had it kept safe in the old icehouse. The lock was forced and the coffin broken open.'

'If they insisted on keeping the coffin on the property, they should have expected some trouble or other,' said Mrs Parry. 'I never heard such a foolish idea. But are you going to tell us some heathenish tale of a Black Mass?'

'Oh, no, ma'am. Though near as bad. The gardens at Oakwood House run down to the shore . . .'

So Wilfred related his news again while we listened in horror. When he finished, and before we could ask any questions, he concluded with: 'And now, ladies, I really have to go back to the inn. I'm sorry to have caused any distress.'

He ducked his head, turned and ran out of the back door. Within minutes we heard the thud of the pony's hooves retreating.

'Barbaric!' declared Aunt Parry, summing up the general impression.

'Do they have any idea who did this dreadful thing?' I asked the Dennis family.

'They're saying Davy did it!' Jessie was back, bursting into the kitchen with hair dripping pump water. 'Only he never did. 'Tisn't fair the way they blame Davy for everything. And now he's gone.' Tears began to roll down her cheeks again, mixing with the trickles from her hair.

'Davy lodges with— with Wilf's aunties,' said Jacob Dennis. 'They said he went out night fishing last evening. He's not returned.'

Mrs Dennis asked timidly, 'Will you have some tea, ladies?'

'For myself, coffee!' decided Aunt Parry. 'It is stronger. How about you, Elizabeth? Yes, coffee for both of us. Bring it to the breakfast table – and bring the brandy. I need a restorative after hearing this ghastly news.'

Neither of us was in the mood to eat much by way of breakfast, not even Aunt Parry, so we had buttered toast with our coffee, and Madeira cake to accompany the brandy.

We had spoken very little during the meal. But when we had finished I spoke my thoughts aloud. 'The coroner will have to be told. It will cause enormous distress to all who knew Sir Henry. It's the sort of lurid story the newspapers like. Reporters will flock in, even come down from London. That will make things so much worse for the Beresfords. Poor Agnes, I feel for her.'

'In my opinion, it is the bishop who must be informed,' said Aunt Parry. 'There are set rituals for driving out evil of this sort, and he must see they are carried out.'

After this we neither of us felt like discussing it further, and retired to make our separate morning toilettes.

A little later, around eleven o'clock, we heard the sound of a carriage on the road behind the house. Shortly afterwards Mrs Dennis appeared carrying a small silver tray on which lay a visiting card.

'It is Mrs Beresford, ladies,' she told us in a hushed voice.

I turned the little card over and read, written on the back, 'I am leaving and would like to say goodbye.'

'Goodness!' cried Mrs Parry. 'Do ask her to come in.'

Agnes was wearing travelling dress and looked pale and quite ill. We begged her to sit down and Aunt Parry demanded of Mrs Dennis whether there was any champagne in the house.

'It is the best restorative!' she stated.

Unfortunately, there was no champagne and Agnes protested that, in any case, as she had a long journey ahead of her, she would take nothing.

'I am going to Bournemouth,' she told us. 'My old governess has retired and been living there for a while now. I expect to stay with her for a little until arrangements can be made to take rooms. This is until— until matters can be fully resolved. You will have learned what happened last night.'

'A dreadful business!' declared Mrs Parry.

'You will understand, then, that I cannot remain at Oakwood House. It is quite out of the question! Andrew must stay because he has much to do, but I cannot. I feel that I should and support my husband, but last night's events were . . . Well, after all that has happened, the— the bonfire was . . .'

Her voice shook and she looked down at her hands, clasped tightly in her lap.

'I am sure it is best that you stay in Bournemouth for a little while,' I assured her. 'Forgive me, but may I ask, have you received any more little tokens, like the roses or the fan?'

'No, there have been no more of those, thank goodness.' Her voice had been subdued but now a note of passion entered it. 'I never wanted the coffin kept in the old icehouse! It was too— too grotesque. Just knowing it was there was bad enough. Now . . .'

'Since there is no champagne, you should take a small glass of brandy,' advised Mrs Parry.

'No, really!' exclaimed Agnes. 'Dear Mrs Parry and Mrs Ross, I am so sorry to leave you here and pray that nothing more happens.'

'I would return to London today,' announced Aunt Parry. 'But Mrs Ross is determined to stay, as Mr Ross is nearby, engaged in investigating the whole dreadful business.'

Agnes rose to her feet. 'I must go or we shall be very late getting to Bournemouth. Miss Jessop, my former governess, should be expecting me. Andrew sent someone to the telegraph office this morning to alert her to my arrival.'

We listened to the carriage roll away and Aunt Parry turned to me. 'Elizabeth,' she said. 'I mean no criticism of Inspector Ross. But that Agnes Beresford should be frightened half out of her wits, and driven from her own home, is intolerable. Something must be done!'

'Yes,' I agreed, 'it must.' Silently, to myself, I added, *And I must do it*. Neither of us paid much attention to lunch, I cannot even remember what it was, but after we left the table Aunt Parry retired to rest, with a cold compress on her brow.

'It has all made me quite ill!' she informed me.

'I am just going to walk down to the church in the village,' I told her.

She made no reply other than a weak wave of her hand.

'You go along for your walk, ma'am,' said Nugent. 'I'll take care of madam.'

I set off but did not get very far, only to the gate out of the property, when Jacob Dennis appeared and asked, 'Off down to the church, I hear, ma'am?'

'Thank you, Jacob, yes.' He still hovered so I asked, 'Can you tell me the name of the vicar?'

'That's Mr Appleton, ma'am. He'll be at the vicarage, ma'am, and that's in a lane tucked away behind the church. I'll walk down with you, and show you.'

'I'm sure I'll find it.'

'No trouble, ma'am,' he assured me earnestly. 'I'm about to walk down to the village myself, anyway.'

'Charlie, the postman, has told you that some village children threw stones at me, I think?' I guessed.

'So I believe, ma'am, and I'm very sorry for it.'

'Jacob, I don't need a guardian!'

'Bless you, ma'am,' he replied cheerfully. 'I am sure you don't. But, speaking for myself, I'm in need of a pint. All that shouting and wailing earlier, I'm sorry you and the other lady were disturbed by it. My wife and I are really distressed that Mrs Beresford has left to stay a while in Bournemouth. We all hope she'll return. The loss of the

Beresfords from Oakwood House would be very bad news for the neighbourhood.'

'If your daughter is broken-hearted because of Davy Evans running off,' I said, 'I must admit I'm inclined to think that, at least, could turn out for the best. If the relationship is over, I mean. Evans is not of good character, and must be quite a bit older than Jessie, I imagine?'

'Why, my girl is only sixteen!' Jacob nodded. 'And you're right. Of course Davy is too old for her. He'll be thirty, I believe, at Christmas. He was a Christmas baby, you see, and they're supposed to be lucky. But that doesn't mean I want him trying his luck with my daughter.'

He didn't know it, but he had just given me a very useful piece of information. I sought a little more.

'Jacob,' I asked, 'I know you've gone fishing with Davy in his sailing boat. Do you think it is possible he has reached France?'

'Well, he's a good sailor, is Davy,' returned Jacob, after a moment's thought. 'But it's a long crossing from here to the French coast. That's where he'll be heading, I dare say. If he left yesterday evening, and without the fog, he'd only just be in sight of the French coast now, I reckon. But it was a bad night. All clear this morning, but out at sea it must have been desperate bad visibility.'

I asked no more questions as I realised how uneasy Jacob Dennis was. Supposing Davy did reach the French coast, I thought there was a strong possibility he'd find a welcoming committee in the form of the French police. The information would have been telegraphed to them by now; and word put out. Even if Davy did have smuggling connections with France, the nature of his action, taking the body from the coffin and setting it on a bonfire, would horrify them, and they'd not be pleased to welcome him.

When we reached the church I saw it was the scene of some activity. It wasn't taking place within the church but at the side of the building, where an outer flight of steps by the outside wall led down below ground level. As I watched, a man's head appeared in a disconcerting way beside a tombstone. He then rose into view, a bit at a time, carrying a large basket filled with a jumble of items. It resembled nothing so much as a ludicrous resurrection. Following that of Sir Henry's body, it was quite frightening. I stopped.

'Just hold on a moment, ma'am,' said Jacob. 'I'll find out what's going on.'

He pushed open the gate and strode towards the man with the basket, who set down his burden to greet the visitor. I watched as he talked with Jacob, both joined by a second man who came up, like the first one, from below ground level. I realised there must be a way into the building, probably into the crypt, by outer steps.

After a few minutes' conversation, Jacob returned to me. 'Now then, ma'am, it's a good thing we stopped to ask, for Mr Appleton is not at the vicarage. He's driven over to Oakwood House to help with the arrangements with the coffin.'

'Sir Henry's coffin? Is he . . . is the body . . .'

'Back in the coffin, where it should be!' said Jacob cheerfully. 'Only it's been decided to store it in the crypt of the church until the funeral.'

'I can't think why it wasn't there in the first place and not in an icehouse!' I snapped before I could stop myself.

The second man to come up the steps from crypt level had joined us, slapping dust from his coat. 'Quite right, ma'am,' he agreed. 'The problem was that the crypt was so full of all kinds of junk and bits and pieces, it hardly seemed decent to put Sir Henry there at the time. It's been used as a storeroom for as long as I can remember. But now we're clearing it out a bit, and making a respectable area for the coffin to rest there, until the funeral. My name is Colman; I'm the verger here.' He bowed. 'Jacob's told you that Mr Appleton has gone over to Oakwood House, I believe? They're going to bring Sir Henry over here, after the vicar has said a prayer or two, to make things right, as it were.' He shook his head. 'Terrible thing, desecrating a body like that!'

'Well, then, Mr Colman,' I said, 'perhaps, as verger, you can help me. I'd like to consult the registers of marriages and baptisms. Are they kept here in the church or at the vicarage?'

'Indeed I can help you, ma'am. The registers are kept in a cupboard in the vestry, all safely locked away. But I have all the keys on this ring here.' From his pocket he produced a formidable set, like a gaoler's, and held them up, jangling them for effect.

There was no need to negotiate my way down the worn outer stairs into the crypt, thank goodness. Colman opened up the north door and we made our way through the church to the vestry. The records were kept in a venerable cupboard of blackened oak.

'Any particular year, ma'am?' asked Colman, opening the cupboards with a flourish. The smell of aged books, leather and glue, and dust filled the air. 'There's a fair old number, as you see.'

'My goodness, there certainly are!' I exclaimed. The cupboard was full of volumes, the history of this village and its inhabitants from very early times. But thanks to Jacob, I had a good idea which year I needed. 'Eighteen thirty-nine,' I told the verger, 'and eighteen forty.'

I suspected I did not need the records for thirty-nine, only those for forty. But I could feel Jacob's eyes watching me and wondered if he guessed what I was about. It did no harm to confuse him a little, muddy the water, as it were.

'Well, let's see,' said Colman happily. He was obviously proud of being in charge of all this. 'Marriages, you say? Here we are.' Two thick volumes landed on a table with a thump. 'And here's the births.' Another two thumps. 'I dare say you'll find there's enough light to read by from the window there, but there is a candle, if you need one . . . And do you want me to stay and help?'

'No, thank you, Mr Colman. I've very much obliged to you for taking this trouble. I'll come and find you and let you know when I've finished.'

He appeared relieved. 'Thank you, ma'am, only we've got to get back and finish making ready the crypt before Sir Henry arrives.'

'I'll give you a hand,' offered Jacob.

'Good of you, Jacob,' said Colman and the two of them set off together back to the crypt.

I thought that Jacob Dennis was a wily old fox. He now knew what my errand in the village was, in some detail. He had the perfect excuse for remaining at the church while I made my searches. Then, when I came to tell Colman I was done and he could lock up the records again, Jacob would declare himself ready to leave and I'd have his company wherever I went next. This might all be for the purpose of protecting me from stone-throwing urchins. But it also meant he knew what I did. Add that to my question as to the age of Davy Evans, and Jacob was shrewd enough to guess exactly what I was about. Ben had been finding it difficult to make his investigations unobserved. So was I.

It was very quiet in the vestry. Whatever the men were moving in the crypt beneath my feet, I could hear nothing of their efforts. I opened the heavy tomes carefully to read the handwriting of record keepers long dead. Most entries were basic: names and dates. It did not take me long to find what I sought, beginning with the register of marriages performed in that church. There, neatly entered, was the name of Isaac Evans, his occupation given as 'itinerant labourer', who married Tabitha Dawlish 'of this parish', in July 1840.

Now I moved on to the register of baptisms, and the entries for later that same year. Sadly, many mothers were entered as 'deceased'. But I found, on December the twenty-fourth, David, a male child, born to Isaac Evans and his wife, Tabitha. Born on Christmas Eve, Davy Evans was a 'Christmas baby', as Jacob had said. Tibby Dawlish had therefore already been four months gone with child, or very nearly, at the time of her marriage. She, at least, had survived childbirth. What, however, I wondered, had happened to Isaac Evans? Why had she resumed her maiden name?

I closed the books and sat for a while, deciding what I should do next. I thought I knew what had happened, but I couldn't prove it. All I could do was ask. I stood up and went to find the verger. When I left the vestry, and entered the main body of the church, I saw with relief that I did not have to go outside and negotiate a way down the mossy, slippery steps. The door to the crypt inside the church stood open and safer steps led down. Now I could hear noises coming up from below, suggesting some heavy piece of furniture was being dragged across the floor. I went down to investigate and found myself in a fantastical place, its vaulted roof hung with ancient cobwebs, dimly lit by lanterns placed here and there. There were stacked chairs and old pews, boxes of books, brass candelabra in dire need of a polish and fragments of medieval statuary, the better pieces perhaps brought down here as long ago as Cromwell's days to save them from being smashed. Other pieces, worn and battered, must once have been on the exterior of the building. The stone faces, with all the damage, stared at me curiously: saints, angels, likenesses of medieval stonemasons, a wyvern's-head waterspout . . . The only natural light filtered in from the door behind me and from that to the outer staircase. Jacob, Colman and a third man were pushing an ancient cope chest against the far wall. I recognised it for its purpose, as it was a quarter-circle in shape. The semi-circular cape, the cope, would be folded to make the quarter-circle before being put away. I wondered if there was a cope still inside it or whether it was empty. But now was not the time to inquire. My presence had been spotted.

'Well, ma'am,' said Colman, coming towards me and dusting his grimy palms together. 'Any luck? Did you find what you were looking for?'

'Thank you, Mr Colman, it was all very interesting.' Not exactly an answer to his question, but I did not want to volunteer more information about my search than I had to.

'Ready to go, then, ma'am?' said Jacob. 'I'll fetch my coat.'

'Oh, please, Mr Dennis, I can find my own way back, so there is no need. You can stay and help here.'

'Oh, we're pretty well finished,' said Colman unhelpfully. 'We've cleared all that end, see?'

One end of the crypt had indeed been cleared and trestles set up ready for the coffin to rest on. I suddenly wanted very much to get out of there. I thanked Colman again and turned to leave the crypt as I had entered it, from the interior of the church. I did not want to walk through the crypt, past all those stone eyes, and rise up through the ground on the outer stairway to emerge among the gravestones.

I was anxious to get away now, before any other villagers saw me there. However as bad luck would have it, just as Jacob and I met up again in the churchyard (he had come up the outer stair), a rumble of wheels and clatter of hooves announced the arrival of a closed carriage and, riding behind it, Andrew Beresford. Beside me, Jacob took off his hat, and stood with head bowed in respect. I did not want Beresford to see me, so I stepped back quickly behind the thick trunk of an ancient oak tree. I was able to peer round this and observe the coffin taken into the church. When the vicar and Beresford had gone inside I came out of my hiding place, feeling rather sheepish, and found Jacob watching me quizzically.

'I did not want Mr Beresford to think that I— that I was taking undue interest at such a sensitive private moment,' I said firmly.

He nodded. 'Will you be going home now, ma'am?'

'No, but you go home, Jacob, or go on down to the public house and have your pint. Please let me pay for it.' I fumbled in my reticule for a coin.

He accepted the coin with a nod of thanks and tucked it into his waistcoat pocket. 'If you're going on down to the village we can walk together, ma'am.'

We stared each other out for a moment. I had to give in. He was not going to leave me.

'All right,' I said, somewhat ungraciously.

We walked up the lane from the church to the main street of the village. Here we paused and I tried one more time to be free of him.

'If you want your pint of ale, Mr Dennis, please go to the public house.' He didn't move. I decided face-to-face challenge was best. 'I mean to call on the Dawlish sisters. So you need not come.'

'Very well, ma'am, I'll just sit on that bench outside their cottage and wait for you there.'

I sighed and gave up. 'You mean to look after me, Mr Dennis.'

'Yes, ma'am, I do. These are strange days.'

Jacob settled himself down on the wooden bench where I'd first encountered Aunt Tibby and Aunt Cora. He took out his clay pipe and pouch of tobacco and began to fill the pipe in a leisurely way. He had time enough, he knew. I walked up to the door and knocked.

Cora Dawlish opened it. She stood looking at me with unfriendly eyes, her sturdy frame blocking the way. 'What do you want, Mrs Ross?'

'I want the truth, Miss Cora, as you know I do. I would like to speak to your sister.'

She hesitated, but from the room behind her I heard Tibby call, 'Bring her in, Cora.'

She stood aside and I walked in to their dark, cramped parlour. Tibby sat by the hearth in a rocking chair.

'I have just come from the church,' I said. 'I have been looking in the registers of marriages and of baptisms.'

I expected her to show anger, or fear. But she seemed hardly to have paid attention to my words.

'Did you see *him*?' she asked fiercely. 'They drove by here.'

'If you mean Sir Henry's coffin, yes. I saw the carriage arrive with it, and the vicar, and Mr Beresford riding behind. They have taken it to the crypt. It must not be disturbed again, Tibby.'

'It will not be,' she said.

'You have a married name, Evans, but you do not use it, even though Davy Evans, who is your son, lives here with you.'

Cora had seated herself in the far corner in another rocking chair, and watched us, tilting the chair back and forth. It creaked faintly. I was left with a wooden chair on which to perch.

Tibby said, 'I did not choose to take the name Evans. The marriage was his doing, Meager's, to save his reputation from further damage.'

'Tell me about it, Tibby.'

There was a short pause during which only the faint creak of the rocking chair in the corner broke the silence.

Then Tibby heaved a deep sigh. 'Very well, I will tell you, because you will give me no peace until you know it all.' She gave a strange, crooked little smile. 'The truth-seeker chose well, in marrying you. He found one who thinks as he does. He cannot abide the notion that old sins should remain secret; no more can you. Only remember this: there are things that are better never spoken of.'

'There are deeds, Aunt Tibby, that are better not committed. But once they are, they can never remain hidden forever.'

'Now you call me "Aunt Tibby"!' She gave an unexpected cackle of laughter and shook her finger at me in reproof. 'Let me tell you then, since you are so very anxious to know, how I came to kill Henry Meager.'

Chapter Eighteen

Elizabeth Martin Ross

'I WAS Miss Madeleine's personal maid,' she began, then paused and looked at me inquiringly.

'Sir Henry's wife,' I said. 'I have seen her portrait.'

'To me she will always be "Miss Madeleine". It was an evil day when she married into that family. I know the portrait you spoke of. It does not do her justice. It shows only her looks, not the beauty of her character. She was good and kind and loving. She even loved that brute she married. He beat her. I saw the bruises, so I know. He blamed her for being childless. He said he needed a son and she should give him one.'

'Did she know he had children himself, elsewhere, out of wedlock?' I asked.

She sighed and shrugged her shoulders. 'Well, there was Robert Harcourt, the Frenchwoman's child. I think she knew about him.'

'You believe it's true, then, as Robert Harcourt himself told my husband, that Sir Henry was his father?'

'Of course he was!' Tibby snapped. 'And when Sir Henry

told his own father that the French lady was carrying his child, he was ordered to put her away; and so he did. Everyone was afraid of the Old Indestructible, including his son!

'It was the Old Indestructible, Sir Hector, who set the pattern of how to deal with such inconveniences. He bought the Frenchwoman a husband, old Mr Harcourt the ship's chandler in Lymington. In that way her child had a name and a respectable family background. Later, after old Mr Harcourt and Sir Hector had both died, Sir Henry would ride over to Lymington from time to time, to visit the widow. He also paid for the boy's education. All this I fancy Miss Madeleine knew, because Sir Henry did it quite openly.' A look of anger crossed Tibby's face. 'It was perhaps the first time money bought Henry Meager out of an awkward situation; but it would not be the last.'

I thought of the entries I'd read in the registers of marriages and births. Isaac Evans, itinerant labourer. His compliance would have cost far less than that of old Mr Harcourt, the Lymington chandler.

'Your son, Davy, is Sir Henry's child,' I said.

She raised a hand to silence me. She would tell the tale in her own time; and not be hurried. 'No pretty girl was safe from him. The tenant farmers knew to hide their daughters. Then Miss Madeleine fell sick. She had the disease of the lungs, consumption, as they call it. There was talk of taking her to Switzerland where the air is said to be very good for such illnesses. But she became too weak to travel.' Tibby paused. 'It was during that time that

Sir Henry turned his attention to me. He would have no refusal. The night my dear lady died, she took my hand as I sat by her bed. She had realised that I was with child by then. She said, "I am very sorry, Tibby. I would have protected you, if I could have done."

'She fell asleep a little after that and never awoke again. He had her room cleared as soon as she was buried. Everything must go. I don't know where all her gowns went. Her jewellery was sold, I believe. He didn't ask me if there was anything of hers I wanted as a memento, so I took something for myself.'

I said, 'You took a little painted fan.'

Tibby Dawlish smiled. 'Yes. You see, truth-seeker's wife, you have a nose for secrets.'

I said, 'It was wrong of you to frighten Mrs Beresford as you did, slipping into the house and leaving first the roses, and then the fan, on her piano. She had done no wrong. She was already terrified enough because Sir Henry's coffin rested nearby. Then it was followed by the dreadful business of taking the body and setting it up atop the bonfire. That was unforgivable.'

'That was not my doing!' she snapped sulkily. 'I left the roses and the fan on the piano, yes. But I did not do it for malice. I did it because I was sorry for her and wanted to show her I bore her no ill will. The roses I cut from bushes in her own garden. I thought she would've realised that. The fan was Miss Madeleine's, I admit. But Miss Madeleine would have been Mr Beresford's aunt by marriage, so it seemed fitting Mrs Beresford should have it.'

'Perhaps you didn't mean to frighten her, but you did!'

I said sharply. 'Now, after all that's happened, Mrs Beresford has been driven from her own home.'

'Wrongdoing breeds more wrongdoing. Ask your husband!' The words were spoken belligerently by Cora Dawlish. She had been sitting so quietly in the corner that I had forgotten her; and the suddenness of her intervention made me start. 'If you must ferret your way into other people's business, you must accept what you find. If you don't like it; then perhaps it would have been better to leave well alone!'

It was a harsh sentiment but there was some truth in it, I had to admit.

Tibby Dawlish made no comment. Perhaps she had not even heard her sister, so intent was she on telling her own tale. She took it up again now.

'After Miss Madeleine died, when Meager saw that my pregnancy was showing, he did as his father had done for the French lady. There are men who travel around the country together in a group, seeking work, as you may know. They go from farm to farm, sleep in a barn, stay a few weeks, then take their money and move on. There was such a group working on Sir Henry's land at the time. Sometimes their women, poor wretches, travel with them. But there was one of those there at that time who had no woman of his own. Isaac Evans was his name. So Meager paid him to stand up in the church and marry me. He made this cottage available to us to live in, rent-free. Rent-free it has remained until this day, though Isaac did not linger long. He left within a few weeks of the wedding. He was a travelling man by nature, and liked the freedom of the road. From time to time, while Davy was a small child, I'd receive a little bag of coins, handed to me by a complete stranger, an itinerant like Isaac. He would tell me, "Isaac sends you this!" He was not a bad man.

'My sister—' Here Tibby acknowledged Cora's presence with a nod of her head in the direction of the corner. 'My sister had also been working as a maid, for a lady in Winchester. When I grew near my time, Cora left her position and came to live with me here to look after me while I was lying in.' Unexpectedly, she smiled. 'Davy was a fine baby, was he not, Cora?'

'He was,' agreed Cora.

'The vicar at that time was old Mr Burrell,' Tibby continued. 'He was a bachelor who lived with his nose in his books, and had an interest in botany, as he called it. He would go wandering about, all over the heath and the fields, with his nose nearly to the ground, looking for some kind of moss.'

'I learned much from him about the properties of plants,' said Cora so quietly I fancied she spoke to herself. 'He had big books with pictures of the plants in them, all coloured and beautiful. He was pleased I was interested and took time to explain it all to me.'

Tibby continued, 'I don't mean Mr Burrell wasn't a good parish priest and a kind man. But I think he was afraid to offend any Meager in case he lost his living. Because of this he made no fuss about marrying Isaac and me.

'I believe his conscience troubled him, though, after Isaac left. He needed a housekeeper, so Cora went to take up that position. She went to the vicarage each morning and came home here at night. He had no wife or kin; but with Cora looking after him he was very comfortable. When he died, he left her an annuity.'

'And some of the plant books,' said Cora.

I wondered if the old man had left her the books or she had just helped herself to them, as Tibby had to the fan.

'It was after that I stopped using the name "Evans" and went back to being Dawlish,' said Tibby.

'So,' I said, 'Cora has a modest income thanks to Reverend Burrell; and Sir Henry let you have the cottage here rent-free.' I almost added that between them they had done pretty well, but of course it was all guilt money. Sir Henry had rid himself of an awkward problem. Burrell had salved his conscience because he must have realised that the child, Davy, was not Isaac's. He had been complicit in the deception. Perhaps he had convinced himself that, in agreeing to marry Tibby and Isaac, he was doing the only thing he could to help both Tibby and the child. For both of them the future would otherwise have been very uncertain. When Isaac deserted his new wife within weeks, Rev. Burrell must have been dismayed.

I asked, 'Tell me about the night Sir Henry died.'

'I must go back before that, about two months ago, it was.'

Tibby began to rock herself back and forth again in the chair and now adopted a slightly sing-song way of talking. I recognised it as the traditional pattern of speech of the storyteller since time immemorial. With her chair creaking back and forth before me, and Cora tilting the companion rocker by the far wall, it was as if the room moved around me and only I stayed still. I began to feel a little nauseous.

'Mr Pelham, the lawyer, came down from London because Meager wanted to bring his will up to date. By then, Harcourt had been working for him for some time as estate manager, with a house provided, and no doubt a good salary. Meager always looked after the Frenchwoman's child.'

I thought, yes, he did look after Robert during his life. Perhaps, if his own father had allowed it, he would even have married the Frenchwoman when he first brought her home. But he did not and he would not, even in death, ever have declared that Robert was his child. And without that declaration, spoken or in writing, there would always be a doubt.

'He didn't look after, as you call it, your son, Davy?' I asked aloud.

'In a way he did, but it was a poor way compared with what he'd done for Robert Harcourt. He paid for no schooling for Davy. He gave him work from time to time. Word had gone round, as it does, that Sir Henry meant to leave a little bequest to all the servants at the Hall, and a decent bequest to Robert Harcourt, for being his manager. So, I thought to myself, he ought to leave something to Davy, since all the others, his kin or not, would be remembered.

'I was walking up on the heath one day, looking for herbs for Cora's medicines, while Mr Pelham was here. I saw Sir Henry, riding alone, and coming towards me. I stepped out into the path, so that he must stop.

'"Well, Tibby," he said. "What is it?" He spoke coldly and carelessly, but I reckoned he knew what I'd ask.

'So I told him. I knew Lawyer Pelham had come to update the will. It was common knowledge the household servants would be remembered, and that Harcourt, as estate manager, would receive a more generous amount. Even though the truth of Harcourt's birth was supposed to be a secret, both of us knew he was Sir Henry's son. Would it not be right and fair that he should leave something to Davy, who was also his son? I was alive to testify, under oath if need be, that he had fathered my child. It would not force him in law to acknowledge Davy; but it would embarrass the Beresfords.

'He gave a great shout of laughter that rang out across the heath. Then his face grew cold and stern again. He leaned forward in the saddle and said, "I have done more than enough for Davy Evans, and for you. All I have done for you both was for the sake of my late wife who was very attached to you. Mark you! I was not required to do *anything*. As the mother of a bastard child you would have been driven out of the village. Who knows where you would have gone, or how you would have supported yourself. You would have had to give your infant to the workhouse or to a baby-farmer; and everyone knows babies in their care have a habit of dying pretty quickly. Davy has lived to reach manhood, and you have kept your good name, because of my generosity towards you both.

'"In addition, I have allowed you to live rent-free. I have seen that Davy has work. As a magistrate, I have kept him out of gaol. Don't imagine I am unaware that he does more than fish from that boat. He meets out at sea with smugglers who bring tobacco and brandy from France."

'"Yes," I said. "And you smoke the tobacco and drink the brandy."

'"You can say what you like, Tibby," he said. "No one would believe you. Davy is a bad lot and everyone knows it. If you started any rumour, I'd have you out of your cottage, you, your sister, and Davy, straight away. I'd see he got no more work. If necessary, I'd see him sent to gaol for smuggling. Don't forget!"

'Then he rode on. I knew he meant it. I wasn't sure that he would not send Davy to gaol just to spite me, but I had to be sure that could not happen.' She looked me full in the face. 'There is a saying, isn't there? About someone "signing his own death warrant"? Well, that is what Henry Meager had done.'

'Why did you seek to draw me into it?' I asked her. I looked towards Cora, who still sat impassively in the far corner, by the window. 'When I first arrived and found you sitting with your sister out there, before the cottage, you, Miss Cora, said I brought death with me.'

Cora shrugged. 'I knew what my sister intended. And I also knew that as soon as he died, people in the village would want to blame someone at once. For this reason I directed their thinking towards your presence. They would not think *you* had killed him, of course! But they would blame you for bringing death; and it would keep their minds busy.'

'And they did blame me,' I snapped. 'The children threw stones at me!'

Ann Granger

'Well, then,' said Cora complacently, 'it worked.'

She levered herself to her feet in a rustle of clothing and went to the window. There she turned her back to me and to her sister, signalling that she had said her part and would say no more. She fixed her stare along the length of the front garden and towards the road. I thought perhaps she was looking to see if Andrew Beresford would ride by again, on his way back from the church, after seeing his uncle's coffin safe in the crypt.

'On that day,' Tibby began again, very quietly, so that I had to ignore Cora and turn back to catch what she was saying. 'The day of the dinner party to which you and Mrs Parry went, I'm talking of. It was a good day for what I needed to do. The servants were so busy. I slipped into the house. I knew it like the back of my hand from the days when I worked and lived there. I went upstairs to what had been Miss Madeleine's room. I knew no one went there. The staff were superstitious about it – and *he* would never go there.'

'You are adept at slipping in and out of other people's houses,' I said. 'You entered and left unseen from Oakwood House, after leaving the items on the piano.'

'Who notices what a servant does?' she retorted. 'They are all trained to be quiet and not intrude. Why, one of them might come into a room with a coal scuttle and make up the fire, rattling the tongs, yet no one pays the slightest attention. Or bring dishes to the table. A hand takes away the dishes from one course and puts down the dishes of the next and not one of the people sitting round the table, drinking and laughing, is aware of it. So I walked through the house, as I had done years ago, and went to Miss Madeleine's room.

'I waited there, thinking about my dear lady, and about all the mischief Sir Henry had done in his life, and would go on doing if he wasn't stopped. At last the guests had gone and he, Meager, had gone to bed. It was peaceful. I knew about the pistols in the library drawer. I went down, broke the lock, took a pistol and loaded it and then I went up to his room. He was asleep. I shot him, threw down the pistol and went back to Miss Madeleine's room. In the morning, when the staff were busy, and the kitchen door unlocked, I made ready to leave. Lynn, the valet, made it even easier for me. He'd found the body and went screaming about the place, attracting everyone's attention. I walked out and came home here.'

She sat now, silent and looking at me in a kind of triumph. But I felt suddenly certain that, though she'd told the truth until the last little piece, she was lying about firing the pistol.

'You conspired with your son,' I said. 'You laid the plan with him, told him where to find the pistols and to wait in Lady Meager's room until the moment came. But he fired the fatal shot.'

The triumph was wiped from her face and she scowled at me. 'No! I killed Meager.'

'I don't believe you, Tibby,' I replied firmly. 'You seek to save your son from the gallows, even if it means you are judged guilty yourself.'

'It does not matter whether you believe me or not,

truth-seeker's wife! It is what I say happened, and I shall say it before the judge.'

'You could not have built the bonfire or put the body on top of it.'

'No, Davy did that. It wasn't any part of my plan. But when they left the body in the icehouse, it was asking for trouble. The Beresfords should not have been surprised when trouble came.' She gave a little nod of satisfaction.

'It was unspeakable! He will answer for it and for everything else, poor Robert Harcourt's death and everything. You planned that, too, I suppose? Who tied the wire across the path? Davy? I dare say it was he who did it, under your direction. And did he also remove it? Or were you waiting in the bushes to dart out and remove it before others came?'

'I wanted to leave matters tidy,' she said complacently.

'Have you no understanding of what you've done?' I asked. 'You brought up your son to hate both his father and the man who was probably his brother. To hate them to the extent that he conspired to kill them: to commit both patricide and fratricide. These are horrible crimes; all right-minded people would be appalled by them. Even those who are rogues and criminals in other ways would not commit such awful deeds.'

'What do I care what others think? If vengeance cannot be done through the law, then it must be done in other ways. A father who does not recognise his child is no father.' A mocking look entered her eyes. 'I have shocked you.'

'The law is not about vengeance,' I argued. 'It is about justice.'

'What I did was justice. The law would not have given me that. I had to make my own.'

'Then let us talk of Robert Harcourt.'

Tibby scowled at me and then looked down at her hands clasped in her lap. 'What of him?'

'He did not deserve to die!'

Tibby looked up at me and I was astonished and appalled at the expression in her eyes. 'He *had* to die. He was too dangerous to leave alive.'

'But for brother to kill or conspire to kill brother . . .'

'When did Robert Harcourt ever treat Davy as a brother? He hated the very idea! Harcourt had already told me, more than once, that when Sir Henry was gone he – Harcourt – would make sure that Beresford turned me, my sister and Davy out of this cottage and chased us away. Where should we have gone? Harcourt said he would inform the authorities about Davy's business with the French smugglers. Another magistrate wouldn't have turned a blind eye. Oh, he was a fine-looking fellow, Harcourt, and thought a great deal of himself, too. I dare say he impressed *you*, Mrs Ross. But once Sir Henry was out of the way, there was nothing to stop the Frenchwoman's son from carrying out his threats.'

I was moved to argue. 'You really believe he would have informed on Davy? After all, if he realised Davy was probably his half-brother . . .'

She leaned forward in the rocking chair, bringing its motion to a halt and herself, its occupant, crouched, almost as if she would spring out at me. 'Oh, Harcourt had long ago guessed the truth about Davy's real parentage. He knew we lived rent-free. He saw how Meager gave Davy odd jobs of work and chose to ignore what he did when out in his boat, and anything else Davy did that might be breaking the law. And Harcourt resented it, you see?

'Besides, if ever Meager had acknowledged Robert Harcourt as his child, I would have spoken up about *my* son. Told the world! Sir Henry might brush aside my threat to speak out, as he did when I stopped him up on the heath. But Harcourt really feared I might do it, and he didn't fancy that one bit.'

It was cruel reality, but I understood. Harcourt's pride had been his downfall. It was one thing for him to boast that his true father was the squire. It wouldn't have been the same thing to be spoken of as only the half-brother of Davy Evans, the local ne'er-do-well. Oh, Davy's silence could be bought, no doubt. But Harcourt would pay all his life for it. He could not afford to leave Tibby and her son in the village. He had to chase them away.

Tibby was speaking again. 'Harcourt earned a good living from Sir Henry. He was a conscientious estate manager, I'll give him that, so he was confident Mr Beresford, the heir, would keep him on. That should have been enough! But no, he had taken it into his head that Sir Henry should acknowledge him publicly.' She snorted.

'Tibby,' I asked cautiously, 'did Harcourt guess you and Davy plotted Sir Henry's death?'

'Well, he wasn't a complete fool, was he?' she snapped. 'Other than in sticking to his demand that Meager admit he was his father. Even before your husband ever arrived here, and that fellow from Southampton was still poking about at the Hall making his inquiries, Harcourt spoke to Davy. He said, "I know you and your mother are responsible for this! If the police don't get to the truth of it, I shall tell them so."' She relaxed and leaned back, setting the rocking of the chair in motion again. 'Harcourt was a threat to Davy. He had to be removed.'

It was how she saw it; and I knew I couldn't shake her belief that what she'd done was in some terrible, twisted way, right. But I might break through that wall of self-justification in another way.

'Tibby,' I said, staring at her in dismay. 'Don't you realise Davy will hang for his part in all this?'

She shook her head. 'Davy is safe away. You won't catch him. He will be in France by now.'

I was so exasperated at my inability to pierce the armour of complacency she had clothed herself in that I seethed with frustration. Somehow, in some way, I would pierce that shield.

'What of that ghastly bonfire? Whoever planned that awful act of desecration, it was designed to drive the Beresfords from Oakwood House. You thought that, when the inheritance was settled, they would move to the Hall; and you did not want any of that family living in the Hall. The body being stored in the icehouse made it easy. Davy is responsible for the bonfire and taking the corpse from the coffin. It was *you* who left the roses and fan on the piano, to frighten Mrs Beresford, not to do something nice for her. But Mr Beresford has told my husband that he and his wife have no intention of living at the Hall. They will rent out the house to a tenant. So you see, what you did in the matter of the roses and the fan was not only cruel, it was unnecessary.'

Tibby looked sulky and sat in silence. It was broken, not by her, but by her sister who spoke from her place at the window.

'He has come here.'

'Mr Beresford?' I asked, surprised.

Cora turned from the window. 'No, your husband.'

I had been so intent on listening to Tibby's tale that I had paid no attention to the noise of wheels and hooves outside. But now I heard the heavy thump of men's feet approaching, and there was a thunderous knock on the door.

Cora went to open it. I saw Ben standing at the threshold and, behind him, Hughes from Southampton.

'What are you doing here, Lizzie?' Ben asked in surprise.

I looked at Tibby. She nodded and ordered sourly, 'Tell him!'

'Miss Tabitha Dawlish,' I said to Ben, 'is, in reality, Mrs Evans, née Dawlish. The marriage to Isaac Evans is recorded in the register of the church here. I found it earlier today. Davy is her son and his father was Sir Henry Meager. Meager paid Evans to marry her.'

Ben looked towards Tibby. 'Is this so?'

'You may read it for yourself in the register, as she told you,' said Tibby. 'She is a good detective, your wife. And if you want to know who killed Meager, then I did. I have told your wife so, and now I tell you.'

Ben looked at me again. 'So she says,' I told him. 'I am not certain myself that she's telling the truth. I think she wants to save her son from the gallows.'

Tibby spoke again and this time there was a note of triumph in her voice. 'You will not find Davy. You can do as you wish with me. I have little time left and will not live long enough to hang.'

Hughes spoke unexpectedly, his soft Welsh tones striking a new note in the room. 'We have found your son.'

Tibby's face drained of colour. 'No! You're lying! Davy is safe away in his boat.'

'We are not lying, Miss Dawlish, or Mrs Evans, as you please.' There was a note of resignation in Ben's voice as he confirmed what Hughes had said. My heart sank.

'The fog thickened at night out at sea and early today a packet ship out from St Malo ran down a sailing boat they hadn't seen in time and couldn't avoid. They realised what had happened and made out the figure of a man clinging to the hull. They managed to get him out of the water and aboard their vessel but, despite their efforts to revive him, by the time they reached Southampton he had died. The body is in the morgue at Southampton. I have seen it there and I recognised your son. We have come here today to ask you to come with us to Southampton to confirm the identification . . .'

'*No!*' Tibby leaped up from the chair with a dreadful screech. The chair began to rock violently behind her as if it, too, rejected Ben's news. '*You lie, truth-seeker! Davy knows the waters hereabouts! He has crossed the Channel before! He has reached France!*'

'No, Mrs Evans, he did not. Please, come with us now. I do not know exactly what you have told Mrs Ross, but you have not made any confession to me. Please do not repeat it now, as in the light of what you will find at the morgue, you may wish to withdraw—'

He broke off as Tibby drew a strange ragged breath, making a sound that was not quite human nor animal. It resembled the desolate cry of the wind moaning through a gap in the eaves on a stormy night. She leaned forward and seemed to somehow shrink into herself, but then pushed herself upright in a desperate effort. It would be her last. She staggered forward and collapsed at the same time.

Cora cried, 'Tibby!' and ran forward to catch her sister. With Tibby clasped in her hands, Cora gasped, 'It is her heart! Dr Wilson told her it would be her heart . . .'

Chapter Nineteen

Elizabeth Martin Ross

'SOMETIMES,' I said to Ben, 'when people talk about right and wrong, they make it sound so simple. In reality it's a complicated thing. Take Isaac Evans. He took money to marry Tibby Dawlish. That meant Tibby and her child were saved from the stigma of illegitimacy. But then he deserted her. He could have argued that he'd abided by the deal he had made with Sir Henry Meager. On the other hand he had not abided by the deal he'd made in the church with Tibby before God. Yet he sent Tibby a purse of a few shillings from time to time. She remembered him kindly.'

We were back in London and seated in our cosy little house, after supper. It was so good to be home.

'You are a romantic,' said Ben bluntly. 'I'm a police officer and I'm not swayed by Tibby's kindly thoughts of the absent Evans. I could put to you a different version. In sending his wife a few shillings from time to time, Evans avoided a charge of deserting and failing to support his family.'

'You are telling me the law would have gone searching high and low to find an itinerant labourer?' I argued.

'I don't know, because the matter didn't arise. A police officer deals in facts.'

Ben was sounding obstinate and I'd get nowhere with my argument, or worse, I'd end up defending Tibby's taking of what she thought of as Justice into her own hands. 'Did anyone ever find the wire that was tied across the path to bring down Harcourt's horse?'

'Now that's a curious thing,' said Ben. 'There is a pond upon the heath behind the village.'

'I know it,' I said. 'I met Cora Dawlish nearby.'

'Well, Hughes has informed me that recent hot weather caused the water to sink to a very low level and various items were recovered from the mud. They included a tangle of wire. It was known the police wanted to find any abandoned wire, so it was reported. That doesn't mean it was the wire tied across the path. But it's a possibility. It might suggest that Tibby Dawlish or Evans, as you please, was hiding in the bushes by the path waiting for Harcourt to ride through, and scurried out to remove the wire after Harcourt was thrown from his horse. Or that Davy removed the wire, and passed it to his mother to take away before he ran out to announce he'd found the body.'

'It is very annoying,' I said after thinking about this, 'not to be able to prove *everything*.'

'Often we are lucky to prove *anything*!' Ben smiled. 'I do enjoy a lively discussion with you concerning police work, Lizzie.'

'Superintendent Dunn wouldn't approve,' I said. 'You need women in the police force. I've told Mr Dunn so.'

'He hasn't forgotten. Ever since you told him that, Dunn has feared that female influence will find its way into the workings of Scotland Yard. However, I do know he has much respect for you, my dear.'

'Don't butter your words,' I told him. 'I know you fear it as much as he does.'

'I wouldn't dare to argue. Am I going to walk into my office one day and find you sitting at my desk?'

'No, not me. But one day, some other woman will sit at that desk!'

There was a pause. 'Meager must have been an odd fellow,' said Ben, wisely changing the subject. 'He doesn't appear to have had much to recommend his character in so many ways, yet he took steps to support his illegitimate children, Harcourt and Davy Evans. Possibly even the girl, Susan Bate, for whom he did the best he could. It is unfortunate that he did not treat the two sons he fathered out of wedlock more evenly. In that, I fancy, he was influenced by Robert's mother being an "old flame", shall we say?'

I added, 'But Davy was only a servant's child, not that of an old love. Besides, she reminded Meager of the wife he'd treated so unkindly. Little wonder Davy grew up to resent the difference deeply. His resentment was fanned by what his mother told him. Mother and son both longed for vengeance.'

Ben nodded. 'That was where Harcourt made his big mistake. He should not have threatened them with expulsion from their cottage and informing on Davy's illegal activities.'

Struck by a thought, I asked, 'What will happen to Susan Bate now? If the Beresfords don't move into the Hall, a new tenant might not want to employ Susan.'

'I can give you news of Susan,' Ben told me. 'Hughes wrote to tell me she is now working for Mrs Garvey at the Acorn Inn. Mrs Garvey is a kind woman and will look after her.'

Ben looked thoughtful. 'With the best will in the world, one makes mistakes. When I first met the assembled staff in the kitchen of the Hall, they were all clearly very distressed. But Warton, the butler, seemed out of his mind, ranting about the end of the world and the scarlet woman . . . quoting other bits of the Book of Revelations as well. The cook told him to be quiet. I thought, at the time, she was embarrassed at his performance and the loss of dignity. But I fancy now Warton saw what had happened as a judgment on Sir Henry's life. Sir Henry had sinned in the ways of the flesh and now he'd been punished. The cook was worried Warton might start spilling out all the family's murkier secrets. She wanted to defend the reputation of her late employer; and told him pretty sharply to stop. My error was in not taking Warton's claims seriously. Then, of course, the wretched Lynn fainted, and Warton was forgotten.'

He sighed. 'A little later Warton stopped his ranting and followed me. He waited in the entrance hall to see if he could speak to me. But I was anxious to hear what Harcourt had to say, and I ignored the poor old fellow.'

'The family portraits told a story, too,' I mused. 'Did you really not see a likeness to Harcourt in the portraits of Captain Sir Hector Meager?'

Ben smiled. 'And did you, Lizzie, not see a likeness to Davy Evans, especially in the early portrait of Hector Meager, with the sea in the background?'

'I didn't give Davy a thought in that respect,' I had to confess. 'Perhaps Davy also inherited his skill as a sailor from his grandfather?'

'Perhaps. However skilful he was, trying to reach France was a desperate throw of the dice. The Channel crossing at that point is probably the widest. Given fair weather and daylight conditions, it would still have taken him hours. He set sail at night, with the fog gathering. That was fool-hardy in the extreme, but he had left himself no other option.' Ben gestured widely with his arm and fell silent.

I wasn't yet ready to give up my pity for Evans. 'I can't think kindly of Davy,' I said. 'But I don't like to think of the moment he saw the larger shape of the packet boat loom up out of the mist and tower above his little sailing boat.'

'He probably heard it before he saw it,' Ben replied. 'The packet boat is steam-driven and the sound of its engines would have travelled through the murk. But Evans couldn't be certain exactly where it was, or manoeuvre fast enough to avoid the danger, when it did appear, like a phantom ship in legend.' Perhaps Ben did not want to be thought fanciful, because he added briskly, 'If you want to feel sorry for someone, why not pity Robert Harcourt, one of those Davy and his dreadful mother conspired to murder?

Rightly or wrongly, Harcourt believed himself Meager's son. For myself, I'm inclined to believe he was. If you think of Davy, you now think of him facing death on the sea. If I think of Harcourt, I remember my first sight of him, standing on the steps of the Hall, looking for all the world like its owner, not the estate manager. Also, I remember him laid out dead in that small back bedroom. And all, really, because he wanted to be acknowledged as a gentleman's son. I can't say I've ever felt any such ambition. I'm a collier's son and proud of it.'

'And Cora Dawlish? What will happen to her?' I asked.

'She has not been charged with anything. She may have known what her sister intended, but she has withdrawn any sort of admission she made to you. She now says she was only teasing you when she prophesied you would bring death.

'The sisters' cottage was searched by Hughes's men in the vain hope of finding some evidence of what Tibby planned. But Cora Dawlish had made sure there was nothing to find, before Hughes got there. There were scraps of burned paper in the grate. Little could be made of them. They might have formed a diary. Even so, if Tibby had made any mention of her plans in it, well, it had gone up in smoke.'

'As Davy meant Meager's body to do!' I couldn't help but say. I was immediately sorry I'd said it, because I saw Ben's expression alter at the memory. I hadn't seen that body atop the bonfire, but he had.

'As Tabitha Evans and her son are both dead, the matter is closed.' More gently, Ben added, 'Put it all behind you, Lizzie. I don't forget the criminals I've encountered and the crimes they've committed. But I don't dwell on them, either. If I did, I'd not be able to do my job. We can't rewrite the past.'

'The matter may be closed,' began Aunt Parry. 'But in a most unsatisfactory manner, I may say. No one has stood trial. Sir Henry's character has been maligned and there is not a shred of evidence that anything that strange old woman said was true. I shall always remember Sir Henry as a charming gentleman.'

It was the following afternoon and, once again, I took tea with her in Dorset Square. Things had come full circle, you might say. But clearly recent events were not closed in Aunt Parry's mind and I was to hear about it.

She tilted forward in a rustle of taffeta. 'However Inspector Ross may choose to view events, none of it will ever leave *my* memory! Your husband's view is formed by his experiences dealing with ruffians and criminals all the time. His finer feelings have been blunted. For a sensitive person such as myself— '

What? She was as sensitive as an armadillo.

'It remains, and always will do, a dreadful business! What particularly annoys me is that it altogether ruined my attempt to restore both my health and yours, Elizabeth, with a visit to the coast for sea air. The entire adventure has left me exhausted.'

'Yes, I am sorry your plan did not work out as you hoped,' I agreed meekly. If she suspected any irony in my reply, she did not show it. Her mind was running on a different track.

'And it all came to pass because of a will,' she went on. 'No matter what had happened years before, the tale didn't *have* to end in two murders! However you look at it, and whatever roots the story had, it was Mr Pelham's arrival to deal with the revision of Sir Henry's will that precipitated events.'

'I dare say you're right, Aunt Parry.' Perhaps she was.

'Of course I am right, Elizabeth.' She sat back in her chair and gazed thoughtfully at two macaroons remaining on a plate, and sighed.

'Wills cause no end of trouble,' she went on, 'especially when people allow themselves expectations of any sort. I remember, when I was a girl, my father had a curate. He wanted to get married. He was a nice enough young man, sincere in his beliefs and pleasant in his manner, but he had no money. The young lady he wished to wed had no money either. However!' Aunt Parry raised a pudgy forefinger. 'She had an aunt. The aunt was elderly, in poor health, and regarded as wealthy. She lived in a fine house and in some style. She was childless. It was generally believed that her niece, the girl the curate wanted to marry, would inherit. She had indicated several times that was her intention. So the young couple married on what little money they had, and waited for the aunt's demise. And die she did.'

'And she hadn't left her fortune to the niece, the curate's wife?' I asked.

'Oh, yes, she had, just as she'd promised she would. But there wasn't any fortune. The aunt had been living on credit for years, keeping up appearances by all kinds of trickery. Her jewels were paste, the originals sold years before. The house was mortgaged to the bank and it took possession of that. Other creditors were waiting in line with their demands. All that the niece received, when the will was finally settled, was a chipped dinner service and a long-case clock that didn't work. Counting one's chickens before they are hatched, as the saying goes, is never a sound principle. Shall we finish the macaroons? And then, perhaps, we can talk about taking a little trip later in the year. Tell me, Elizabeth, how would you fancy a tour of the Lake District?'

Accompany Inspector Ben Ross on more adventures in ...

THE MURDERER'S APPRENTICE

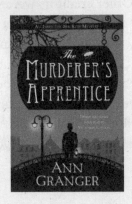

It is March 1870. London is in the grip of fog and ice. But Scotland Yard's Inspector Ben Ross has more than the weather to worry about when the body of a young woman is found in a dustbin at the back of a Piccadilly restaurant.

Ben must establish who the victim is before he can find out how and why she came to be there. His enquiries lead him first to a bootmaker in Salisbury and then to a landowner in Yorkshire. Meanwhile, Ben's wife, Lizzie, aided by their eagle-eyed maid, Bessie, is investigating the mystery of a girl who is apparently being kept a prisoner in her own home.

As Ben pursues an increasingly complex case, Lizzie reveals a vital piece of evidence that brings him one step closer to solving the crime...

Available now from

HEADLINE

THE DEAD WOMAN OF DEPTFORD

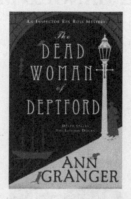

On a cold November night in a Deptford yard, dock worker
Harry Parker stumbles upon the body of a dead woman.
Inspector Ben Ross is summoned from Scotland Yard to this
insalubrious part of town, but no witness to the murder of this
well-dressed, middle-aged woman can be found. Even Jeb Fisher,
the local rag-and-bone man, swears he's seen nothing.

Meanwhile, Ben's wife Lizzie is trying to suppress a scandal:
family friend Edgar Wellings has a gambling addiction and no
means of repaying his debts. Reluctantly, Lizzie agrees to visit his
debt collector's house in Deptford, but when she arrives she
finds her husband is investigating the murder of the woman in
question. Edgar was the last man to see Mrs Clifford alive and
he has good reason to want her dead, but Ben and Lizzie both
know that a case like this is rarely as simple as it appears...

Available now from

HEADLINE

THE TESTIMONY OF
THE HANGED MAN

A hanged man would say anything to save his life.

But what if his testimony is true?

When Inspector Ben Ross is called to Newgate Prison by a man condemned to die by the hangman's noose, he isn't expecting to give any credence to the man's testimony. But the account of a murder he witnessed over seventeen years ago is so utterly believable that Ben can't help wondering if what he's heard is true.

It's too late to save the man's life, but it's not too late to investigate a murder that has gone undetected for all these years.

Available now from

HEADLINE

A PARTICULAR EYE FOR VILLAINY

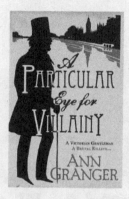

When Mr Thomas Tapley is found bludgeoned to death in his sitting room, his neighbour Inspector Benjamin Ross of Scotland Yard is immediately summoned. Little is known about the elusive gentleman until Mr Jonathan Tapley, QC, hears of the news and the truth about his cousin's tragic past slowly begins to emerge.

Meanwhile, Ben's wife Lizzie is convinced she saw someone following Thomas Tapley on the day he died, and she discovers that he received a mysterious visitor a few days before his death. As the list of suspects begins to mount, Ben must unearth who would benefit most from Tapley's unfortunate demise.

And don't miss the other novels in the series:

A Rare Interest in Corpses
A Mortal Curiosity
A Better Quality of Murder

Available now from

HEADLINE

THRILLINGLY GOOD BOOKS FROM CRIMINALLY GOOD WRITERS

CRIME FILES BRINGS YOU THE LATEST RELEASES FROM TOP CRIME AND THRILLER AUTHORS.

SIGN UP ONLINE FOR OUR MONTHLY NEWSLETTER AND BE THE FIRST TO KNOW ABOUT OUR COMPETITIONS, NEW BOOKS AND MORE.